MW01114326

Dirty

DNA 2

BLAQUE

Copyright 2018 BlaQue
Published by:
Fade 2 BlaQue Ink LLC
Washington, DC
www.pinkangelpublications.com

All rights reserved. Without limiting the rights under copyright reserved above. No part of this book may be reproduced, stored in or introduced into a retrieval system, or transmitted, in any form or by any means (electronic, mechanical, photocopying, recording, or otherwise), without prior written consent from both the author, and publisher Pink Angel Publications, except brief quotes used in reviews.

This work is a work of fiction. It is not meant to depict, portray, or represent any particular real person. All the characters, incidents, and dialogues are the product of the author's imagination and are not to be construed as real. Any references or similarities to actual events, entities, real people, living or dead, or to real locales are intended to give the novel a sense of reality. Any similarity in other names, characters, entities, places and incidents is entirely coincidental.

This book is licensed for your personal enjoyment only. This book may not be re-sold or given away to other people. If you would like to share this book with another person, please purchase an additional copy for each recipient. Thank you for respecting the hard work of this author/publisher.

Editing: Fade 2 BlaQue Ink

Formatting: GhostwriterInc @ Ghostwriterinc2016@gmail.com

BLAQUE

Dirty
DNA 2

CHAPTER ONE

Chuck Brown and the Soul Searchers

"Bustin' Loose"

NiQue

"Push baby. You're doing great!" Dread said. He was standing on the side of my hospital bed like a cheerleader who was serious about their role. The only things missing were the bull horn and the pom-poms. I could barely understand shit he was saying. I really wanted him to shut the fuck up and let me concentrate on getting the fucking baby out of me.

We were in Washington Hospital Center, and I was giving birth to our daughter. Dread was amped up about the baby. That is the only reason I didn't kill it in the first place when I found out I was pregnant. Having a baby was not on the agenda as far as I was concerned.

The whole pregnancy has been a nightmare. I can't believe people do this shit more than once. There was no way I was going to let this nigga get me pregnant again. As far as I was concerned, they could pull out my whole womb and give it to someone who wanted to have babies.

There were nurses running in and out of the room and they were all starting to get on my damn nerves. White jackets and two pieced cotton uniforms make me uneasy. I hated being in the hospital. It didn't matter why I was there; I just didn't want to be there. I would rather have this kid on a park bench without all the hoopla, at least then I wouldn't have to be near all those damn doctors. Having doctors around meant me running the

3

risk of people finding out what was really up with me, and I didn't want any of their asses all up in my business!

"Ms. Watkins you are almost there," the nurse said without taking her eyes off my chart.

She was between my legs, looking at God knows what, and I wanted her to do something other than talk about, "almost being there." I wanted this shit to be done and over with! The doctor walked in, and the nurse who had taken up residence between my legs moved over so he could move into her spot.

"Ms. Watkins are you ready to have your baby?" he asked.

That was a stupid ass question. Of course, I was ready! I was ready to have my body back. I was sick of a baby stealing all of my attention and invading my space. I nodded my head and hoped he wouldn't ask any more dumb ass questions. The doctor started ordering me to bear down and push.

It was about damn time too!

I took a deep breath and pushed while Dread and one of the nurses held my legs up; damn near pinned to my chest. Not only was the baby an unexpected monkey wrench to my plans, but it was fucking with my comfort level as well. I screamed from the intense pain as the baby tore at my insides on its way out. It felt like the little bitch was tearing my insides apart.

"Ms. Watkins, the baby's head is almost out," the doctor said.

Fire was ripping through my pussy, at least that's how it felt. I just don't see how people could say giving birth is a beautiful thing. There was nothing beautiful about the experience at all for me. You get fat and wobble. People always want to touch your stomach—even strangers. You're moody and emotional and you have to deal with nine months of being poked and prodded by doctors who constantly tell you what to do, eat, wear, and they even have the nerve to tell you how to sleep! *What kind of shit is that?* Then you have to go through the pain! And that shit ain't no joke.

DNA 2

I decided that I would pay—whoever I had to—to tie my tubes. Hell, they could not only tie them, but burn them and bury those bitches in a shallow grave as far as I was concerned. There was no way I was subjecting myself to that kind of excruciating pain ever again; all that, "having babies" shit was for the birds.

After four more minutes of pushing, little YaSheema Nicole Evans was born. She weighed eight pounds and nine ounces. She had a head full of curly reddish-brown hair and was the spitting image of Dread. I was so exhausted from all the work I had put in that I didn't even want to hold her. No bonding moment for us. I was just so damn happy the whole ordeal was over and I could move on to my next mission, my wedding.

Since we found out we were having a baby, we had put the wedding plans on hold. Sure, I wanted to get married, but I didn't want to walk down the aisle fat and out of shape. That shit ain't cute no matter how you slice it. When I saw my baby's face for the first time, I didn't react like other new mothers who cooed and want to love up on their babies. I wanted her out of my sight and out of my way. Dread, on the other hand, was taking pictures and holding her every chance he got. I thought it was kind of sickening. No one was paying me any mind, and secretly that was pissing me off even more.

The only thing good about the entire pregnancy was the fact that Dread catered to my every need. Not to mention, the sex was off the hook; when we had sex that is. I already had plans for when I got out of this hospital! I was going through withdrawals from not being able to smoke weed and drink, but the fact that I couldn't pop a pill was killing me. I had been trying to keep my secret under wraps without self-medicating, and it took a lot of concentration, on my part, not to let on that Pajay was lurking around inside my head. It was easy to keep her under control as long as I had Xtasy coursing through my system. Some days were tougher than others in making sure she stayed in check.

I was grateful that Dread had been on the road promoting his upcoming album, so I was free to let Pajay do her own thing. No one knew I was fighting a never-ending battle with her and I was doing my best to keep her from getting us killed. Dread had insisted that he come back to DC for the last month of the pregnancy, so he wouldn't miss the birth. Before he had left, we had purchased a home in Laurel, Maryland. Neither one of us wanted to live in the city any more after all that had happened. Plus, with his growing success, we would have people in our business 24/7 if we hadn't moved.

I tell you one thing though; I was getting sick of Detective Gatsby on my ass about YaYa. I knew that if he kept pressing us out, I was going to have Pajay end his life fast, just so we could have some peace of mind. He was hell-bent on finding out who had killed that selfish bitch YaYa, and I was sick of everything being about her! Even in death, it was all about her!

I had to act like I was normal for two more days until they released us from the hospital and then I could call my man Tye, who always hooked me up with the triple stack Xtasy pills for a cheap price. Once I could get my hands on what I needed, I could try and deal with being a mother. There was no way I could be a mother, soon-to-be wife, and deal with Pajay, all while being sober. That shit was damn near impossible without having my pills to keep Pajay in check and keep people from finding out how fucked up I really could be.

CHAPTER TWO

DJ Flexx

"Southeast Anthem"

Neko

It has been a year since my sister, YaYa, was murdered. Even though she and I hadn't known each other very long, I loved her unconditionally; flaws and all. She had more flaws than I cared to count, but she had a special place in my heart.

Since the day my mother, Christa, introduced us, YaYa was my heart. She had taken me into her home and welcomed me into the family with open arms. She gave me the family I always dreamed of having; rich and powerful. My father, Darnell, was a notorious drug dealer in DC and he had it all. I had come up big time by connecting with my birth father and my sister. I had gone from literally living on the streets with my crack head mother, to living in the lap of luxury with my father and sister; virtually overnight.

So much shit had happened after the day YaYa and I met that I knew our meeting was both a gift and a curse. From the disappearance of our mother, to the death of everyone who seemed to come in contact with her, YaYa seemed marked. The more time that passes, the more I suspect YaYa had something to do with my mother's disappearance. If my sister knew about what happened to my mother, she never let on about it.

It was like death followed my sister. It didn't matter to me though. She always treated me good; and all I wanted was for us to make it out of the city alive. Funny thing is, after YaYa died the killing seemed to stop. Whoever was hunting her and the rest of my family got who they were after and then they just ceased. They targeted their prey and then they went away quietly. Pajay, the mystery person who had supposedly stalked my father and sister, just seemed to disappear off the map. Hell, she was never really on the map because I didn't know who she was or what she looked like. There were no records of her, so the police didn't look into her being a suspect. It was like none of it ever happened. I couldn't be sure if she even existed.

The police had found my mother's body a few months back. She was found by a bunch of patrons who were enjoying a cruise up the Potomac River on the *Spirit of Washington*. When they found Christa's body, I really felt lost. I was hoping against all odds that she was out there somewhere alive; even if she was never really a mother in the first place. It was like I was the parent and she was the child. Now I was all alone trying to cope with the shit I had witnessed in the short period of time I had been united with my long-lost family.

After YaSheema died, the money my father left her was then left to me since I was the last surviving relative to come forward. Some people thought that the money would make me happy. In all actuality it just made me bitter. I knew that money was a part of the reason my sister was dead. Had we not been waiting around for that money, we could have left town. Whoever the mystery person was who was haunting her would have never caught up to her and she would still be alive.

Although I didn't mention it to anyone, I had the sinking feeling that NiQue knew more than she was letting on too. I think she was afraid to tell what she knew. Right after they found YaYa's body, she started fucking with that nigga, Dread. I felt like that shit was tacky and dangerous. He had come between NiQue and YaYa and that caused some obvious friction between the two of them. Now that nigga Dread was a different matter! I think that nigga knew what happened to my sister. It was too fucking convenient that as soon as he found out my sister was knocked up with *his* baby, that's when she went missing.

He kept claiming that he didn't have anything to do with it. NiQue came with some bullshit story about being with him when he found the letter that YaSheema supposedly left at his house. It's all just too suspect to me. They are sticking to their story that they had found out YaYa was pregnant via the letter. Since NiQue and YaSheema were like family, the police believed NiQue. They said Dread's alibi was air-tight. I didn't know who was more foolish, NiQue for sticking by that dude, or the police for believing that lame ass story!

Only one person believed that there was more to it than we could see with the naked eye. That detective, the one who hunted me for the death of my father and the first attempt on Oscar's life, believed that Dread had something to do with it. He and I had called a truce so that we could catch whoever was responsible for turning my world upside down. I guess Detective Gatsby felt like he could have done more to protect YaSheema. He was always two steps behind whoever committed the crimes.

I tried to put what I could of my life together again little by little. I was always left behind to pick up the pieces. I am just grateful that life has finally returned to normal for me; or at least as normal as it could be after all of the shit that went down. For a long time I wondered if I was destined for a lifetime of tragic shit going on. I have been trying to keep my nose clean and stay out of trouble. I don't want any static. I have been laying low and waiting until someone talks. Someone is bound to run their mouth about the shit. The murders were too high profiled for niggas to keep quiet. When niggas get comfortable, they get sloppy.

I don't know what made me stay in DC after I buried my sister. I then had to cremate what was left of my mother. A nigga could never catch a fucking break except for the fact that a young nigga was rich! I took the money Pops left me and YaYa and opened up a detailing shop and started flipping that shit. I remembered one of the last conversations YaYa and I had before she died. We discussed what we would do with the money so we could try and fly right and not have to do what our father did to survive. I even have a little thing going with that broad Pinky. I am sure if YaYa were here she would not have approved of it, but shorty is thorough. Pinky got a lot of shit with her, but she holds her own, and don't be trying to involve a nigga in her shit. I know her line of work ain't what you would call, "normal," but it was no different than any of my family members who formerly employed her.

Pinky knew how to treat a nigga. She knew how to cook, clean, and fuck! She kept to herself and stayed out of a nigga's way when he ain't want to be bothered. She made her own ends and I had to admit I felt safe around her. She was good with her hands and she was mean with her Nina. She proved that the first day I met shorty over a year ago. My introduction to Pinky was wild, but her lifestyle is much wilder. I ran into Pinky at YaYa's funeral. She stayed in the back of the funeral home. I noticed her when we were filing out to head to the cemetery. I could never forget her and those hot pink dread locks. She was the only person at the funeral who was daring enough to wear hot pink to a funeral. You had no choice but to take notice of her. The whole suit hugged her womanly curves just right.

Pinky was the kind of woman that was etched in a nigga's mind forever. That bitch was built like Nicki Minaj without all that surgery shit. She is 100% natural! Someone in the heavens was rooting for us fellas, because she was bad as shit. She has the perkiest titties and the juiciest round ass. Her face was sweet and as angelic as a teenager. She was pushing thirty and had big, brown doe eyes, and cute little freckles that made her look harmless and youthful. Her looks were only for show. They were meant to throw a nigga off his guard.

Dirty
DNA 2

There was nothing angelic about her though. The only thing she was sweet on was me and my dick; and even when we would fuck, I wondered what made her tick. She was so mysterious. I would find myself trying to concentrate on fucking her, and my mind would drift off into if she would kill me if she had the chance. All she did was "work," which consisted of taking clean up jobs niggas contracted her for. She was a paid, trained, killer! She also danced at *The Stadium Club* to keep what she really did under wraps. Hell, she probably would have preferred it if I didn't know about any of the shit she did. Had I not been on the scene when she finished a job for YaSheema before she died, I might not have ever known what she really did for a living. She only pulled about two hits a month; and she would chill, shaking her ass, smoking weed and riding on her motorcycle the rest of the time.

Our shit was good though. She ain't want too much from me; and I ain't want anything from her. We vibed like that. I didn't ask her too many questions and she didn't ask me shit either. I liked it that way because I didn't want to get too attached to anyone else and have them turn up missing or dead.

Sometimes, when I didn't hear from Pinky for a few days, I would find myself worrying about her, and then like a light switch, I would turn off my feelings. I guess I really was my father's son. I kept Pinky around in case I needed to employ her in the event I ever found out the niggas who did that shit to my family. I would gladly pay her to handle their asses; and I knew she would charge me for it whether we were sexing or not. I couldn't blame her though. Business is business. I expected the service, and she would expect to be paid. Fair is fair! I wasn't going to knock baby girl's hustle!

I have been trying to keep my mind focused on making money. I used to see NiQue all the time until she and that nigga Dread moved out of the city. We talk, but not often because I don't like the fact that she is all up in that dude's face. I felt betrayed when she told me she was pregnant with his baby, and then she dropped a bombshell on me by telling me they were getting married. I couldn't believe she even wanted me to give her away. I thought she had lost her fucking mind!

There was no way I was giving her away in a wedding I didn't approve of, let alone that she was marrying a nigga I suspected of foul play against my sister. She would have to find someone else to do the honors because I didn't even know if I was gonna go to the wedding or not. They definitely didn't have my blessings, and I damn sure wasn't going to pretend I was happy about their union.

Dirty
DNA 2

CHAPTER THREE
Backyard Band (BYB)
"Everyone Falls in Love"
Detective Gatsby

I could barely see the old worn desk that sat beneath piles of paper, stacks of folders and evidence I had been studying that I hadn't returned to the evidence room. Containers of partially consumed food and bottles of soft drinks that I didn't bother to toss into the trash cluttered the room. I had begun to live in my little match box of an office; running from my own nightmares and trying not to let the "what-ifs" clog my already fucked up mind.

Too many cases of my cases were falling by the wayside and the chief wasn't too pleased with my work performance lately. I was obsessed with catching a killer who couldn't be caught. The last time I felt that way about a case, I ended up in mental hospital; only to get out and murder my own mother and father. There was no way I was trying to see inside of the booby hatch again.

The Clayton-Reynolds case had grown cold long ago, but I wouldn't let it go. I kept running into dead ends and I was running out of leads. I knew there was something I was missing, but I could not put my finger on it. There was one piece to the puzzle and I swore the piece missing was Ronald Dread Evans. I knew I was borderline obsessed; but I couldn't help it! Thoughts of breaking the case wide open consumed me. I couldn't shake the guilt I felt for not keeping YaSheema alive. Had I done just a little more, had I held Ms. Clayton for questioning when I started to bring her in, maybe she would be alive.

I took a sip of my coffee from earlier in the day. It was cold, and rather disgusting, but it was the only thing I trusted to drink that was on my desk. Everything else was suspect. I pulled out the pictures of YaSheema Clayton from the folder that sat on top of the enormous pile of stuff on my desk. This is how it started every time. I would pull out the pictures and stare at them, vowing to catch the killer or killers that seemed rather elusive.

A whole year had gone by since YaSheema's body turned up in Blue Plaines, and there had been no break in the case. The shit had grown cold and I was still trying to play a never-ending game of "who done it." I knew I had better either let it go, or fuck around and lose my job trying to chase down the bastards who had sliced, diced, and gunned down her whole family with the exception of her brother, her best friend and the boyfriend.

When the bodies started dropping in the young girl's circle I thought she was the one behind the hits, until she turned up missing. I didn't know who was telling the truth and who was covering for whom. I knew one thing; whoever took out almost everyone close to her was playing for keeps; and the fact that they were still out there was playing on my sanity. I needed closure on the case; not just for YaSheema, but also for the people she left behind that cared about her. She deserved justice for all the shit she had been taken through before she died. Maybe I was more involved in her case than I should be simply because I felt guilty for not being able to save my own family. I didn't give a rat's ass how many new cases were dropped on my desk; I always made the Clayton-Reynolds case a high priority.

Dirty

DNA 2

CHAPTER FOUR

Junkyard Band (JYB)

"Sardines"

Dread

I was so excited that we were finally bringing our baby girl
home. I wasn't so sure NiQue was happy about it though. Don't
get me wrong, she seemed happy to be coming home, but she
was acting like if she could have left our daughter in the hospital
she would have. No questions asked. I had read about that postpartum depression shit in some of the baby books I had bought
her. She barely read the titles of those muthafuckers. They were
taking up space on coffee tables, being used as coasters, or
discarded altogether. It seemed like once she found out she was
pregnant she started to change. I didn't know who the fuck she
was half-the-time and she was nowhere to be found the other
half of the time. NiQue was always real moody and she acted
like she didn't want me around. She seemed happiest when I was
out on tour and she wasn't thrilled about having to be a parent.
Some days I would catch her mumbling to herself.

I thought once she moved out of the city and away from the
stares of the people accusing us of some shit we ain't do, maybe
she would return to normal. She was the one who suggested we
move to Laurel. I told her I didn't think it was a good idea if we
spent that kind of money on a house so far from my studio in
the city, but she insisted we leave. She even gave up more than
half of the down payment on the million-dollar home. I didn't
question her behavior. I just went along with her moves to make
her comfortable. I felt like I owed her that for keeping that Fed,

Detective Gatsby, off my back. Bad publicity was something I didn't need.

All I wanted to do was the same old shit I was doing before meeting her or YaSheema. I wanted to make my music. That was the decision I was fighting before YaYa turned up missing. For me, all a nigga wanted to do was smoke and do the music thing. Those were my only priorities. I keep blaming myself for not just telling YaYa I would go with her when she asked. Had I just told her what I was thinking when I had the chance, she might be alive today. I regret not just being straight up with her off the break. Now she and the baby are gone.

I felt like I was being given a second chance. I thought it was a sign from God to make my wrongs right. I wasn't chasing females and trying to fuck anything moving that wanted to give me some pussy. I was trying to be different from what I had been in my past. That shit was easier said than done. In the beginning, I felt like fucking with NiQue would always give me a small piece of YaSheema to remember. I'm starting to think that is the furthest thing from the truth. My career is going great, as far as my home life, not so much.

CHAPTER FIVE

Lil Benny and the Masters

"Cat in the Hat"

Neko

I was just closing up the shop for the night. We always made a killing on the first and the fithteenth of the month. Paydays always gave us the best benefits. This first was no exception to the norm. All that good government money from all the "baby mommas"—doing their baby daddies a solid by hooking up their rides—was much appreciated by me. All day long we were packed and the money on the first stayed flowing.

I was sitting in my office that was housed in the back of the shop. I was smoking a blunt and kicking it with my man Shadow. The *NBA* Play-offs were on and I had my money on OKC to take home the ring.

"Nigga, I don't give a fuck who wins this shit. The *Lakers* ain't make it to the play-offs." Shadow said.

He knew I had money on the game with a few niggas in the shop, and the way it was looking I was going to lose my money. It was some short shit, but a nigga hates to lose money.

"You know that ole, soggy pamper-wearing, LeBron is going to cry his way to a ring." He laughed.

"Man, you know the Refs were paid to make sure that nigga put a ring on it. Ole, Beyonce-song singing-ass nigga." I added cracking up laughing.

The weed had us high as shit, and we couldn't figure out if we were coming or going. As we tried to decide if we should make a move or not, there was a knock on my office door and Natalie, my receptionist, stuck her head in to announce I had a visitor. I nodded my head to let her know to let my guest in. She stepped aside, and in walked NiQue. *Damn she looked good too!* The baby weight went to all the right places. I knew I wasn't crazy either because I heard Shadow gulp hard. Natalie gave NiQue a once over again, wrinkled her lips as if to say, "whatever" and asked me in a vicious tone was there anything else she could do for me before she left for the night.

I knew Natalie would react like that because that crazy Jamaican bitch was stuck on a young nigga. I fuck her every now and again off the late night, and she has been acting like she is my girl. I always kept baby girl on reserve for those times when Pinky had jobs to do out of town or when she was on her period. Natalie would speak that Patois shit and find her thick ass hips and healthy thighs on my dick when I couldn't get any pussy from Pinky.

"Naw, baby I'm good." I said to Natalie while never taking my eyes off of NiQue.

Natalie slammed the door behind her and I eyed NiQue from head to toe. She looked different. She was almost pulsating with sexiness. I had never looked at her like that before, but something about the way her ass sat up in her painted-on jeans made my dick jump.

"Damn, Neko! Where have you been hiding her?" Shadow said, standing to get a formal introduction.

"Nigga fall back…this is NiQue. She is like family." I said, trying to recover from staring at her too long. I knew it was obvious that I had been caught off guard by her appearance.

NiQue always looked good; that was a given, but the way she looked after dropping that baby put me in the mind of Faith after Biggie got her pregnant. NiQue was thick in all the right places, but not "too thick." Her thickness was in her hips, and her breasts were full and inviting.

"I am trying to make her a part of my family too! She can be my next baby momma!" Shadow said laughing but meaning every word he said. That nigga already had five kids and three baby mommas. He was a *Maury Show* waiting to happen.

"Let me holla' at my folks." I said ushering Shadow out the door.

NiQue stood by the desk and there was an awkward silence between us. I hadn't talked to her much since I found out about the baby and the wedding. I still had my suspicions about her man. She sashayed over to where I stood and hugged me.

"How have you been Neko?"

"I've been coolin'." I said trying not to look at her lustfully.

"That's good. I haven't heard from you. I got to thinking about you and I thought I would pay you a visit," she said.

"I've been trying to stay focused on making this shop work." I said trying to refocus my attention on anything other than her cleavage which was spilling out of her tight blouse. I felt almost dirty looking at NiQue with lustful eyes, and I didn't want her to see that she was making me feel uneasy. She had taken a seat in the spot where Shadow had once been. I could feel her waiting on me to say something else.

"I had the baby," she said breaking the silence.

"I kind of figured that. You ain't walking around looking like you swallowed a watermelon whole." I said jokingly. "I would have thought you would bring here to meet her uncle Neko."

"She is with her father. That is where she is most of the time. I am trying to get adjusted to having a baby. You know, it's a lot to deal with, although I am trying." she said, sounding like she was trying to convince herself more than me.

"Well, they say babies are a lot of work. I guess that is why I don't have any yet, and it may be a long time before I jump out there and have any."

"You know, you never responded to the wedding invitation. I know you said you didn't think you could commit to giving me away at the wedding, but are you going to at least come?" she asked.

I took a seat across from her behind my desk and stared at her like she had lost her mind. Every time we spoke it was about the fucking wedding and what part I would be playing in it.

"NiQue, I already told you, I don't approve of you marrying that nigga. After all that has happened, I just can't see myself being there, joining in on your wedded bliss when I ain't even sure if that nigga should be walking the streets a free man, let alone down an aisle with my family. I fight the urge to put a slug through his dome every night."

I had gone too far. I hadn't meant to let that last part slip out, but it did. We really didn't have any proof that Dread was connected in YaYa's death, so I should have kept that part to myself. There was just something tugging at me, telling me there was more than meets the eye when it came to Dread.

I looked at NiQue and she looked a little sad that I had not changed my mind about even attending the wedding. Her eyes were filled with disappointment. I wanted to be there to support the last person on earth that I had some kind of connection too, but I couldn't condone her marrying Dread. I couldn't see handing her over to the devil with no regard.

"I understand. I know in time you will see that he didn't have anything to do with what happened to YaYa. I was with him when he found out she was pregnant. I don't know why you don't believe him. As a matter of fact, I don't know why you don't believe me," she said sadly.

I don't know why I felt like everything out of her mouth was all an act for my benefit, but I was unmoved by it all.

"NiQue, I will make it to the wedding. Giving you away...I am not sure about that part. Let me think on it. I will let you know," I said.

DNA 2

NiQue smiled at the idea of me hopefully walking her down the aisle. I couldn't front. I did want to have a relationship with NiQue and the baby, but all that socializing with Dread was out!

She stood to leave and I made my way around the desk so I could walk her out to the front of the shop.

"Oh, there was another reason for my visit. I almost forgot. I am looking to get into some business ventures. I have been kind of strapped for cash since we bought the house and had the baby. I was wondering if you knew anything about where I could get my hands on some powder and pills at wholesale prices." She asked like she was asking if she could borrow five dollars.

"Naw, I don't know anything about any of that. You know that was all of Pop and YaYa's arena. I try to stay away from shit like that." I said. I had my shit with me, but I wasn't going to involve her or anyone else in it. I tried to keep my street business quiet. The less people who knew anything about it, the better off I would be.

"Is there anything I can get for you? I can give you some money if you need it. I thought with your man being on tour, you should have plenty of paper stacked." I said.

I was concerned that Dread was keeping her around, but not taking care of her the way she needed to be taken care of.

"I have a little something put away, but I like watching my money grow you know!" she said.

She winked at me and left out of the building. I watched her as she got into her brand-new Mercedes Benz SLS AMG. I couldn't help but wonder where she would put a baby in that car being that it was a two-seater. I admired the paint job. It was money green with flecks of gold. I guess her man wasn't doing too badly if he had her pushing that Benz. I closed and locked the door to the shop and turned the sign to read, *"CLOSED."*

When I started to head towards the back of the shop where my office was located, Shadow popped out of the waiting area, snacking on chips from the vending machine.

"Damn nigga, announce yourself!" I said. I was startled because I had forgotten that he was still in the building.

"What? I thought we were going out or something. Maybe hit up the strip club. You never know, you might find the future Mrs." he said, laughing while stuffing his mouth full of chips.

"Aight let me finish closing up and maybe we can hit up *Proud Mary's* on the waterfront." I said chuckling. I shouldn't have had to close up my own shop, but Natalie had a serious case of the ass and a major attitude. Just to spite me, she most likely left right after NiQue walked in.

A couple hours later, Shadow and I found ourselves on the waterfront in Fort Washington, listening to the sounds of the female go-go band, Bella Donna. Proud Mary's was a quaint little spot right on the waterfront. It featured different bands every night of the week. The bar was small, but the food was good and the drinks were even better. The entertainment wasn't bad either. Shadow had found a table out on the deck, which was by pure luck because normally the place was standing room only. We were doing 1800 slammers, talking shit, and watching the bitches prance around in next to nothing.

"Man, you ain't got no swag!" Shadow said obviously feeling his liquor.

"Imma go to the big boy's room and imma show you what swag is. Just because you got them ole' pretty boy eyes don't mean shit." Shadow said as he stood to go handle his business. I laughed at him and watched as he disappeared in the crowd, smacking women on the ass along the way.

The waitress made her way back to the table and I ordered another round and some buffalo wings to feed the liquor. I couldn't help noticing her tight short shorts and tight tank top. Her nipples were as hard as glass from the late spring breeze.

"You like what you see?" she said while she was gathering up the empty glasses.

"I might." I said eyeing her plump ass.

"Good, because if the price is right you can see more!" she said licking her glossed lips in a suggestive way.

"I'm a big tipper." I challenged her.

"Good. I like my tips big. I get off in about forty-five minutes. Meet me in the front of the club." she said as she finished gathering up the rest of our empty glasses and headed to the bar to put in the order for the wings and drinks. I watched her back field in motion and couldn't help but stare. My concentration was broken when I noticed Shadow making his way back to the table with a vexed look on his face.

"What happened, you took a shit and they ran out of paper?" I said fucking with him.

"Naw. I saw that little shorty from your shop, NiQue. I tried to holler at her and she looked at me like she ain't know who I was. I even called her by her name and she told me I had the wrong person. Baby girl looked confused as hell." he said taking a seat.

"Maybe she didn't care about who you were!" I said laughing at him.

"I called her by her name and she said that wasn't her name." Shadow said looking confused.

"Maybe it wasn't her."

"She was wearing the same shit from when she visited the shop. Maybe she is drunk or something. I could never forget an ass like that." he said laughing and dismissing my comment.

The waitress came back to the table with the drinks, breaking up the conversation. Shadow turned his attention to her and forgot all about his supposed encounter with NiQue. We sat out on the deck until I saw shorty motion towards her wrist letting me know it was time for her to get off.

I told Shadow I would catch up with him later, and then made my way to the front of the club just in time to see a Mercedes SLS AMG, the exact same color as NiQue's, pulling out of the parking lot. I knew it had to be her because there weren't too many folks pushing that kind of car, especially not in that color. That color was custom and I am sure the odds of another person having it was next to none.

Ms. Waitress walked up on me and I forgot all about the car and NiQue. Thoughts of fucking Ms. Waitress on the top floor of some swanky ass hotel while she put um' on the glass entered my mind.

"You ready to spend?" she said seductively.

"Yeah, a nigga got some extra ends." I said as we walked to the car, arm in arm, like we were old lovers.

Dirty
DNA 2

CHAPTER SIX

Pure Elegance

"One Leg Up"

Dread

I don't know where NiQue slipped off to. She had been pulling
disappearing acts a lot lately and I was getting sick of it! She
knew I had a show, and yet she darted off and I hadn't seen her
for hours. I had just laid the baby down for the night. I hated to
leave YaSheema here with the nanny again, but I didn't really
have a choice. I could not miss my show.

Funny thing is, Joseah, the nanny and I were talking earlier
and she let me know that NiQue had been pulling the same shit
with her too. NiQue would claim to be running to the store and
get ghost for hours. Not to mention, when she would come back
she would be "different." I tried to get Joseah to elaborate on
what she meant by, "different" but she wouldn't though. She
just told me, in her Spanish accent, that she didn't want any
trouble, but that I had better watch my back because NiQue
couldn't be trusted and may have been sneaky.

I kissed the baby on her forehead and pulled her door shut
behind me; careful not to disturb her. I only had about thirty
minutes to get myself ready and head out so I wouldn't be late. I
wanted to talk to NiQue before I left because I would be flying
out in the morning to a gig in Atlanta. I was supposed to be
performing at this year's A3C festival as one of the DMV's
hottest up and coming performers. Once again, NiQue was
gone, and I doubted if I would see her before I left in the
morning.

BLAQUE

Crack had booked me for a performance for some bitch's birthday party at the Stadium Club. These days I was charging ten thousand a show, and to keep up with NiQue's spending habits, I would most likely have to up my fee again. She was blowing through money like it was water.

I hurried myself to the master bedroom and showered. I pulled out a fresh pair of white linen pants and a pink *Hugo Boss* polo. The broad I was performing for requested everyone be in those specific colors or else I would not be wearing anything pink. If she wasn't paying I wouldn't be caught dead in a pink shirt. I splashed on some *Hugo Boss* cologne, dressed, and hurried to find Joseah. I let her know that I was leaving and that I would be leaving again in the morning. I could tell she wasn't happy about both me and NiQue always being on the go, but there was nothing I could do about it. I quickly wrote her a check for a thousand dollars which was two hundred more than I normally paid her per week. She took the check from my hands and went about her business making bottles and washing the baby's clothes. Any reservations she had about me leaving were gone with the extra ends she received.

I felt bad being away from baby YaSheema, but I had money to make. I left the house and headed into the city to the studio to meet up with the rest of the guys before we were to head to the club. Once I got to Cap Citi Entertainment Studios I saw Crack, and a few others, standing outside waiting in front of the limos that were supposed to take us to the party.

"Wassup Dread?" Crack said when I pulled up beside them.

"You know, same old shit." I said out of the window while nodding to my niggas from the Cap; Vito, Butta, Coogi, Fats and NATO.

They all got into their respective cars and drove to the club. When we pulled up we could tell the inside was packed. There were people all over the place in pink and white, waiting to get inside. The suburban car doors that held our security staff swung open, and Big Jeff, Bilbo and our head of security, Ox; all got out and made their way to our cars to usher us inside.

When we started making our way to the front, you could hear people screaming and chanting my name. That shit would never get old for me. All my life I wanted to make music people would feel, and now I was doing just what I had set out to do. Once we were inside, Crack, Ox, and I, made our way to the back of the club, while the rest of the fellas headed to our VIP section. I was supposed to be performing three songs and the birthday girl, who was some high-paid stripper bitch named Pinky, requested that I perform my hit song, "Make It Drop" while she performed on the stage. I didn't care what she did, as long as she was paying.

"I'm going to see if I can find Pinky." Crack said. He left the dressing room, and Ox and I blazed a J of loud. I sipped on a *Corona*. I tried not to drink before I had a show. I liked to stay on my toes and stay professional at all times. Smoking was another situation. I did that any and every day of the week so that shit didn't matter.

After about ten minutes, Crack came back, followed by a brick-house chick with an ass so phat she could turn a gay nigga straight. She was dressed in a white dress that left little to the imagination. The dress barely covered her ass. You could clearly see her hot pink thong and bikini top through the thin fabric. Hot pink *Red Bottoms* pulled her outfit together, and she topped it all off by sporting pink dreads that were pinned up in a neat, curly Mohawk.

"Hi, I'm Pinky. I am so glad you could make it." she said while extending her hand to shake mine.

"Nice to meet you baby girl. Happy birthday. It looks like you have one hell of a turn out." I said referring to all of the folks inside and outside the club.

"Yeah, I don't do anything unless I do it big." she said smiling.

BLAQUE

Her voice was like honey and she smelled just as sweet. I could feel my dick rising to attention just looking at her. I hadn't had any pussy in over three months. NiQue was holding out on me and I was getting tired of begging her for pussy that was supposed to belong to me.

Pinky walked further into the dressing room and proceeded to spread lines of coke on the dressing table. I watched her ass jiggle underneath the dress she struggled to keep from rising up over her creamy unblemished behind. She took a seat in front of the drug, rolled up a hundred dollar bill and snorted a line. Once she was finished, she turned to offer us some. We all declined her offer. She shrugged her shoulders and tooted the rest of the lines. Pinky sniffed a couple of times, wiped her nose and stood up.

"I guess it's show time." she said and we all left the room.

We followed her to the back entrance of the stage. She was standing so close to me I could feel her body radiating heat. The lights dimmed throughout the club and the DJ was announcing Pinky to the stage. There were two spotlights centered in the middle of the stage that illuminated a pole that I am sure had seen better days.

"That's your marker on the stage." she said pointing to the place where the light shone in white.

"The other one is mine. Wait until the beat for Make It Drop comes on and make your way to your marker and I got the rest," she instructed. Before she made her way onto the stage, she adjusted herself in her dress again and then strutted onto the stage. The crowd began to go wild at just the sight of her.

"I have a very special surprise for you all tonight! You all could have been anywhere else in the world, but you decided to help me celebrate my birthday. DMV are you ready?" Pinky announced into the mic she had been given by the infamous DJ Khalil when she took the stage.

28

DNA 2

From all the extras around the joint and the free-flowing party favors being given to the people in attendance, I knew Pinky had spent upwards of about one hundred thousand dollars to put the party together. I was silently kicking myself for not charging her more for me to perform. I was more than sure she could afford it. The song, "Novacane" by Frank Ocean came blasting through the huge speakers and Pinky handed the mic back to DJ Khalil.

Watching her in motion reminded me of a cat by the way she moved across the stage. Each step she took seemed to move to the rhythm pulsating through the speakers and to say I was captivated by her was an understatement. She turned her back to her audience and made her ass jiggle just enough for the fabric to rise on her dress, exposing the pink thong.

The beat changed up and I heard my queue. I made my way to the stage and started to perform my song and Pinky went wild. She swung her long legs around the pole and slid down it and into a split once she hit the floor. She got up from the floor, walked over to me, and started gyrating and dancing all on me. I was mesmerized to say the least. Her movements were hypnotic, reminiscent of a mixture of that Latino chick Shakira and Beyonce all rolled into one. As I watched her body pulsate instinctively to the music, I couldn't help but think of the effects of throwing a stone in a calm lake and watching it ripple. That's how she moved; melodic and erotic.

The crowd was going crazy. They were throwing money by the fistfuls onto the stage. As I watched the crowd making it rain on her, I knew how she was able to pay me without a problem. If she made money like that every night, there was no way her pockets would be anything other than stacked. What amazed me even more than the amount of money niggas and bitches were throwing on the stage at her was that fact that she hadn't even gotten totally naked yet. She was still in her dress, but it was hiked above her waist while she was twerking her coke bottle hips.

The song changed up again and my lyrics to, "Whatever Happens Here" ripped through the speakers. Pinky seductively came out of her dress and gave one hell of a strip tease. She unfastened the straps on her bikini top and let her bosom fall free. She pranced around the stage performing movements that forced onlookers to sit and stare. I tried to keep up with her movements and perform without letting on that I would much rather be in the audience enjoying the show than being a part of it.

I made it through the song and there was a pause in the music. DJ Khalil was filling in the gaps as a team of guys brought out a blow-up pool onto the stage. It looked like it was full of strawberry milk, but I couldn't make out what was actually inside the baby pool. I was so entranced in everything happening around me that I almost missed Pinky giving me my props on the stage. I snapped back to reality and saw all of my boys heading to the stage. They were followed by several fine ass females that all lined up on the stage as well. I had no idea what Pinky had in store but shit just got interesting.

The same guys who had brought the pool out with the pink substance in it were wheeling out a cart with different flavors of ice cream toppings. There were cans of whipped cream, chocolate syrup, caramel syrup, strawberry syrup, nuts, cherries, sprinkles and something that looked like butterscotch. I found out real fast what was about to happen next. Pinky announced her next set.

"Fuck having a birthday cake. Imma let these horny mutha fuckas turn yours truly into a human sundae!" she yelled into the mic.

The crowd roared with excitement. The lights dimmed again. I was preparing to do my last song when Coogi snatched the mic from me and Pinky grabbed my hands. She pulled me towards the toppings on the cart.

"I think our very special guest should do the honors." Pinky said while she snaked her way out of her thong. She stepped into the pool and stretched out in it. Her legs were spread wide eagle; exposing her neatly-waxed pussy. She inserted two fingers inside herself before another chick joined her in the pool.

Now I have seen a lot of shit in my travels on the road, but I have never seen any shit like that before. Vito urged me to take the chocolate syrup he was holding and be the first to use it on Pinky's naked body. Something deep down inside of me told me to decline and get the fuck out of there; but if the bitch was going to pay me to cover her body in toppings, then so be it. I would dump whatever she wanted me to on her as long as she was paying for it.

The music started again and Coogi's song, "Hood Star" floated through the air. That's when I knew the shit was all a set up. They knew I wasn't going to be performing all of my songs that night. I fought off the angel on my shoulder telling me not to get caught up in the nonsense, but I couldn't help it. This bitch was fine as fuck.

I heard DJ Khalil in the background saying, "This just went from a birthday party to a bachelor party!" he laughed as he told me congrats on my upcoming wedding. I could barely make out what he was saying because I was too busy coating Pinky, and the other bitches who had accompanied the Cap Citi Boys up on the stage, with *Hershey's* syrup. They were all over each other putting on a hell of a show in that little ass pool. The girls were licking the toppings off of one another. There was nothing but titties and ass and sweet sticky shit all over the place. The bitches were fingering, licking, and fucking each other with fierceness. The niggas in the audience were making it rain dead presidents all over the stage. There were bills big and small, raining down from every direction.

BLAQUE

When I tried to back away from the orgy in front of me, Pinky rose from the pool and asked me to follow her back to the dressing room. I was hoping she had my money so that I could get out of there before the shit happening on stage had a chance to ruin not only my soon-to-be marriage, but also my career. Scenarios like this one had a way of landing niggas in the tabloids and fucking up happy homes.

I took one more look at the festivities on the stage and against my better judgment, I exited, stage left, with Pinky. We didn't say one word to one another as we walked to the dressing room. The only noise that could be heard was the sound of Pinky's stilettos clicking, forcibly, against the wooden floor as we headed in the direction of the club that looked like it was reserved for "happy endings."

I was having a battle inside my head. I just wanted to get my money and get the fuck out of there before the "show" landed me in trouble. It was bad enough NiQue and I had barely said more than ten words to one another in the last three days, but there were also too many temptations lurking inside the club walls. I wanted to run from them, but I wanted to experience them as well. Once we were inside the confines of her private dressing room, Pinky grabbed a towel from the rack and headed into the bathroom. She was covered in all sorts of stuff from her performance and was going to take a shower to remove the evidence from the show.

"Are you coming?" she seductively asked as she peeked from behind the bathroom door.

"Coming where? I only want to get my money and then I am going to bounce. I am sure my wife is waiting on me to come home. I got to get it moving."

She stepped from the door that was concealing her naked body and a cloud of steam from the shower followed her.

"I think we both know you ain't married just yet. Even if you were married you would still do what you are about to do!

DNA 2

It's a man's nature. You all are visual creatures. That's what stimulates you." she said while making her way over to where I was planted next to the door.

Everything inside me said, *get the fuck out of there, and fast*. My mind and heart were screaming for me to leave. My dick, which was at full attention, was telling me to stay and see how warm, wet and tight her pussy was.

Pinky took my hand and led me to a chair where she had thrown her white dress and thong. She pushed my six-foot frame into the chair and began to straddle me. I knew she could tell from the bulge in my pants that I didn't want to leave. Not without fucking her. Slowly she gyrated her body across my lap. Veins, already engorged with blood, intensified, and my hardness thickened in strength. As her body moved, Pinky took one of my hands, which was still covered in syrup, and placed the pointer and middle fingers into her mouth. Seductively and intimately she sucked clean all of the gooey, sweet syrup from my fingers.

She had me in a trance. The way she made my fingers touch the back of her throat made my dick throb. The bitch had no type of gag reflex at all. I kept trying to think of any and everything unappealing; anything that would keep from saying fuck it and pull my dick out and fuck her like I knew she wanted me to.

She took my fingers out of her mouth and placed my hands on her breast and I could feel her nipples harden at my touch. Before I knew it, Pinky got up and unfastened my pants. She was watching me with careful eyes. She was waiting for me to object. I wanted to stop her, I really did. But the words, "Stop, No, and Don't" wouldn't make their way to my lips. She took my dick out of my pants and did just what the devil on my shoulder wanted the whole time. She parted her lips and took all of me in her mouth. This bitch was a pro with it too! She was sucking my dick like she loved a nigga and it felt amazing.

"Oh shit!" I moaned.

Her tongue snaked its way down the shaft as she sucked and immediately, I felt like I was in heaven. It had been a long time since I had anyone give me any head, and even longer since someone did it with so much enthusiasm. I fought the urge to cum with each stroke of her moist mouth. Any anxiety I felt about letting that shit go down was gone. I had silenced that little angel bitch on my shoulder.

I couldn't handle it anymore. "Get the fuck up and bend over!" I growled.

Pinky shot to her feet like lightening and bent her round ass over the chair. Forcefully I entered her from behind with every inch of my being. My body trembled with the first stroke. Her pussy was tight and hot. Just the way I liked it. I fucked her fast and hard. Pinky kept up with me thrust for thrust. She was throwing it back on me and I felt all my frustration and aggravation surging through me and gathering in one central location, the tip of my dick. I fucked her like I was mad at her and she loved every minute of it.

I forgot all about NiQue and whatever she was out in the streets doing. I forgot about my three-month-old daughter at home and all of the drama in my twisted world. There was nothing loving about the sex Pinky and I were having. It was angry and cold, but it felt so good to be taking out a year's worth of pain on someone without catching a charge.

"Nigga take this pussy like you own it! I'm about to cummmm!" she cried.

I felt her wetness dripping all over me with the smacking of her ass against my stomach. I couldn't hold it anymore, it was too late. The explosion had already happened while I was deep inside her walls. I pulled my dick out of her wet tunnel and finished cumming all over her ass and back.

Pinky stood upright with a satisfied grin on her face. She walked over to a desk that sat in the corner and opened it. Pulling out a thick, white envelope, she smiled again before handing it to me. I didn't need to open it. I knew it was my money. No words were spoken. She simply headed back to her bathroom and left me standing there like a trick. The guilt started to eat at me instantly. I knew I was fucked up for what I had just done and not to mention…I had fucked a stripper raw. I guess the devil had won after all.

BLAQUE

CHAPTER SEVEN

Rare Essence

"Overnight Scenario"

NiQue

I came home with what I needed to make it through the next few days.

"I can't believe you keep trying to force feed me this shit!" Pajay said angrily. She was mad that I was always trying to think of new ways to get rid of her.

Truth is, whenever she was around shit just didn't go right. Quite frankly, I was starting to get sick of her ass always doing shit that I had to explain later. She was always doing something to get "us" in trouble, and then when I needed her to help clean up the mess that she had made, she was nowhere to be found. If I could have my way, Pajay and I could go our separate ways and I wouldn't have any complaints about it.

"You might as well stop thinking of getting rid of me. I ain't going anywhere!" she taunted.

I wish I could just cut her out of the picture altogether, but there was no telling what she would do if I tried. Making my way to the kitchen, I poured myself a glass of orange juice and popped an Xtasy pill before chasing it with the cold juice. Natural juices had a way of making the *high* come faster and harder.

"I wish you would be quiet and let me think." I said to her.

I downed the rest of the juice and put the glass on the counter. Joseah walked in, catching me of guard and scaring me in the process. I damn near jumped across the room when I noticed she was there. My eyes searched hers, and I hoped she

37

hadn't caught me talking to Pajay again. The strange look on her face told me that she heard something. I just didn't know how much she had heard.

"Señorita Watkins, Señor Evans said he would be leaving in the morning. He said he has a show in Georgia. I checked on the baby and she is sleeping. Do chu need anything else before I go to bed?" She asked.

"No, that is all Joseah. Oh wait; did Mr. Evans say when he would be returning?" I questioned her. I didn't need any more surprises.

"Señor Evans said he will be in tonight and then he was leaving in the morning. He did not say when he would be coming back from Georgia. You no look so good. Can I get chu something?" she asked again.

I was secretly trying to see how much time I had to myself.

"No, thank you Joseah," I said.

She eyed me suspiciously and then left the kitchen. I swear she was talking shit under her breath as she walked away. I decided to let it go because as much as I hated to admit it, we needed her old ass. She kept the baby well taken care of and I definitely did not need or want to be a full-time mother. I was already trying to play mother to Pajay, who was constantly running wild. Once Joseah left the kitchen and I heard the door close to her room, Pajay spoke up.

"That smart-mouthed bitch is gonna catch it one day. I don't give a fuck what she thinks she does around here. We pay her to watch that bratty ass baby and nothing more. No one asked her for her fucking opinion. Chu no look so good!" she said mocking Joseah's broken English.

"Shhhhh, she might hear you!" I said in a hushed tone trying to quiet Pajay who seemed to be growing agitated.

"I don't care who hears me. I meant what the fuck I said. She better watch herself!" Pajay said.

I shook my head trying to ignore Pajay bitching in my ear like a bully. I made my way up the stairs and down the hallway towards my room. Stopping short of my intended destination, I decided to look in on the baby. As I walked in her room I could see her sleeping peacefully. She looked so beautiful. A sharp pain pierced my heart and I wished I could love her the way I was supposed to be loved; but Pajay was not going to let that happen without a fight. Instantly I was reminded of how I had to damn near beg Pajay to allow me to keep my own baby when I found out I was pregnant with her. Pajay wanted no parts of a baby and she tried everything in her power to keep me on the go, ripping and running the streets to keep me away from her.

I kissed her tiny little hand and pulled her pink blanket up over her. She smiled in her sleep and it made me feel guilty. I know I wasn't doing right by her, but if I spent too much time with baby YaSheema, Pajay would do something foul to her. That was a fact and one I couldn't ignore. It wasn't that I was intentionally trying to ignore my baby; I was keeping my distance in order to protect her. Deep in my soul I wished I could tell someone what I was going through. Way back when, I used to have YaYa to talk to, but Pajay decided that was a relationship I didn't need. Over the years I had other friends to talk to when I was lonely. They were in my life for support when I needed them and they weren't all bad. Carlie was always there for me when my surrogate brother Mike would repeatedly rape me. She would hold my hand and tell me we would make it through. She would comfort me. There were many nights I wanted to kill myself, but Carlie wouldn't hear of it! She would hold me and tell me it would be ok. She was there for me when it seemed like nothing in my life would ever go right.

Then there was Cree. She was an older woman who reminded me of what a mother was supposed to be. She was as sweet as apple pie and would never dream of hurting anyone. When I needed motherly love and it was nowhere to be found, Cree gave me that. Then, Pajay showed up that fateful day and silenced them all. I had just learned that my whole existence was a lie. I was so angry with everyone I thought loved and cared about me. They had all lied to me. Pajay stepped up at the lowest point of my life and vowed that whoever wronged me would pay. She was, and is, my protector of sorts; but in an evil way.

From the day she entered my life I knew she was nothing but trouble, but I let her in my world anyway, because I didn't want to be alone. She promised that she would take care of me and together we would deal with everyone responsible for fucking me over. The day Pajay arrived was the same day that Carlie and Cree disappeared. I so desperately wanted them back in exchange for Pajay. She was ruthless. She always said that the bad things she did was to right the many wrongs people had inflicted upon me. I couldn't tell. It seemed like she was only out for self-gratification and that shit scared me.

There have been many times when I thought about talking to someone about Pajay, but she quickly deaded that idea. She told me that we didn't need anyone but one another. For years I believed her. That was a huge mistake because she was trying to ruin my life and everyone I loved in it. I never wanted to kill YaYa; Pajay did. She said we had to be happy, and in order for "us" to feel that way, YaYa had to go. I think Pajay thrived off of other folk's misery and pain.

I could forgive almost everyone who had hurt me, including my own father, who had abandoned me to play Daddy to my sister YaYa instead of me. Pajay could not forgive him though. So instead, she plotted on them all, set them up, and killed them one by one. She was ruthless, cruel, and uncaring. Her motive was always centered on revenge. She found joy in tormenting others. I, on the other hand, just wanted my family to love me. Yet Pajay was always in my ear telling me that "they" we were the evil ones, so much so, that I started to believe it.

The Xtasy was starting to kick in and I needed to lie down. I left baby YaSheema's room and closed the door behind me, making sure Pajay was nowhere near my daughter. There was no telling what she would do to her if I wasn't careful. I was always looking over my shoulder fucking around with Pajay. No matter what I did, she was always lurking somewhere in the shadows. Watching my every move. The only time I could shake her was when I was high.

The only person who ever knew about me taking Xtasy was YaYa. Even she didn't know the reason why I had to stay intoxicated. It wasn't because I liked to be high. It was because it was the only way I knew how to keep Pajay at bay. Something about the combination of the drug made her defenseless. When I was sober she would reign supreme. She would leave a trail of murder, mayhem and chaos. When I was high, she couldn't fight.

After I got pregnant and couldn't pop the pills like I needed to, Pajay would be there in the middle of the night nagging me. Begging me to get us out of the house and find her something to get into. I would try to reason with her, telling her that we had no business out in the streets doing God knew what with God only knew who. Pajay's vice was sex. She craved it. She didn't care who she got it from either. I thought that if through the pregnancy I let her have her way with Dread she would leave me be. That didn't work out as well as I thought it would. The disease I had acquired during the pregnancy, *Hyperemesis Gravidarum*, a form of severe morning sickness that had to be treated with medication, left me drained and not wanting to be touched. I was sick all the time. I couldn't hold anything down, not even water. I lost so much weight the doctors had to hospitalize me for the first three months of the pregnancy until they were sure both the baby and I would make it. I thought being in the hospital would keep Pajay on the straight and narrow. I thought me threatening to tell the doctors that she was there would keep her from doing something crazy. But she didn't scare easily.

BLAQUE

It wasn't long after we were admitted that she was up to her old tricks. She had a torrid affair with a bum ass janitor from the hospital. She fucked him on the regular during her whole stay and he left us with a bad case of the crabs. Pajay didn't give a fuck though. She just kept going.

I tried to reason with her. Letting her know people were looking at us strange. They couldn't figure out how in the hell I had gotten crabs being in the hospital. I tried to play it off and claim it must have been the dirty sheets or the toilets weren't cleaned properly. I blamed it on everything but the real cause of the matter. Shit was so out of hand. I would catch her masturbating in my hospital bed daily. I prayed no one would catch her.

She had taken shit to the extreme. I was constantly thinking about killing myself and then I would start thinking about the life growing inside me and all I had already lost. I prayed for a new beginning. If I took my own life then YaYa, Daddy, Oscar and all the others would have died in vain. They died because Pajay had to control everything and those closest to me controlled their own lives and destiny. Since she had no control over what they did, she tried to take control by taking their lives.

I headed to the shower and let the cool water beam on my skin. If there was nothing else I loved about our house, I loved the shower. I had it custom designed to my liking. There were water spouts from each of walls and then there was the huge umbrella shower that hung overhead. I could control the water temperature of each spout along with the pressure. The shower was the only place I felt like I could wash my sins away. It was the only place I felt clean.

Dread designed everything else in the house because I simply didn't care what else he did as long as we were together. He hired a team of people to come in and design everything with the exception of the bathroom and the baby's room. I decorated the bathroom and he designed our daughter's room.

Dirty
DNA 2

The shower was refreshing. I turned off the water and wrapped an over-sized *Ralph Lauren* towel around my body and went to lie down. Even though I had just taken a cool shower and it was nowhere close to being hot in the house, I could feel the sweat forming on my face. That was the Xtasy signaling the beginning of me "rolling." I rolled over and reached in the nightstand for a piece of chewing gum so I wouldn't grind my teeth all night while I was high. I popped the chewing gum in my mouth and lay there staring at the ceiling. I knew sleep was not going to come because that was one of the effects of the drug, restlessness. No matter how tired you felt you were wired.

I wondered if Dread was going to come home and secretly I hoped he wouldn't. We hadn't made love in months and the strong drug was making me feel like I needed to be touched. I am sure he would appreciate it. We hadn't been intimate since before the baby was born and she was three months old. The doctors blamed my lack of intimacy on PPD. Postpartum Depression was what they called it and I let them because I was scared of getting pregnant again and having to go another nine months with Pajay calling the shots.

Tossing and turning in the huge circular bed, my body was so tired from all of the ripping and running, but my mind was wide awake. I got up and grabbed a book from one of the large bookshelves connected to the entertainment stand in the room. I thought if I read I would bore myself to sleep. I picked up a novel from one of those hood writers and started reading it.

I got through the first couple of chapters of a book called, "I Am Her, The Mistress" by some chick named V. Brown. I was no reader, but the booked had me hooked. V. Brown's words kept me entertained. The gritty sex scenes and wild shit her character was wrapped up in had me going. The book had me feeling like my life wasn't as bad as I thought it was. It could have been like the bitches in the book. Just when I thought I would be ok, Pajay spoke up startling me from the story I was reading.

"You know you shouldn't keep trying to get rid of me with the shit you keep putting into our body. You ain't learned yet? I ain't going away!" she laughed wickedly.

I didn't know what to say. I guess the Xtasy wasn't as strong as the last batch I had copped. There was no way she should have shown up so quickly. That triple stack pill should have bought me at least two days of no her!

I grabbed for my purse and took out the baggie that contained the rest of the pills I had bought from Tye. I popped the pill in my mouth and dry swallowed it in hopes of getting rid of Pajay. All I could do was hope I didn't fuck around and overdose. You never knew what was really in those pills; it was a gamble every single time I took one. There was no telling what the bootleg pharmacist had concocted together and formed into the little blue pill before passing it on. I had already taken a chance by getting the pills in the first place. I had run into Neko's friend, Shadow, and had to try and act as if we hadn't just met a couple hours earlier. Of all the places to have to meet up my connect Tye! I just knew I was busted and that greasy nigga Shadow was going to see what I was doing and tell Neko I was copping Xtasy pills in the club.

"This is my body and I can do whatever the fuck I want to it!" I yelled at Pajay.

Just as I was getting ready to hurl insults at Pajay for trying to, once again, tell me what to do, in walked Dread.

"Who are you in here talking too?" he questioned me. He was looking all around the room trying to see if I was alone.

Shit, he almost caught us again. I thought to myself. I was sitting in the middle of the bed with the baggie of blue pills wrapped tightly in my hand, careful not to let him see it.

Dirty
DNA 2

"Oh, hi baby. I was fussing because the doctor told me today that I needed to lose a few pounds." I said, looking into his eyes to see if he believed me or not.

"I waited up for you. I was hoping we could spend some time together before you headed for Atlanta in the morning." I tried to change the subject.

"I'm tired. All I want to do is get in the shower and go to bed." he said dryly.

I could feel my blood starting to boil. The Xtasy had me feeling frisky and this nigga didn't even want the pussy. I watched him disrobe and head straight for the bathroom without giving me a second thought or look. He closed the door and I heard the shower start.

"See, I told you this nigga ain't to be trusted. We have been holding out giving him the pussy and now he don't want it. I bet him and his ratchet friends have been out sticking dick to anyone who will take it." Pajay said interrupting my thoughts again. She was always barging in where she was clearly not wanted.

"Mind you're fucking business." I whispered. I sat there trying to figure out how I was going to get in my fiancé's good graces.

Dread exited the shower in nothing but his towel. He had beads of water dripping from his body and I wanted him so badly to not only acknowledge me, but to desire me the way I desired him. He roamed through the oak dresser and found a wife beater t-shirt and some boxers. Finally, he spoke after what seemed like an eternity.

"I am gonna' go check on the baby and head down to the studio for a little while." he said as he walked out of the bedroom door.

I felt like he was trying to avoid me and using the baby to do so.

"I told you his sneaky ass is up to something. You better start listening with your head instead of your heart. Fuck him. We don't need him! We

can do so much better than him!" Pajay said irritated with the situation.

She finally stopped nagging and I was thankful that my second little blue pill was kicking in. As it made its way through my veins Pajay eventually left me too. I was all alone and I hated it. Hot, fresh tears formed in my eyes. I swear I could hear my heart breaking. I lay there crying and hoping against hope that I hadn't fucked up one of the few good things I had left in my life.

CHAPTER EIGHT

Northeast Groovers (NEG)

"Booty Call"

Detective Gatsby

I had been tailing Mr. Evans from his Laurel, Maryland home into the city. I had followed him right to his studio in Southeast, DC. I knew the area very well. It wasn't my jurisdiction, but I had followed him there so much that I knew where he was headed even before he got there.

Ronald "Dread" Evans was not making shit easy for me. I had tailed him, his security, and his label mates back through the city and to the infamous *Stadium Club*. Since they were all out in full force, my guess was that either they were there to have a little fun, or they had a performance. Once they were inside I could not gain access to the club because it was a private event. There was a huge crowd out front of the club. They were all dressed in pink and white. Even if I could use my badge to muscle my way into the club, I would have stuck out like a sore thumb. I wasn't dressed in pink or white and I would have probably been the only over-fifty white guy in the club.

I found a parking space and shut down the engine of my old Impala and waited to see if anything transpired. Scantily-clad women paraded around in front of the club. It was like a meat market out there. I figured if nothing else I could entertain myself with the sights outside. The bouncers were sheisty as hell. I watched them make their nightly pay plus some. People were desperately trying to get into the affair, which meant the bouncers were clocking dollas on the side charging people astronomical prices just to get in. Some people were allowed in and some were turned away.

47

BLAQUE

A group of average-looking women approach a big bouncer and he literally laughed at them and sent them on their way. It was the bouncer's routine to turn away anyone that wasn't willing to pay $200 they were trying to con out of people on top of the $300 fee to step foot in the door. Money talked for the event and if a person didn't have it they weren't getting in. I shook my head at the happenings. Another group of young women approached the burly bouncers, the only difference was that the second set of women were all drop-dead gorgeous. The leader of the group stepped up and whispered something in the bouncer's ear. She stepped back and did a little spin, and I could see the smile forming on the bouncer's hungry lips. The young girl grabbed his crotch and licked her full pouty lips. The bouncer must have known that was his queue, because he immediately motioned for another burly bouncer to take his place at the door. He said a couple of words to his partner and proceeded towards the alley.

I didn't have to see what happened. I already knew. The woman gave him some type of sexual gratification in exchange for entrance to the club. About twenty minutes later the girl appeared from the darkened alley and the bouncer followed closely behind her. Her group got excited when the twosome made their return to the front of the club. The bouncer took his post again without another word, and quickly allowed the whole group of young girls inside. I am sure none of them paid cash to gain entrance. I never saw money change hands. I knew something better than cash was exchanged in that alley.

I was almost tempted to go and question the bouncer about the young girl's skills. It had been so long since I had even had a woman that it was comical. I hadn't had any pleasures of the flesh since my sweet Anona was taken from me at the hands of my own father. I am sure people thought I was just a cop who maintained a normal and healthy life. What they didn't know was that was far from the truth.

48

I tried to refocus my attention on the happenings outside of the club and not let my mind drift to thoughts of Anona and the baby. I lost more than my future wife and child that fateful day. I lost my parents and I know I lost a piece of my soul and my mind as well. Those events changed me. Death will do that.

I wiped the tears forming in the corners of my eyes on the sleeve of my worn shirt that had seen better days. Bile built up in my throat as it often did when I drudged up the memories of my lost love and the betrayal of my parents. Searching around the mess on the floor of the car, I found what I knew would be a flat ginger ale, and I took a sip of the warm substance to soothe the sick feeling that was trying to take hold of me.

My life had turned into nothing but failures. After losing my wife and child, I couldn't seem to do anything right. I swore this time would be different. I would find and capture the person or persons responsible for killing off the entire Clayton clan. It was my new mission in life. No matter how long it took me, I would see to it that I brought their killer or killers to justice. Nothing would deter me from seeing the case through to the end, and once it was all over, I would retire, collect my gold watch and pension for my many years of dedicated service on the force.

I must have sat out there for hours waiting for my target to make his way from the club. I had fallen asleep in the car; drunk from the pint of *Jack Daniels* I consumed while waiting for my mark. Awakened by loud voices from the crowds of people exiting the club and spilling onto the streets, I glanced at the clock on the dash and saw that it read nearly four a.m. Once again, my suspect had eluded me and I could not find him in the crowds milling about in the streets. Ironically, I saw the same group of young women who had gained entrance to the club by way of "favors" their friend had given to the bouncer. They were headed in the direction of my car. Shrugging my shoulders, I figured I would give it a go. I was feeling the effects of the alcohol I had downed earlier. Once the group was close enough to my car, I stepped out and blocked their path. They were chit chatting about the happenings in the club and barely noticed me.

"Khalia, that bitch Pinky sure can party. Did you see she had the entire club rocking?" One of the girls said.

"Can you believe she had the entire Cap Citi Mob there?" Another one squealed in excitement.

"Excuse me Miss, can I speak with you for a minute?" I asked the obvious ringleader.

She was even more beautiful than I thought. She was the color of ebony and the hot pink short shorts that hugged her coke bottle frame had me feeling woozy with desire. She was about 5'7" and bowlegged. Her long, curly hair fell down her back and stopped right above her huge ass. *Damn...I loved DC women.* There was nothing like the black women who dwelled here. They came in all shapes, colors and sizes. I could feel myself getting worked up just looking at her. I knew I had to stay calm if I wanted my plan to work.

"No, you can't speak to me grandpa." she said harshly. She eyed me up and down and tossed her long, curly hair and started to walk away. She was fiery and it was turning me on.

"I bet if I let my fellow boys in blue know what you did in that alley to get in the club you would have something to talk about." I said, flashing her friends who were definitely paying attention, my badge.

She stopped dead in her tracks and spun on her heels.

"What, are you gonna try and bust me now or something?" she asked looking from me to her friends to help her out.

They were of no help and had nothing to say. They gave her the "you are on your own bitch look."

I knew my plan was working.

"I figure you can either talk to me about what I want to know or talk to the judge first thing Monday morning about tricking in the alley to get in the club. Your choice." I said trying to get her to consider leaving her friends to not only give me the information I wanted, but give me what my body craved.

"Ya'll go ahead. Let me see wassup with him." she said dismissing her friends who were more than happy to leave her there with the burden of getting a cop off of her ass alone.

Not one of them tried to stay and defend her and make sure she could hold her own before they all walked off. They left her there, alone, with what they didn't know was really the big bad wolf. As soon as they were at a good distance from us, I walked around to the passenger's side door of the car and opened it for her. She got inside and folded her arms defensively across her chest that heaved up and down in pure anger. I got back in the car on the driver's side and began my interrogation.

"I just need some information on what happened in the club tonight." I said smoothly.

She seemed to be buying it, and slowly began to calm down. "What kind of information?"

"What was that rapper guy, Dread, doing in there?"

"He performed with the stripper, Pinky. It's her birthday and he was one of the special guests."

"Nothing else happened?"

"Ummm, no. Pinky performed, Dread performed. That was it. Was something else supposed to happen?" She asked me with a little too much attitude.

"Look, I will ask all of the questions. You are to just answer them!" I said a little more harshly than I had intended to.

The girl fidgeted around nervously in the cracked leather seat. I was staring at her brown thighs and wondering how she would look with them wrapped around me. Her low cut, pink, mid-drift top was revealing her perky breast and I was hoping she was going to taste as good as she looked. I hated dirty bitches.

She saw me eyeing her cleavage and she placed her hand on the door handle, ready to try and make a break for it in case I tried anything.

"Look mister, I told you everything you wanted to know. Please let me go. I am sure my friends are over there waiting on me to join them." she said with her voice trembling.

Her eyes darted over in the direction in which her friends had gone. Silently she prayed that she would make eye contact with one of them and they would come for her. They weren't coming anywhere near me or my car just because I was a cop. They were most likely under-aged little tramps that had no business out late at night at an establishment like that anyway!

"Sure you can leave once I get what I need from you." I said looking at her lustfully.

"What do you need from me?" she asked stuttering. She was becoming more and more uneasy and it was turning me on.

"I need whatever it is you gave that bouncer to get inside that club."

I could see the alarm spread across over her face. I was getting a sick thrill out of the whole situation. It was a sense of power. I was the predator and she was the prey.

"I don't know what you thought happened back there, but it wasn't like that." she stammered.

"Yes, it was." I said knowingly.

I started the car, pulled out of the parking space, and drove to the alley where I had seen her take the bouncer. It was dark and deserted. I shut down the engine and motioned for her to come closer. She wouldn't move and it started to aggravate me.

"How the fuck could you suck and fuck that slimy ass bouncer and not do it to keep your ass out of trouble?" I growled, mad that she didn't want me the way I wanted her.

"I didn't do anything with him!" she tried to explain.

I grabbed her by her throat with one hand, and unfastened my trousers with the other and pulled out my dick. She squirmed around trying to free herself from my grasp. She clawed and scratched at my hands and wrists which were prohibiting air from reaching her lungs. The more she fought, the more I tightened my grip around her neck. I could feel her going limp. I didn't want the bitch to die. I just wanted her to suck my dick! I loosened my grip on her neck. She took long gulps of air into her lungs; reminding me of a fish out of water. The tears were flowing down her face causing the mascara she was wearing to stain her cheeks.

"I will do anything you want me to do! Just don't hurt me!" she said between sucking in the air that she so desperately needed.

I let her neck go and grabbed the back of her head and brought it down forcefully to my lap.

"Please don't make me do this!" she said sobbing.

"Suck it bitch; and you better not bite me or I will blow your fucking head off!" I said gruffly.

She began to suck my dick and I pushed her head down further making her gag on it. She tried to pull away and I delivered a blow to the back of her head causing her to graze my dick with her teeth. I winced in pain and retaliated at the same time. I grabbed a fistful of her hair and pulled her head up out of my lap, bringing her face to face with me. Then I open hand smacked the shit out of her.

"Bitch I said, don't bite me. If you bite me again I will kill you! Now suck it and no teeth!" I demanded.

Blood was trickling from the corner of her mouth from the force of the back hand slap I gave her. She sniffled and put her head back in my lap and this time she sucked my dick like her life depended on it. I let my seat back, closed my eyes and enjoyed the pleasure I was receiving. That was a serious mistake. I should have never closed my eyes.

I saw flashes of my dead wife's body lying in a pool of blood. I could hear her begging for me to stop the assault on the young girl. Then I saw my father laying there laughing at me and egging me on.

"Go ahead son; you know these nigger bitches like it rough. You know that nigger bitch of yours had some great pussy!" he laughed.

My eyes sprang open and I saw my father raping Anona, the woman who was to be my wife. She was dressed in her white wedding gown with her pregnant belly protruding from the front of the dress. She was fighting and screaming for him to stop raping her. When our eyes connected, she mouthed the words, 'Help us.'

I grabbed the young girl out of my lap, and when I took a good look at her she wasn't the same young tenderoni I had forced to perform fellatio on me. Instead, I saw my mother's wicked face. She was screaming obscenities at me like she had done many years ago for wanting to marry a black woman.

"Shut the fuck up you hateful bitch!" I screamed at who I thought was my mother.

She wouldn't stop. she continued throwing insults at me and my wife.

"You are no son of mine wanting to marry this gutter trash! We didn't raise you to bring this trash into our family. We taught you to take the trash out!" She kept repeating those words over and over again until it rang so loudly in my ears that there was nothing more that I wanted than to silence her.

I pulled out my service pistol and began to beat my mother's wicked image until there was nothing but quiet.

The poor girl was balled up in the passenger seat of the car. Her face was bloody and badly beaten. Her teeth we scattered around the piles of trash on the floor like *Chicklets*. There was no doubt about it, she was dead. My heart began beating so fast I just knew it was going to explode out of my overweight chest.

"Oh my God, what have I done?" I cried.

DNA 2

There was no way I could explain away my temporary insanity and live to tell about it. They would fry my ass for that shit for sure! I had to get rid of her, and get rid of the evidence. I reached across the dead girl's body and opened the passenger side door, quickly pushing her body out of it. She hit the dirty pavement with a thud. I pulled the door closed, started the car, threw it in reverse, and sped backwards to the entrance of the alley. Once I got to the beginning of the alley I looked in the rearview mirror to make sure no one would see my car leaving from the scene of the crime.

The streets were clear. It looked like the club goers had all called it a night and I was free and clear of being noticed. I whipped the Impala out of the alley backwards and got as far away from the scene as I possibly could. *I had fucked up royally!*

My head was swirling. My mind was going in so many directions at one time that I was getting whiplash. I sped through the streets trying to get as much distance between me and that alley. When I was sure I was a safe distance away, I pulled over. Frantically, I searched the car for evidence that may have been left behind. That's when I saw it, the bloody purse that was in the young girl's lap. I went through it. Inside I found her wallet. I went through it and found sixty dollars in cash and her identification. Her name was Khalia York. She was only seventeen years old. I stuffed the money in my pocket and returned the ID to the wallet where I had found it.

She had no fucking business being anywhere near that fucking club! Not only was she of no age to drink, but she wasn't even old enough to legally get inside either. My body shook with fear from what I had done to an innocent child. Within moments I had turned into a pedophile, rapist and a murderer. I finished going through her personal belongings feeling more and more horrible with each passing moment. Inside her purse were pictures of her and random people. I stopped at a photo of the young girl. She was dressed in her cap and gown from her high school graduation. She was standing with another young woman. It wasn't their faces that stood out to me. It was the image of Neko Reynolds, who stood between them that made my heart sink.

Somehow, the man I had vowed to help capture the killer of his entire murdered family knew the young woman whom I had just killed. There was no way I could face him. He had already gone through so much. There was no way of telling who the girl was to him, and her death might be the news that would send him over the edge. I was not going to be anywhere near him when he found out there had been another murder close to him. For all I knew, another murder could very well be the final straw that would cause him to flip out and commit a murder himself for sure!

CHAPTER NINE

Mambo Sauce

"Welcome to DC"

Neko

I woke up to Pinky entering my condo using the spare key I had given her. I looked at the alarm clock on the nightstand and it was after four in the morning.

"Good morning sexy." I said into the darkness.

It was still dark outside so I couldn't see her, but I knew it was her. No one else had access to my home besides her. I trusted no one else enough to give them a key.

"Hey baby. I didn't mean to wake you." she said in her husky voice. Her voice reminded me of the singer Mariah Carey-Cannon with its deep sultry tone.

I knew she had worked at the club and I figured she was coming over because it was her birthday and she was expecting her gift.

"Hey birthday girl, how does it feel to be a year wiser, a year better, and a year older?" I asked her.

"It feels the same. Not too much different from any other day."

"How was the club tonight?"

"I made a killing!" she said moving about the room navigating her way through the darkness.

I felt the bed lower on the opposite side. I could smell the warm, vanilla sugar *Bath and Body Works* scent emanating from her voluptuous body. She cuddled up to me and we drifted off to sleep.

I woke up a few hours later and Pinky was still fast asleep. I eased out of the bed and decided to fix her breakfast. I headed down the hallway and peeked in the den at the thirty-one helium balloons I had hidden inside. My plan was to surprise Pinky with her gift, which was a platinum pink, diamond heart Necklace, along with breakfast in bed. I knew she would love the necklace simply because it was pink. I also planned to take her shopping for a new bike and let her pick out a custom paint job which I knew she would want. I was going to foot the whole bill. I was thinking dinner for two at the *Melting Pot* and then back to my place for a long session of her thanking me for her gifts. I had to admit, ole' girl has a special place in my heart. I knew she did her and I did me, but we had a special type of bond with one another.

I fixed breakfast and placed it on a tray and headed back to the bedroom. I knew Pinky would be ready for some serious love making after she saw the pink balloons attached to the box containing the necklace. Before I could get down the hallway with the tray of food and the balloons, I heard Pinky screaming. I ran the rest of the way down the hall trying not to spill anything on the carpet. Once I made it to the room, Pinky was sitting straight up in the bed and staring at the television which she must have turned on after I crept out of the room.

"What's wrong?" I asked.

She had fresh tears pouring from her big doe eyes, tracing the path of each one of her light brown freckles. She didn't speak, she just pointed towards the television and I immediately dropped the tray of food that I tried so carefully to preserve in my sprint down the hall.

The words, *"BREAKING NEWS"* were flashing across the screen and *Fox 5 News* was reporting the murder of Khalia York. A picture of the girl was shown over top of the live footage of the crime scene. I stepped over the mess I had made on the floor and rushed to turn up the television.

Dirty

DNA 2

"The body of a seventeen-year-old girl, identified as Khalia York, was found behind the infamous Stadium Nightclub. She was the apparent victim of a robbery gone horribly wrong. Police are not releasing any other information until the victim's family can be notified. If you have any information in regards to this case, please contact Crime Solvers at 202-555-5555."

I switched the television off and scrambled to get to Pinky's side of the bed. She sat there not moving, as though time had stopped. She was still staring at the television screen that was now blank. I held her in my arms and rocked her. I tried whatever I could to get a response from her, but she would not budge. I had never seen her vulnerable before. I knew the heartache she was feeling. I knew it all too well. The loss of your sister is a tough pill to swallow.

BLAQUE

CHAPTER TEN

Critical Condition Band (CCB)

"Butterfly"

Dread

I hated being late. I was heading out the door to the airport to my show in Georgia. Joseah was following behind me trying to help me pack up last-minute items that I had forgotten to pack. The baby was wrapped tightly in her arms and the situation seemed so odd to me. NiQue should have been the one doing all of the things that Joseah was doing.

"Señor, when will you be returning home?" she asked.

"I should only be gone for about a week or so."

"Señor Evans we need to talk and it is very important that we speak!" she said frantically.

"Joseah, I am in a rush. My flight leaves in an hour and a half and I have to get to BWI. If I miss this flight, I will have to hear a bunch of crap from Crack." I said sifting through different jewelry pieces.

"But, señor…"

I interrupted her before she could protest and make me even later than I already was.

"We will have to talk about it another time Joseah; really I cannot do this right now!"

"Chu wife is acting strange and I am worried about what she will do to the baby!" she blurted out.

I stopped looking through the pieces of assorted chains and focused on what Joseah was saying. Just then NiQue walked in the kitchen and Joseah stopped in her tracks. All conversation and whatever Joseah was going to say ceased. I could tell she was shook. I had to admit the look on NiQue's face was enough to knock an elephant over with a feather. I was curious where Joseah was headed when she said she was worried about what NiQue would do to the baby.

"Good morning!" NiQue said in a sing song manner.

Joseah held the baby even closer to her bosom and would not move. I could tell there was something going on between them, but I didn't know what, nor did I have the time to try and sort it out.

"Morning babe, can you help me grab a few things before I head out? I was supposed to pack up some other promotional stuff last night, but I ended up in the studio and well, you know how that goes." I said to NiQue.

I went to her and gave her a kiss as a peace offering for the way I had acted the night before. I purposely slept in the baby's room because I felt horrible for sleeping with that stripper bitch.

"Sure, what do you need?" NiQue responded.

"Can you get me a breakfast sandwich whipped up and a glass of OJ? I hate eating that airport food."

"Why can't she do it? Ain't that what we pay her for?" she said glaring at Joseah.

"Damn ma, aren't we cranky this morning; and "no" we pay her to care for the baby while we handle business." I responded trying to smooth over the bad vibes rising in the kitchen.

"I have been meaning to talk to you about that. I think we should take care of the baby more on our own so she won't get attached to being with a stranger." NiQue said throwing major shade.

Joseah clutched the baby even tighter and the tension was so thick in the room you could cut it with a knife. I knew something had gone down with the two of them, but neither would say what had happened. I didn't exactly have the time to try and figure it out either. My time to get out of the house and make that flight was ticking down and I didn't have the time to break up the girl fight NiQue and Joseah had going on. NiQue walked pass Joseah and rolled her eyes. She went on to do as I asked and fixed me a breakfast sandwich.

I finished stuffing the promo cd's and posters into the carry-on bag I planned on taking with me. Joseah gathered the YaSheema's bottle and headed out of the kitchen to feed and change her. I finally sat down to enjoy the turkey bacon, egg white and cheese sandwich that NiQue made for me. I turned on the television that was in the kitchen and flipped through the channels before settling on the news. Nothing but the same old shit was happening in the world until there was a breaking news report about a murder at the Stadium Club the night before.

NiQue started in again on why Joseah needed to be fired and I shushed her. I turned up the volume on the 32" flat screen that was built into a nook in the wall of the kitchen and focused in on what had happened at the club. The reporter was giving up information on the young woman whose body had been found by an employee of the club. The body was badly beaten, and the employee found it when they took out the trash from an event held there just hours before.

I shook my head at the senseless violence, and silently thanked God that I had left the club when I did. I damn sure didn't need the press on my ass about some youngin' getting robbed and left for dead at one of my venues. I didn't pay the news flash any more attention. Quickly, I washed down the rest of my sandwich and was getting ready to put my plate and glass in the sink when the reporter began an interview with another employee of the club who happened to be the victim's sister.

The glass and the plate slipped from my hands and shattered on the floor when I saw Chyan "Pinky" York's sad, but beautiful face. According to the reporter she was the sister of the victim. I couldn't believe what I was hearing and seeing. NiQue came in the kitchen to see what the noise was about and what had me shook. When she saw the image of Pinky on the television her mouth fell open.

"Oh, my goodness. Babe you know her? She used to work for my brother and YaYa's father." NiQue said.

I nodded, too stunned to speak. Truth is I didn't know she had worked for YaYa or NiQue's family, but I did know her. NiQue stood there staring at me and waiting for me to say something.

"It was her birthday celebration we performed at last night. I didn't meet her until I performed last night" I said trying to hide how I really knew the shapely pole queen.

"The way you are acting I thought you knew her personally." NiQue said suspiciously.

"Naw, it just caught me off guard to see that it was her sister that was murdered. That's all." I stuttered.

"Well, believe me, whoever did that shit to her folks better relocate from the city. That bitch is one of the wildest bitches on the map. She used to work for my...I mean, YaYa's father; and if I know one thing about her, she will make whoever did this to her family pay dearly!" NiQue said excitedly.

"What do you mean she is one of the wildest bitches on the map?" I questioned.

"Pinky is a paid killer. When I said she worked for YaYa's dad, she used to put in that work. If you needed to have a nigga's head hit, she was the one you called. She is a regular ole' assassin." NiQue said nonchalantly. She spoke of the woman being a killer as casually as someone would talk about the weather.

I sat there wondering how in the hell had I not known who she was! I got to thinking about how close to my own family she was and I was instantly shaken because of it. What if she spoke with NiQue and told her how we met? What if she found out that my future wife was associated with her former employers. I knew she looked a little familiar, but when you have seen so many chicks on the regular, you tend to forget where you knew them from. The faces kind of ran together after a while.

Then it hit me like a ton of bricks. I had seen her at YaSheema's funeral! She stayed to herself and she stood in the back of the funeral parlor. You would have missed her if it weren't for those pink dread locks. How the fuck could I forget?

NiQue was busying herself with cleaning up the mess I had made with the glass and plate. I sat there daydreaming about the night before and wondering how I hadn't put it all together. I shrugged it off and gathered my stuff, making my way to the foyer to catch my flight. NiQue ran behind me.

"Baby, can I take you to the airport? I didn't get to spend any time with you last night and I think I am starting to get a handle on this PPD shit." she said. She hugged me and it felt so good. It felt like my relationship with my fiancé was returning to normal. I hugged her back and tilted her chin so we could engage in a kiss. Something we hadn't done since before baby YaYa was born. I was glad I could see the old NiQue in her eyes. I was a creature of habit, and I hated change. I was thrilled to know she was putting forth an effort to make us work.

"Sure babe!" I said, dropping my bags at the door remembering to kiss my daughter. NiQue headed out the door and I let her know I wanted to kiss the baby bye. I made my way up the steps and into the nursery where I found Joseah sitting in the rocking chair holding my baby girl who was the spitting image of me. I kissed YaSheema who was cooing like she was carrying on a conversation and then I gave her back to the nanny who looked more than afraid. She looked petrified that I was leaving.

"Señor Evans, chu no believe what I say to chu; but chu wife is evil and when chu return I will be leaving my position. I don't want to be responsible for what she might to do to me, chu, or the baby." she said firmly.

"Joseah, she has been under a lot of stress lately and we really need you. I hope you will reconsider leaving us, but if you do decide to leave, I understand."

She nodded her head like she understood what I was saying. I didn't have time to try and hash things out with her. I had other shit to do. I made my way back down the steps grabbed my bags and headed out the door to my truck where NiQue was waiting to drop me off at the airport. Something told me to hold off on the trip to Atlanta; but the showcase was what my career needed to get me in the *XXL Freshmen Top Ten Edition.* I closed the door not knowing it would be the last time my home would be normal!

Dirty

DNA 2

CHAPTER ELEVEN

Backyard Band (BYB)

"Unibomber"

NiQue

I dropped Dread off at BWI and it seemed like we were going to be able to work through the rough patch we were going through. The night before he was a little hesitant to be in my presence, which was totally understandable because of the way I had been treating him the past three or so months. But the morning had gone well, and it seemed as though things were looking up for us; that is until Joseah had to stick her nose where it didn't belong.

"I'm glad you and your nigga are making nice with one another." Pajay said sarcastically.

I almost swerved off of the road when she interrupted my thoughts. I focused my attention on driving and attempted to ignore her banter. I knew she didn't mean what she had said about me and Dread.

"I hope the two of you don't make any more of those disgusting, little, bastard babies. It's going to take us months to get that baby weight off." she said sucking her teeth.

"Pajay watch your mouth! That is my daughter you're referring too. She is not disgusting, and she has nothing to do with your pointed anger." I harshly scolded her. She was really testing me. I knew once she had caught Joseah trying to drop a dime on us that she was going to be in rare form. And as expected, I was stuck listening to her ass going off.

BLAQUE

"I wish you would stop being so damn naïve. What are you going to do about that babysitter? She keeps butting in where she doesn't belong?" she asked.

I hated to admit it, but Pajay was right; Joseah was going to have to be dealt with. She had caught me, one too many times, talking to who she "thought" was myself. I was just trying to get my life in order, and I was not going to have her destroying what I had worked so hard to get. I pushed the pedal down to the floor and shot up 295 South. Music pumped loudly in my ears as I tried not to think about what had to be done in order to keep my home life in order, and my relationship peaceful. We pulled up in front of the house and my mind was made up. I hit the doorway and didn't say a word to Joseah who I knew was somewhere in the house. I went straight towards the baby's room to make sure she wasn't anywhere near Joseah. I climbed the steps to her room being careful not to make too much noise. I pushed the door open to the nursery quietly and the baby was snuggled under her pink blanket. I left as fast as I had come, pulling the door shut behind me. She was safe.

"You know you are full of shit and you aren't going to really go down there and handle that old bitch. You depend on her to be the mother that you ain't never had but always wanted." Pajay said trying to hype me up.

She was taunting me. Her voice was making my adrenaline pump faster through my veins. It was as if Pajay knew exactly how to make me mad and push me into situations just, so she could react. She was a shit starter and I hated her for it too! She had a way of proving, time and time again, that I was weak. Pajay would take me to new levels of anger. Forcing me to the brink of insanity, she had a way of taking me there and then right before I would do some unthinkable shit just to shut her up, I would think of the consequences and back down. I would think about possibly going to jail or even ending up dead. I would reconsider the shit I was doing and that's when Pajay had full control. She would step in to finish the job I was too chicken shit to go through. Then like the sucker she really was, she would leave me to clean up behind her mess.

"Leave me alone Pajay. If this is going to work, I need you let me handle it." I said trying to get her to shut up and let me think. *"If this is going to be done, it's going to be done my way this time. Only fools act off of impulse, and when you don't think things through, you end up with the Feds at your door. Then they call in those doctors who wanna analyze us! Do you want that?"* I asked.

Pajay quieted down a bit, but I knew she was there; waiting and plotting how she was going to upstage me. She was sneaky like that. I entered the den and looked around for what I could use to aid me in getting Joseah out of our lives. I spotted the phone cord and snatched it from the wall. I left the den and headed to handle this shit once and for all. I got to the bottom of the steps and went to the left. Joseah was always on the lower level of the house when she wasn't in the nursery with the baby. I checked each room and when I came to the kitchen, there she was with her back to me washing the dishes I had left in the sink after making Dread's breakfast.

A deep breath escaped from my lips as I charged at her full force. I swung the telephone cord over her head, around her fleshy neck, and I yanked her backwards; causing her to lose her footing and fall backwards. Her overweight body hit the floor with a thump. The bowl she was washing shattered near her feet. Her head crashed against the floor and bounced off of the tiles like a basketball being dribbled from half court. I went down with her—banging my knees on the floor. I could barely feel the pain shooting up my legs; I was that caught up in what I was doing. Joseah couldn't fight back or try to save herself. Her head hitting the floor had knocked her unconscious.

"Finish it. Kill that nosy bitch!" Pajay screamed. She was cheering me on. It made me want to choke her instead. As usual, something deep within was telling me I didn't have to do what I

was doing. I could have just fired her and sent her on her way. She didn't have to die!

"Don't start this stupid shit! I swear what would you do without me?" Pajay said taking control. She wrapped the cord tightly around Joseah's neck and choked her until the last bit of breath left her lungs. That was the last thing I remembered until I woke up a few hours later next to Joseah's dead body. I heard the sound of the baby crying through the baby monitor that was on the island counter. I looked around the kitchen half expecting Pajay to be there, but she wasn't. The water was still running in the sink from where Joseah was washing the dishes. I got up from the floor wincing from the pain shooting through my knees. I removed the cord from her neck and stuffed it in the pocket of my jeans and limped to get to the baby.

I got to baby Yasheema's room and picked her up to quiet her cries. I was so afraid that Pajay had tried to do something to her while I lay on the kitchen floor. Instinctively, I put the baby in her carrier and went back to the kitchen and got her bottles and put them in the baby bag in the hallway. The garage was next on my "to do" list. I went into the garage, pressed the automatic door opener and walked out to where I had parked Dread's truck earlier. I strapped my daughter in the back seat, got in the driver's seat, and backed out of the driveway as if nothing had happened.

"That's what I'm talking about. Make it all look like an accident. We can tell the police that we came home and decided to take the baby out for a ride because she was fussy. When we returned home, we found the nanny dead, simple as that!" Pajay said like it was just that easy.

I had another body under my belt and it felt awful.

"You need to get rid of the evidence you, dumb ass! You are riding around with the damn phone cord in your pocket. You need to dump that shit and get to a store and buy another one to replace it so nothing seems out of order when the Feds start snooping around the house. You do know they are gonna' suspect us; right?" she said.

Dirty
DNA 2

"Shut up and let me think! Stop fucking ordering me around!" I shouted at her. I yelled so loud I scared the baby who had drifted off to sleep. I pulled the car over on the side of the road and put the car in park. Shuffling through my purse, I finally found my bag of magic blue pills. I needed to think, and I didn't need Pajay looking over my shoulder and fussing in my ear about what I needed to do.

I took two of the pills and pulled back onto the road and drove until I ended up damn near in Baltimore. I pulled into a strip mall and purchased a new phone cord, identical to the one I needed to replace. I found a deli and decided I needed to have folks see me. That way if the police wanted to check into where I had been, my movements could be traced. I ordered a cold cut sub and a large orange juice. I fed the baby and picked at the sandwich until I felt like enough time had passed. Before leaving the deli, I tossed the old phone cord in the trash. There was no way anyone would be looking for a murder weapon way out in Baltimore.

When I arrived back at my home, I pulled the truck into the garage and popped another pill. I had to be sure I wouldn't be getting another surprise visit from Pajay while I cleaned up her mess. Having her around while I tried to pull things off could be dangerous. All it would take was for her to get upset and I could land in the loony bin; or worse, jail.

I carried the baby inside and placed her carrier near the door. I headed straight up the steps to hook up the new phone cord. I made my way back down the steps and unstrapped the baby from the carrier and walked casually into the kitchen where Joseah's body was still laying face up on the floor. She looked like she was sleeping, but I knew better. I put on my game face and grabbed the cordless phone from the counter.

"911. What is your emergency? Do you need the Police, the Fire Department or an Ambulance?" the 911 operator asked me.

I took a breath, it was show time!

"Ambulance. I think my nanny had an accident!" I shouted into the phone.

"What type of accident ma'am?"

"I'm not sure. I just returned home from running errands with my daughter and found her on the kitchen floor." I responded trying to sound shaken.

"Is she breathing?"

"No…I don't think so! Oh, please send someone quick!"

"Ma'am, please try and stay calm. Is there anyone else in the house with you?"

"Oh, God I don't know!" I said trying to sound alarmed.

"Ma'am can you and your daughter get out of the house safely?" the operator asked.

"I can try and go to my neighbor's house." I said.

"Ok, get out of the house and don't touch anything. Help is on the way."

I disconnected the call and headed out the front door to the neighbor's house. I rang the bell and an older white lady opened the door. I explained the circumstances that had brought me to her home and she ushered me and my baby girl inside. Moments later, I heard the wail of the sirens making their way onto my street. My neighbor went back outside and directed the first officer who arrived to where I was.

I sat there in the lady's kitchen with a blank look on my face; rocking the baby, tears rolling down my cheeks. Sympathetically, the officer told me to stay put. I nodded through fake tears and he left back out of the front door of my neighbor's home. The sounds of blaring sirens and more trucks screeching to a halt could be heard. I knew there were at the front of my house. I couldn't take it anymore and went out on the porch and joined my neighbor who was watching all of the commotion unfold.

The paramedics rushed inside my house and my heart started to pound. A light sweat formed on my forehead signaling the start of my roll. At least Pajay wasn't a factor for the time being.

DNA 2

It felt like time was standing still. I stood there for what felt like an eternity before the lead officer made his way over to me.

"Ma'am are you the one who made the call?" the officer asked.

"Yes...what happened...is she going to be alright?"

"It looks like she took a nasty fall and hit her head pretty hard. We will know more once the coroner gets here."

"Oh God, no!" I exclaimed trying to seem as distressed as possible.

"I didn't get your name ma'am." The officer said pulling out a small notepad. He began jotting down something and looked at me waiting for me to give him my name.

"My name is Pajay... I mean ShaniQua Watkins." I stammered trying to cover the fact that I had almost fucked up.

"We will need to ask you a few questions. You will have to come down to the station with us." the officer stated before scribbling more information on the paper.

"Sure, whatever you need officer. May I go inside and get my cell phone? I have to call my fiancé and let him know what's going on."

"Your fiancé? Where is he and what is his name?" the cop asked.

"His name is Ronald Evans. I dropped him off at the airport this morning. He has a performance in Atlanta. I am sure he has called me by now to let me know he got there safely."

"You can't go back in the house ma'am until the coroners have removed the body and the detectives have given the sign that the scene is all clear."

Just as he finished his statement, a black coroner's van pulled into my driveway. Two white females got out of the van and spoke briefly with a man who I assumed was the lead detective. Shortly thereafter, they followed him inside my house.

Through all of the excitement, and the comings and goings in my front yard, I managed to notice a black Impala with DC government plates making its way to the front of my house. I knew that car. I had seen it one too many times. It was Detective Gatsby. His being there meant nothing but more added stress for me.

"What the fuck does he want?" Pajay spoke up. Her voice was faint, but she was audible enough to cause me some alarm.

"This cracker is beginning to be a pain in my ass." she said annoyed with his presence.

I watched him get out of the car and walk up my driveway. He flashed the other officers his badge and they let him through the yellow tape that was surrounding the perimeter of the house.

"Like it or not we are gonna' have to deal with his ass, because if he starts snooping around and giving any of our past information to these other Feds it could mean trouble for us." Pajay said. Then she finally grew quiet.

She had a valid point; if that nosy ass cop stirred up anything it could mean trouble for us all.

Dirty
DNA 2

CHAPTER TWELVE

Rare Essence (R.E)

"Lock It"

Detective Gatsby

I hadn't slept all night. Every time I tried to close my eyes I would see her eyes wide open, staring at me, accusing me. I tossed and turned. I just knew someone from IA (Internal Affairs) would be knocking on my door to question me.

I gave up on the idea of sleeping and paced through my small apartment. I finally turned on my television to see if my latest fuck up had landed on the news. Flipping through the channels, I finally landed on *Channel 8 News*. From the looks of it, not only had they identified the young woman's body, but they had notified her next of kin who was one of the dancers from the club. She was giving a statement and offering a reward to anyone that could give information that would lead to the arrest of her sister's killer. I was just about to turn the TV off when the camera showed a very familiar face on the screen. It was Neko Reynolds. He was consoling the sister of my victim. The sadness in both of their eyes radiated through the screen. The reporter went on to say that the club had been closed the night before for a private function.

I shut off the television. I didn't need to hear anymore. I couldn't take it. That rapper guy, Dread, had been in the club that night and Neko Reynolds was involved with the victim's sister. I knew Neko had plenty of hatred for Ronald Evans, and I was going to use that in my favor to get out of this mess I had created.

BLAQUE

I felt better just thinking about what I was about to do. If everything went as I was planning it to go, I didn't have to worry about anything else. I got dressed as quickly as I could. I would worry about showering later on. I had a mission to complete and I was going to get the job done once and for all.

*****

I pulled up to the Evans' residence and it looked like a full three-ring circus outside. I almost panicked and drove off. Calming my nerves, I finally exited my car. There were police crawling all over the place. I flashed one of the rookie officers my badge. He let me through the taped-off area and I proceeded to look for my target. I had the arrest warrant in my hands and ready to take Ronald "Dread" Evans down on sight. He may not have committed the crime the night before, but he was going to get pinched for it! Especially if I had anything to do with it.

Walking through the massive yard and up the steps, I found the lead detective handling whatever was going on at the residence. To my surprise I found out that the nanny who worked for the Evans' family was dead!

After being brought up to speed by the detectives on the scene of the happenings surrounding in the Evans' house, I proceeded to try to find my mark. I walked back out to the front yard of the house and questioned the officers milling around if they knew where I could find Ms. Watkins. The young cop pointed over to the neighboring porch. I headed in the direction of Ms. Watkins and I could tell she was not happy to see me at all!

"Ms. Watkins, may I have a word with you?" I asked.

"No you cannot. As you can see I don't really have the time to play these mind fuck games with you detective." she snapped at me.

76

DNA 2

"Well, maybe this will help." I said handing her the warrant for her fiancés arrest.

She scanned the paperwork and shook her head, balled up the paper, and threw it on the lawn.

"This has got to be all wrong! Dread didn't have anything to do with that girl's death. He was performing last night! Call his manager and they will be able to verify it!" she screamed at me.

"Ms. Watkins, did you ever stop to ask your fiancé where he was performing last night?"

She shook her head. I knew I had her right then and there. This shit was going to actually work!

"He was performing at the Stadium Club last night for a private event. According to sources he disappeared after his performance. There was quite a bit of time that he was unaccounted for. He had the means to murder that young girl, dump her body, and return home to you like it never happened." I said putting the icing on the cake.

ShaniQua Watkins stood there simmering like a pot ready to boil over.

"Now, where is he? Or would you like to go down for aiding and harboring a wanted man?" I asked her hoping she would give me a reason to slap the cuffs on her ass too. I was willing to lock up anyone; I had too to save my own ass. If that meant busting her too, then so be it!

"I hate to disappoint you Detective Gatsby, but he is out of town on business. He left this morning for Atlanta." NiQue said.

"Now isn't that convenient? A woman loses her life and now Mr. Evans is out of town! How convenient indeed! And now, of all things, we have a dead nanny and it doesn't strike you as funny that he skipped town?" I said, stirring the pot. "I will see to it that we get his ass this time. He keeps slipping away from me, but he won't this time. He got off for killing your best friend's entire family and you still stand firm on protecting that piece of shit. He must have put it on your dumb ass good!" I said, making her hotter than the flames of hell.

"Look Detective Can't Catch Crook, if you want to walk out of here with your own life, you would want to get the fuck outta my face! I am not beyond fucking up a washed-up cop with a hard on for busting niggas for no reason!" she spewed.

She was so feisty it was a turn on. I quickly shook off those types of thoughts because that is what landed me here in the first place; me wanting to fuck some sweet, juicy, black pussy.

I started to go back and forth with her for the hell of it, but I knew it wasn't going to do me any good. I was going to let her win this round, but she was going to have to see me again!

Her elderly neighbor put her arms around NiQue's shoulders and tried to get her to go inside the house. NiQue shook her head. She handed the baby to the older white woman and then she walked up to me. Her full chest was heaving up and down in a rhythmic pattern that you couldn't help but notice. Her eyes were dilated wide as saucers, which struck me as strange because it was bright as a summer's day outside and unless she had them medically dilated it was odd for them to be that way. Her skin was slick with sweat. I knew that look; she was high.

"Detective Gatsby, you and I both know my husband is no killer. He is an entertainer! If you keep up this bullshit of trying to frame him, I swear I will make you pay for it with your life." She stuck her finger in my chest and something about the way she threatened me made me believe that she would do just as she said she would. There was no way she was just going to threaten me and get away with it. My ego would not stand for it.

"Ms. Watkins now you look here! I am an officer of the law and I am doing my job. Now you are more than welcome to run and get your lawyer or whoever you want to get, but you are not going to stand here and threaten me like you have no respect for the law." I said sternly.

"Oh, I have respect for the law, just not for you! And if you don't get the fuck out of here, you will see how disrespectful I can be. I don't need my lawyer to deal with you!" She seethed.

Something about what she said had me shook. I knew she meant ever word she was saying. This ballsy bitch wasn't making threats, she was making promises. I backed away from her because something about her seemed inhumane. I didn't want her that close to me. The sexual attraction I had originally felt was gone now and I didn't want it to come back. This bitch would fuck around and bite my dick off!

"Do me a favor, tell your fiancé he should make this easy on himself and turn himself in or I can make this ugly for the both of you."

I turned to head back over to where the Maryland cops were trying to restore order on the normally peaceful block. I stopped in my tracks, turned around and approached Ms. Watkins again.

"Oh, and whatever you are high off of, you better not let these county cops find out, they will have that pretty baby in foster care faster than you can blink." I laughed and walked away from her.

If she had believed Ronald was innocent, she definitely doubted it now. From the looks of it, he hadn't told her about the location of his show the night before and if I didn't have any other ammo against him, what I had just told her was the shit that sealed his fate.

BLAQUE

Dirty

DNA 2

CHAPTER THIRTEEN

Experience Unlimited (EU)

"Da Butt"

Dread

I was uneasy the entire flight to Georgia. Once I touched down and the captain announced our arrival in Atlanta, I powered my cell phone on and I had fourteen voicemails from NiQue. As I listened to each of them, I noticed they all said the same thing; she wanted me to call her as soon as I could. The five text messages she sent all said the same thing, "Call Me ASAP!" I figured she and Joseah had gotten into another altercation and I wasn't in the mood to deal with ShaniQua's childish shit.

I couldn't get my thoughts in order from all the shit that happened the night before. From fucking that stripper, to her sister being murdered; it was an ill situation and I couldn't get any of it out of my head. Like the nigga that I am, I was happier than a mutha fucker that I had left when I did, or I could have been mixed up in all that drama. Senseless drama was not in my equation. I had been trying to avoid any heat since the cops had left me alone about who had killed YaYa.

I grabbed my carryon luggage and headed to baggage claim. I retrieved my belongings and went out front to meet Ox and Crack who were supposed to be there to pick me up. Before I could get out of the automatic doors, reporters swarmed me. There were lights flashing and people pushing up in my face, all trying to ask me questions. They were all asking something different, and I couldn't make out what they were saying. I was grabbed roughly by Ox who also grabbed my bags, and Big Jeff and Crucial brought up the rear trying to keep the reporters away from me.

Next thing I knew, a huge Chevy Avalanche pulled up to the curb. Another one just like it pulled up behind it. When the doors swung open on the first truck Crack was behind the wheel and Billbo hopped out of the second truck. Billbo, Ox and Big Jeff were trying to keep the reporters away from our vehicles as they ushered me inside. Before the door could fully close, I heard one of the reporters very clearly.

"Mr. Evans did you kill her?"

I tried to see who asked the question, and I wanted to respond by asking a question. I didn't know what the fuck was going on. It looked like a circus in the *Southwest* terminal. Billbo slammed the door shut, moved the crowd back, and got into the truck behind us. I swear we must have driven 75 miles an hour getting out of the airport.

"What was that shit back there?" I asked Crack who was looking straight ahead maneuvering through the other cars on the ramp trying to get out of the crowded airport.

"We will talk about that once we find a new hotel. The hotel we were staying in sold us out to those blood-thirsty reporters." he said narrowly missing an old beat up Honda that had jumped in our lane going well below the speed limit.

"What the fuck are you talking about Crack? Who sold us out and for what? Who do those people think I murdered? What is going on?" I asked confused.

"We will talk about all of this once we get to another hotel. I found a spot in College Park. The whole damn town is sold out for this concert." Crack said, not offering any more information.

We rode in silence until we pulled up to a *Hilton*. Crack ordered me to stay put and out of sight like I was child. Even though I wanted to know what was going on, I wasn't willing to risk everything by trying to find out.

DNA 2

Crack came back with keycards in his hands and distributed them to everyone in the trucks. We pulled around to the back of the hotel and we entered the hotel through a service entrance. We used a cargo elevator in the kitchen used by the room service staff. Once we got to our rooms on the sixth floor, everyone went their own way. I could see from the expressions on their faces that they too had been through some shit today, and I knew I was getting ready to hear all about it. I entered my suite and admired the view of the city. I barely noticed Crack had entered the room behind me.

"Dunny, you want to hit this?" he said pulling a rolled J of Kush from his duffle bag. I laughed to myself. With all the money we were getting, Crack still hadn't invested in any real luggage. I took the blunt from him and sparked it while walking out on the balcony. Cracked followed me out into the humid, sticky, southern air.

"What was all that shit at the airport about?" I asked him taking a pull of the weed into my lungs.

"So you really don't know what happened?" he asked taking the blunt.

"I wouldn't be asking you if I knew."

"Man, that stripper broad's sister got murked last night behind the club. Those reporters back there found out we had a show at the club where it happened. They said something about an anonymous tip being given to them and something about you being wanted for questioning." He pulled the blunt again and passed it back to me. I slowly tried to process what he was saying.

"Do they think I had something to do with that lil' bitch getting her head hit?"

"Yeah man, they do. That is why we had to try and shake them and change locations. Have you talked to your girl?" Crack questioned me.

"Naw, I haven't talked to her yet. She didn't even know where I performed last night. I was trying to avoid her for a minute. She has been tripping lately. I don't know how she is going to take this shit." I said truthfully.

"Well, I think you better tell her wassup before she has to hear it from someone else. She is going to find out; might as well be on your terms that she gets the news. The last thing you need is her finding this shit out from someone else. She might not take it too lightly that you held back some shit like this from her. You know how she can get." Crack said.

I nodded, letting him know he was right. We finished the blunt and I rolled another one. I retrieved my cell phone from my pocket and called NiQue. She picked up on the first ring.

"Hey babe, we need to talk. Are you alone?" I asked her.

"Yes, it's just me and the baby. Dread I don't know what's going on, but you need to get the fuck back here now. Joseah is dead and that asshole of a detective came here with a warrant for your arrest!" she cried into the phone.

"What do you mean Joseah is dead?" I damn near choked on the smoke from the blunt. Maybe I wasn't hearing her correctly.

"After I dropped you off at the airport I went home and the baby was fussy so I took her for a ride to calm her down. When I came back home I found her," her voice trailed off.

"What do you mean you, 'found' her?" My head was spinning. This shit can't possibly be happening again.

"I found her dead in the kitchen. The police said it looks like she fell and she hit her head. They aren't saying much more than that," she was sobbing into the receiver.

"Are you ok?" I asked then it hit me! Did she say that that detective came to the house with a warrant?

"Baby did you say that cop Gatsby came there looking for me?"

DNA 2

"Dread, it wasn't just any cop; it was the one from…" her voice trailed off and I knew she didn't want to discuss it. I knew just what she was talking about.

"What did he say? What did he want?" I asked her firing question after question.

"He said something about you being wanted for murder! He had a warrant and everything. Dread, please come home. I don't want to be alone. I can't do this alone. I can't do this again!" she whined.

"Look, stay inside. Don't leave the house and I will try to get on the first flight that I can back to DC." I ordered.

"There might be a problem with me coming straight back. I ran into some shit at the airport and I am not in Atlanta. I had to change hotels. I am in College Park until I can get out of here. When I touched down earlier today, there were reporters swarming all over the place. It's a wonder that the police didn't pick me up and send my ass back to DC." I said.

"Dread, please hurry home to us. I would die without you!" NiQue cried. She was damn near hysterical and it was breaking me down.

"I got you shorty. On everything I am gonna' get this handled and I will back home before you know it." I said. I was trying to convince myself more than I was trying to reassure her.

"Dread? Why didn't you tell us that you were performing at a strip club last night? Did you have anything to do with that young girl turning up dead? If you had something to do with that shit you need to speak up. *We* can't help you if you don't tell *us* what happened." she fussed into the phone.

I couldn't believe what she was asking me. I looked at the phone like it was a foreign object.

"NiQue you are being real reckless right now. I don't have shit to hide because I didn't do anything wrong, but you are not gonna interrogate me over the phone," I said growing agitated with her.

"*We* would appreciate it if you didn't hide anything from *us* anymore." she said and then the line went dead.

I was so pissed off. She had the nerve to be trying to make me account for every step I took when all she did was disappear and leave our newborn with who she referred to as, "the strange nanny."

I paced back and forth in the hotel room until it hit me! Who the fuck was she referring to when she said, "*We* would appreciate it if you didn't hide anything from *us?*" Didn't she just say she was alone?

I guess I was answering to not only her but the baby too. I threw the cell phone across the room and it slammed against the wall, shattering into several pieces. Crack jumped up like someone had launched a grenade. The sound of the phone crashing against the wall had startled him.

"Dunny, you have to stay calm. I don't know what the fuck is going on; but losing your cool right now is not going to solve anything. We have to figure out what we are going to do. Obviously, everyone knows you aren't in DC because of the mob of paparazzi in the airport and the other hotel. They know you are here in Georgia; they just don't know where!" Crack said. He stood there waiting for me to respond.

I didn't have anything to say. I knew one thing for sure, and that was that I needed to get home and talk to Pinky, so she could clear me of this shit. She was the only person who knew where I was last night after I got off of that stage. She was the one person who held the key to my freedom. I just prayed that her clearing my name didn't ruin my relationship with NiQue.

Dirty

DNA 2

CHAPTER FOURTEEN

All-in-one

"Mandingo"

Neko

Pinky hasn't been the same since she had to go in front of the whole world via the reporters to look for her sister's killer. Even though our relationship has never been one based on the traditional foundation of what a relationship should be built on, I have tried to be there for her. I know what it is like to lose the people you care about most in this world. That common bond was enough to keep us bonded.

I walked in her bedroom where she had been hibernating for the last twenty-four hours since all of her business had been aired out on the news. The only thing the reporters didn't know was what Pinky really did to make serious money. Somehow, that information hadn't gotten out and I am sure she was glad it hadn't. However, with her being on every news channel in the DMV every few hours, it wasn't good for her business. No one was interested in a hit woman for hire who had let someone infiltrate her spot and murder one of her own.

She had the pale pink curtains pulled shut, making it hard for the light to penetrate the room. The only thing she did was watch the television, hoping there was new information on her sister's case. I hated to think that her sister's case might grow cold before the cops even gave it a second thought. I had become an expert at making funeral arrangements, so I didn't mind lending Pinky a helping hand in that regard. All of this shit had seemed so surreal. There was no way this should have happened.

BLAQUE

In the short, few weeks before the murder, Pinky and I had just sent Khalia off to the prom and after that we attended her graduation. She was a good girl. There was no way she could have been caught up in some bullshit that would land her dead in the alley of one of the country's most notorious strip clubs. She was only seventeen! Her life was just starting, and she should have been deciding on which college she would be attending in the fall. Instead, we were deciding on which cemetery to bury her in.

I crossed her large bedroom and shut her TV off. Pinky stirred beneath the covers.

"Neko don't turn that off! What if they have some information and I miss it?"

"Pink, the police will call you if anything changes or if they find out anything more than they already know. You have got to stop torturing yourself."

"I should have been there for her. I know this shit is all my fault. It had to be someone who was out to get me and got her instead. There is no other reason for this. It was retaliation or revenge. I just know it! I have taken out so many niggas...who's to say one of them ain't target, kill her, and dump her at the club to make a statement?" She was going round and round, with her theories and it was rather sad.

Pinky was normally a killer with no remorse. You could never get an emotion out of her unless it revolved around her sister. This shit had her feeling a certain kind of way and it was breaking me down little by little to see it.

"Pinky, there was no way for you to know this was going to happen. Most people didn't even know she was your sister. Please stop beating yourself up about this. This ain't your fault and you already know whoever is responsible is gonna pay!"

She sat up in the bed and I took a good look at her. Her eyes were puffy, and her normally neatly maintained, hot pink locks were half pinned up and half hanging all over the place. She

88

looked lost; and I wished I could immediately take the pain away if it would help her return to normal.

She ignored my statement and disregarded me as if I weren't there. I watched as she fumbled around her bed; ultimately finding the remote and switching the TV back on. She flipped through the channels, surveying each and every news station she came across. I took a seat next to her on the bed and reached out to hold her and she flinched like I was about to hurt her.

"Damn, when did we get here?" I asked.

"I'm sorry Neko, but I don't want to really be bothered right now. I am sure you can understand that with all of this going on, I just want to be alone."

"Well, I don't think it's a good idea for you to be alone right now. You ain't exactly doing to great on your own!" I argued.

She avoided looking at me. I knew she was trying to hide the helplessness she was feeling. Someone as rough as she is can easily be broken; and she was ashamed of it.

I could see through her act. She was trying desperately to hold on to the tough girl act when I knew she really wanted to let go and let the tears loose. I had seen my sister YaYa play this game one too many times. I knew the game all too well.

"Neko how do you know what's good for me?" she said giving up much attitude.

"Pinky, I am not gonna do this with you. If you don't want me here, then all you have to do is say so and I will let you be." I countered.

"I say so!" she shouted.

I damn sure wasn't going to argue with her. I had had more than my share of death and I didn't want to partake in anymore. I knew she was just grieving, but she was not gonna take her frustrations out on my ass just because I was trying to help.

My cell vibrated in my pocket letting me know I had a text message. I entered the password and saw a message from Natalie and dismissed it without looking at it. I knew she didn't want anything but some attention. I would have to deal with her when I finished handling this shit with Pinky.

"You might as well go to whoever that is calling or texting your phone because I want to be left alone!" Pinky said rolling her eyes like she was truly pissed with me.

"Aight shorty. Just call me if you need anything or if you hear anything." I said standing to leave the room.

I got to the doorway and the look in her eyes said, "please don't leave me," but if she was gonna act like this then I was not going to sit around and take her shit. I was just trying to help her the best way I knew how.

"Make sure you call the funeral home too. They said this Wednesday is the first day they have available for the service. I hope you take care of yourself Pink."

I saw the tears welling up in her eyes. She nodded and turned her head, so I wouldn't see her cry again. I shook my head and walked out of her room not knowing what else to do. My girl, who wasn't exactly my girl, was buggin'. I didn't know how to approach her or help her in fear she might flip the script on me. I walked out of her house and headed to my Yukon which occupied her driveway. Once I got inside, I made a phone call. I let the phone ring three times and almost hung up. I felt guilty even thinking about what I was about to go and do, but Pinky forced me to do it!

"Oh, so you finally call me back huh?" Natalie said in her husky Jamaican accent.

"A friend of mine had a death in the family and I was helping them out with the funeral arrangements. So, all that popping off at the mouth shit you can keep to yourself Natalie."

"I'm sorry, I didn't know; I just thought you were trying to avoid me." Natalie said.

"You ain't know ma. Are you home? I am trying to come through and see you. I need you right now baby. It's been a long fucking day and I need what you got." I said smoothly.

DNA 2

"What is it you need from me?"

I could hear her freaked out ass smiling through the phone and that shit turned me on. I cranked the engine of my truck, backed out of the driveway and headed to SW where Natalie lived.

"I need whatever you are offering me baby. I'll be there in twenty minutes. Make sure that thang is ready for Daddy when I get there; aight?"

I didn't even wait for her to respond. I hung up the phone and threw it in the passenger seat and pushed in the direction of Natalie's house. If I never understood, *like father like son*, I understood that shit now. It was all too clear. My Pops was known for keeping bitches on him and I was no exception! I had heard many stories about how Pops always had a bad bitch on his arm! I had to admit my thirst for variety was something deep rooted and I am sure it stemmed from Pop's genes.

I got to Natalie's house in under the twenty minutes I had estimated. I did the breath check and pulled down the visor to make sure I was straight.

I'm a handsome nigga.

My signature grey eyes sparkled with anticipation of beating the pussy up. That seemed like the only thing I really enjoyed since my sister died. As long as I had pussy I was aight. I pushed the visor back into place. I got out of the car, set the alarm, and knocked on Natalie's raggedy ass door. I hated coming to her house because she lived in the ghetto and you never knew if you were gonna get car jacked, robbed or caught slipping.

I heard her shoes clicking across the floor towards the door. When she opened it, she made sure she opened it wide enough for the whole block to see her empty ass, run-down section-eight type house. She was naked as the day she was born. All she had on was a pair of satin blue *Prada* heels. Her long weave was the only thing covering her perky implanted breast. Her makeup was the same color of her shoes and she had on that glittery lotion shit I hated. She smelled like the knock off version of *Versace Bright Cristal.* I hated cheap perfume! You could never get that shit off of your skin without damn near scrubbing until you bled. All I could do was think to myself that if she spent the money she paid for those shoes and those tits wisely, she could afford to live somewhere better than here.

Maybe I should be with Pinky. As quickly as that thought came, it was gone as Natalie she turned around to let me completely in the door. I watched her chocolate ass jiggle with every step she took, and I was mesmerized. I knew she was about to do a nigga proper and I so needed it after all the shit that had happened. I didn't even give Pinky and what she was going through another thought. My thoughts were immediately lost in the rhythmic sway of Natalie's hips. I knew coming to see her was definitely a smart move to relieve some pent-up frustration.

Dirty
DNA 2

CHAPTER FIFTEEN

DJ Flexx

"The Water Dance"

NiQue

I had spent the majority of the night being asked the same ten questions a hundred different ways. These cops were stupid if they thought I was going to implicate myself. They just kept asking me where I had been and how was it that I didn't know anything about Joseah. I made it a point of telling them that maybe they got close to their help if they could afford help; but I damn sure didn't. We paid her to do her job. I didn't need another friend, so I never made it my business to know anything other than her name. Dread handled writing the checks for her and that was fine with me.

"Ms. Watkins how is it, that your nanny lived on your property and yet you didn't know anything about her?" the detective asked me.

"My fiancé handled the dealings with the help. He interviewed her, hired her and he paid her! I had very little contact with her because she wasn't one of my favorite people. As a matter of fact, we had discussed letting her go earlier in the day." I said.

The bald head Fed asked me the same things over and over until I started to become annoyed. They even went as far as asking me to submit to a polygraph. I demanded that they get my lawyer down there, and with those words they finally eased up and let me go home to my daughter who had been with Dread's mother.

BLAQUE

This day had been stressful enough. All I wanted to do was go home, roll a spliff, have a drink, and try to pretend this day hadn't happen. Dread wasn't making shit any better. He wasn't here and now this cop was looking for him again! I was furious he hadn't bothered to tell me that he had been at that club with that stripper bitch. That shit had me feeling a certain kind of way. I was always learning shit second hand.

I called Mrs. Evans to let her know I was on my way and she said she would keep YaSheema for a couple of days. I was more than happy to let her stay there. I had all but forgotten I couldn't just drop her on Joseah and do me anymore. I had better get myself together and quick. I had to learn to be a good mother of a three-month-old who I knew nothing about in a matter of a few days; all because mommy fucked around and killed the nanny. I turned on my *Ipod* and the song, *"Monster"* came pouring through the speakers.

"How appropriate is that, my song upon entrance!" Pajay said.

"Oh no!" I said shaking my head. "I am not in the mood to deal with your ass. I don't have the baby, no Dread, no Joseah, and I damn sure don't feel like your company!" I said to her.

"Don't blame me for your company or lack thereof," she laughed.

"You know you are really twisted and I know how to fix your ass."

I stuck my hand in my purse trying to find my magic pills, but I came up empty.

"Fuck!" I said hitting the steering wheel. I had left the pills in the house. There was no way I could have gone to the police station with a bag of Xtasy in my *Michael Kors* purse. I removed my hand and balled up my fist and slammed it into the steering wheel causing the horn to blow. The driver in front of me moved out of my way thinking I was trying to pass them. I sped up and around the car and the little old lady driving the big Lincoln made me chuckle to myself. I could never understand why old people drove the biggest cars they could find.

94

Dirty
DNA 2

"What are you smiling for?" Pajay said interrupting my comical thought.

"Just sit back and shut up." I said to Pajay, defeated for the moment.

"You don't have the baby, and the in-laws said you could have some time to yourself. Why don't we take advantage of that? Dread ain't home. Plus, who knows who the fuck he is out screwing because it damn sure ain't you." Pajay reminded me.

I let out a loud sigh. I was getting real tired of her. She was a thorn in my side and a real pain in the ass. She only showed face when it suited her, and then when the shit got hot she would roll out untouched; leaving me to fend for myself. The others had never left my side like she did. This game she was playing was getting old.

"So, what's the plan?" she asked again.

"I plan to go home without you sticking around to fuck some shit up for me. Then I plan on taking a long, hot bath, smoke a J and go to bed. This has been one of the longest days of my life and I have to go to the lawyer's office in the morning. Wait…why am I explaining this shit to you?"

"You don't have to explain shit to me because I already know you say one thing and do another. Anyway, where are you gonna get the money for the lawyer? Remember Ms. Fancy Pants you bought this house and now we're almost broke. You know that nigga ain't gonna represent us without cold hard cash! He doesn't take his retainer fees in the form of washed-up pussy!" she laughed.

"Keep it up bitch and I will fuck around and over dose just to get rid of you!" I threatened.

"Yeah go ahead and let me see you try that shit. Fuck me and you fuck yourself!" She spat back. *"I wanna see you make it one day without me. Just one day of weak ass NiQue and the whole world would be chewing you up and spitting you out. You wouldn't survive without me! Besides, I am tons of fun; who wouldn't want me around?"*

The music changed, and Rhianna and Eminem versed back
and forth about an affair gone wrong. I felt like that was what
was happening with me and Pajay! She fucked up and I had to
fix it, but she was right; I couldn't live life without her. I owed
her. She saved me when I had no one else. When everyone else
would rather abuse and then abandon me, she was right there to
right their wrongs no matter how harsh the punishment. She was
the judge and the jury, and no one ever got probation. They
were all sentenced to death.

*"So, what did that sneaky ass man of yours have to say about being at
that strip club? Or did you even ask him?"*

I shrugged my shoulders, not wanting to have this
conversation with her because it was not going to lead to
anything good. Besides it was none of her business

"Yeah, I asked him." I said keeping my eyes focused on the
road. I prayed she wouldn't try to fish around for too many
details.

*"So, what did he say? Let me guess, he didn't have anything to say
about it. I told you not to trust that nigga!"* she said chastising me as if
I were a child instead of the grown woman I am.

"I would prefer it if you would stay out of my relationship
with my man; thank you!" I spat back.

I needed to hurry home and get to my stash to get rid of her
before she started a war with Dread. I was in no mood to deal
with her attitude or her treachery. Pajay sucked her teeth and
quieted down for the rest of the ride towards our upscale home
in Laurel.

*****

I pulled into the driveway and parked the truck next to my
Benz then strolled up the walkway. I noticed the stares coming
from my neighbors who were in their yards tending to their
flower beds and watching their children play. I ignored their

sideways stares and kept it moving right into the house. Once I got inside I went straight to the kitchen and looked at the mess I had to clean up from the incident with Joseah. I instantly started regretting everything that had happened the day before. I stared at the broken shards of glass along the floor and felt horrible for what we had done to Joseah who didn't do anything to deserve an early death.

"That nosy bitch deserved everything she got! She had it coming! Had she minded her own fucking business she would still be alive." Pajay barged in.

"I thought I told you to go away!" I screamed.

"Haven't you figured it out, I ain't going anywhere."

I didn't respond to her stubborn ass. I simply stepped over the broken glass and retrieved a cup from the dish drain and headed for the fridge to get some orange juice. I poured a glass and exited the kitchen the same way I had come in. I walked up the steps feeling drained of all my energy. I went to my hiding spot in my bedroom, got my bag of medicine, and popped two pills.

"You are gonna fuck around and overdose." Pajay said.

I ignored her; refusing to give her any conversation. Instead of listening to her nonsense, I turned on the sound system to drown out her words. Slow, yet steady, motions lead my actions as I walked into the bathroom to run a hot bath. Anxiously, I emptied the remaining bath salts into the steamy water anticipating how good the bath was going to feel. I disrobed in front of the mirror that hung on the back of the door to the bathroom and looked at the bruises on my legs from the fall I took while assaulting Joseah. The salty water of my tears began to gather in the corners of my eyes. I was so ashamed of what I had allowed to happen to that woman. As the water fell from the faucet into the tub, tears started to fall down my face and on to my naked skin in the same manner.

"There is no use in crying over spilled milk. Crying isn't gonna get us anywhere. It damn sure ain't gonna bring her back. You and I both know she was bound to expose our little secrets and we can't afford to have anyone digging in our past. You are finally getting everything you ever wanted. Did you want her to tell your man that you are crazy and talking to people that aren't there? They would lock us away and then you would lose it all! Your man, your house, the baby and your freedom would all be no more. We did what we had to do to survive. Remember that!" Pajay said.

No matter how hard I tried to find some truth in what Pajay was telling me, I could find none. I knew we were no more than cold-blooded killers. This has to end! I said to myself before going over to the vanity and retrieving both a razor blade and my cell phone. I at least wanted to call Dread and let him know what he meant to me before I committed the ultimate sin. I dialed his number and it went straight to voicemail. I pushed the end button on the call and slid my body into the hot water and sat there, contemplating suicide.

"Oh, so you are just gonna try and take the coward's way out and kill yourself?" Pajay spoke up.

I couldn't bring myself to do it because I didn't want my daughter to know I went out like a sucker. I wanted her to know that her mother was a soldier. I couldn't succeed at anything, not even killing myself. My high was starting to kick in and as usual Pajay was gone; at least for the time being, or until she found some way to pull me into another fucked up situation.

I finished my bath, toweled off and crawled into my lonely circular bed after trying Dread's cell again to no avail. This time I hung up and then powered the phone off. I didn't want to be bothered by anyone. I finally drifted off to sleep with images of my sister YaSheema, Oscar, and my no-good ass Daddy dancing through my head.

CHAPTER SIXTEEN

911 Band

"All the Brown"

Detective Gatsby

I was sitting in my office with my feet kicked up atop the piles of crap I had stored there. I was feeling good too! For the first time in a long time I felt like I was making some progress in my life. I was on the verge of breaking this Clayton-Reynolds and York case wide open.

I had that nigger Dread on the run. I had dropped a dime on him through some folks over at the local news stations. I had made a few calls letting them know he was a suspect in the murder of Khalia York. Those nosy bastards loved to have the story first. Too bad I called each and every news station in the area and told the same story to each reporter. I even had taken the liberty of telling them where he was.

It was just a matter of time before there would be no juror who wouldn't know about the case and fry Ronald Evans. Even though I knew he had nothing to do with the young girl's death, I was going to make sure he got the book thrown at him for slipping through my fingers for the deaths of his former girlfriend and her family. As long as he was locked up, I didn't care what I had to do to see this thing through.

Someone was knocking on the door. I planted my feet on the floor and tried to make myself look like I was busy working.

"Come in!" I yelled.

BLAQUE

In walked the sister of my victim. Chyan "Pinky" York, was opposite of her baby sister in many ways. One would never even know they were related to one another. Where Chyan was high yellow, Khalia was chocolate. The only resemblance they bore was their beautiful shaped bodies. Don't get me wrong, both women were gorgeous, but the older sister was a brick house. She looked like she had been sculpted like that. Her ass was so round and juicy you could see it from the front. Her perky double D breasts sat up firm even without the assistance of a bra in the pink tank top she was wearing. Her supple breasts gave way to her washboard tummy and then widened down to her delicious hips and toned thighs.

I licked my lips watching her watch me. I was imaging her giving me a private lap dance in my office. Chyan walking into my office like that reminded me of that Beyonce video, "Dance for You." I could see her dancing around my office just until I bent her black ass over my desk doggy style and fucked her until all of my frustrations were gone. I had to stop fantasizing about women like this. This is how I almost got caught with a body instead of being able to pin it on that fool Dread.

I finally spoke up.

"Good morning Ms. York. Please take a seat." I said directing her to sit in the chair that sat across from me. I could tell she was uncomfortable in my messy office. I would have at least attempted to clean up a little had I known she would be paying me a visit so soon. I had just called her roughly thirty minutes ago, and here she was in front of me looking like a video vixen.

"Hello detective. I hope you called me down here to tell me that you have my sister's killer in custody. I ain't really interested in anything else." she said obviously noticing how I was giving her the lustful eye.

I cleared my throat.

100

DNA 2

"Actually, I do have information on your sister's murderer. I wanted you to be the first to know that we have a suspect." I lied.

She sat at the edge of the seat hanging on my every word.

"His name is Ronald Evans." I said waiting to see if she could make a connection.

After studying her face for a moment, I could tell that she didn't know Dread by his government name.

"You may also know him as Ronald 'Dread' Evans. He is a rapper and we believe he was performing at your place of employment the night of your sister's untimely death."

Her facial expression grew cold. Her face turned red and her eyes narrowed. Something about the mention of the suspect caused her despair and I wanted to know why.

"Ms. York, are you alright? Can I get you anything?" I asked trying to pry without her knowing what I was up to.

"No…no, I am ok. Have you all tried to pick him up? Do you have him in custody yet?" she asked.

"No ma'am. Apparently, he left the state the day after the murder and we are currently going through the proper channels to get him picked up as soon as we can get his exact location. The last bit of information we gathered was that he was supposed to be performing in Atlanta. That is what we were able to gather thus far. As soon as I am able to obtain any more information, you will be the first to know!"

"Good, let me know if you pick him." she said standing to leave my office.

Something about the way she said "if" bothered me. It was as if I wasn't going to do everything I could to see that slimy bastard behind bars. Before she could make it to the door, Clancy from the forensics' team entered my office.

"Oh, I am sorry Detective Gatsby. I didn't mean to disturb your meeting." Clancy said eye balling the hell out of Chyan York. He was about to turn around and leave back out of the door, but she had him captivated. I didn't blame him either she was a lot to take in.

"I was just leaving." Ms York said, throwing her *Gucci* bag strap over her shoulder and making her way out of my tiny office. Clancy didn't speak until we both shook off the effect Chyan had unknowingly whipped on us.

"Damn Gatsby, she is fine as hell! Wait, isn't she the woman from the nightclub killing?" Clancy asked.

I shook my head up and down to let him know he was correct.

"Well, you may have some news for her sooner than you thought." Clancy said smiling wide.

My stomach started to turn because I was hoping whatever he had found didn't link this shit to me.

"We were able to find some DNA under the victim's nails. There was also a bottle of Ginger Ale that was found open lying next to our victim's body. I am not sure if we are able to get any information from the soda bottle because that could have belonged to anyone, but the skin under her fingers is a different story. I have already taken the liberty of running the DNA samples through the system." Clancy said proudly.

I couldn't have been more disgusted with the news. I had all but forgotten about the tender folds of skin that I had kept neatly bandaged. Underneath the bandages were deep gashes where the young girl had clawed at my wrists; trying to free my hands from crushing her wind pipe when she hadn't complied with my demands of a blow job.

I unknowingly started fidgeting with my wrists. Clancy stared at me pulling at the stupid bandages and I immediately dropped my hands in lap out of his view.

"I didn't think we were gonna find anything that would help us take this guy Evans down." Clancy said very proud of himself. "This could be what I need to get that promotion to the Head of

Dirty
DNA 2

Forensics. Think about it, if we bag this rapper guy, it could put both of our careers in fast forward."

"Yeah a promotion would be nice." I said only half meaning it. I started to shuffle papers on my desk trying to look busy. I was hoping that Clancy would get the picture and leave.

"Gatsby, I am sure you have a lot to do. I will contact you once I get the DNA information. It shouldn't take more than a few days before we know something. I put a rush on it because I know catching this guy means a lot to you." Clancy left my office and I sat there dumbfounded, trying to figure out how the fuck I was going to keep him from finding out that that DNA was mine and not Ronald Evans.

BLAQUE

CHAPTER SEVENTEEN

Raw Image Band

"Shake It Out"

Dread

I felt like I was a hostage. I had been hiding out in this hotel in Georgia and wanted nothing more than to go home and be with my daughter. After smashing my phone up, I hadn't heard from NiQue and I am sure the way things were going, she wasn't too fond of me right now. It had been two days and some change since I had spoken with her and even though she would pull disappearing acts on me from time to time, I had never done the same to her and I felt low for doing it now.

I was getting real tired of feeling like I was trapped in this hotel room. The worst part of it was that I had nothing to do with that girl's death. I didn't even know who she was; but people were looking at me like I was the prime suspect. It was all over every news channel and I felt like a caged animal.

Just when I was ready to make a break for it and try to get back to the DMV, Vito and Budda followed by Coogi, Trae and Ox entered into my room. They were carrying take-out bags of food and they were talking about being stuck in Georgia and not being able to make a move until this shit got cleared up. My stomach grumbled. The smell of the take-out wafted over to me reminding me that I hadn't had anything to eat.

"Wassup Dunny? Are you aight?" Vito asked sitting the bag of soul food in front of me.

"I guess man. This whole being stuck in here not knowing what's going on with my wifey and my seed is driving me crazy. She said they found the nanny in the kitchen dead the morning I flew out here, and I have been trying to make heads or tails of all of it." I said hoping he would offer me something out of the containers of food, and better yet a resolution to the madness.

As if he were reading my mind he slid the food over to me.

"We ordered you something. I didn't know if you wanted anything, but I damn sure wasn't going to share my food with you!" he laughed trying to make me feel better about the situation at hand.

I gobbled down the food and sat there with my boys until it was damn near nightfall. The concert was the very next day and I still didn't know if I was supposed to be performing or not. This whole thing with the body in DC was fucking up my career moves, and I wasn't feeling it. I had waited damn near my whole life to get invited to the *A3C Festival,* and now it looked like my whole crew was going to go on without me in fear that I would be arrested as soon as I stepped on the stage to perform.

It seemed like no matter what I did to try and fly right; shit never went my way since I got down with NiQue. I didn't want to blame her for all the bad shit that kept happening, but there was no way to overlook the fact that all of this crazy shit started happening as soon as I started fucking with her and YaYa.

The guys were amped up about going out tonight and I couldn't get motivated or excited about any of it. They were planning to go out to *Magic City* for a night of fun and freak action. I thought it was in bad taste to go to yet another strip club being that all this shit came about because we had been in a strip club. I couldn't blame the guys for wanting to go out though. After debating the situation in my head, I decided against going and stayed in the room.

*****

The guys from the Cap all got dressed and left out, leaving me to my thoughts. Crack had left his cell with me, so I could contact him if I needed anything. I felt like a kid who was being punished and could not leave his room for bad behavior.

I flopped on the bed and decided I would try and contact NiQue. She had played the mad role long enough and I was tired of acting like a stubborn ass little boy. I was going to be the bigger person in the relationship and call her. If for no other reason than to make sure my baby girl was ok.

I dialed her number and the call went straight to voicemail. Hearing the automated message telling me she wasn't available made me feel like I was going crazy. I tried to call her a second and third time with the same result. I finally gave up on calling her and prayed that she and the baby were alright.

I don't know what made me do it, but I went through the contacts in Cracks cell phone and located Pinky's number. I figured since he had set up the performance with her directly, surely, he would have her contact information. There had to be an email, the number to her booking agent or a number to reach her in his *BlackBerry*. Crack was too organized in his business not to have kept something like that for future reference.

I browsed through the contacts until I found what I had been looking for. Her number was listed in his phone under Pinky Stadium Club. I dialed the number. My heart was thundering in my chest and my palms were sweaty as the phone started to ring. One the third ring she answered. It felt like my mouth instantly went dry.

"Hello." she said. She sounded tired and worn out.

I could tell she had been crying and probably had been pushed to the brink of insanity over the last few days. Gulping hard, I tried to gather the courage to speak. I cleared my throat forcing the words from my lips.

"Umm, can I speak with Pinky?" I finally managed to say.

"This is she. Who's speaking?"

"This is Dread…I really need to speak with you. I need you to hear me out. The shit they are saying about what happened with your folks ain't true baby girl. I would never do anything like that to anyone!" I said with urgency. I feared she would hang up or she may have the police standing right there tracing the call. Those pigs could have been listening in on the call and just waiting for me to give my whereabouts. I was paranoid as hell.

"I was framed. Someone else did that horrible shit to your folks and set me up to take the fall. I don't know who did it but I am desperate to find out who is out to slander my name and ruin me. I just need you to believe I ain't do it."

"Believe you!" She screamed through tears. "I don't believe shit you say. You killed my sister and you are going to pay!" she barked.

"Please listen to me." I begged.

"After we left the stage and you and I…well you know…I left the club and went home to my fiancé." I said trying to get her to hear me out. "I had never seen your sister before I saw her picture on the news the next day. You have got to believe me! I wouldn't hurt her or any other person unless they wronged me. I had no reason to kill her!" I blurted out.

She sucked her teeth and I knew she didn't want to hear anything I had to say. For all I knew, she was calling the police and sending them to my location.

"Pinky you know I ain't have nothing to do with this!"

"I don't know shit about you! I know one thing and one thing only. You better either run, or let the police get you before I do! You have no idea who you are fucking with!" she said icily and then the line went dead. I stood there with the phone pressed to my ear with no one on the other end. Hopelessness began to sink in. There was no reasoning with her. There was only one thing left to do, and that was to get home to DC and figure out on my own who was trying to ruin my life. Everything else would have to wait.

*****

Hours later I was finishing up the last of my packing when Crack walked into the room.

"Wassup Dread?" Crack asked. He watched from the doorway as I haphazardly threw my belongings into my suitcases. I jumped from the sound of his voice. I was a nervous wreck. I didn't know who could be after me at this point. It could be Pinky, the police, or whoever was trying to set me up to take the fall for that murder.

"I'm packing my shit to leave." I said never stopping long enough to look at him. I just kept stuffing my belongings in my bags.

"I have to get home! The shit going on is serious and it could fuck up my whole world. I haven't heard shit from NiQue. I miss my daughter. Then there is the shit that happened to the nanny. I don't know what the fuck is going on, but I swear on my life Crack, I'm gonna find out!" I said meaning every word.

"I feel you man. I just hope you know what you are doing. You are risking everything by going home blindly. How are you gonna get there? I know you don't plan on just waltzing into an airport and flying back!"

"No, I don't. That is where you come in old friend." I said setting my plan into motion.

I was getting home and there wasn't a damn soul who was going to stop me either.

BLAQUE

CHAPTER EIGHTEEN

DJ Kool

"Let Me Clear My Throat"

Neko

Over the last few days I had just said, "fuck it" and stayed away from Pinky. I tried everything I could to be there for her, yet she did nothing but push me away. I was getting sick of her acting like she didn't want a nigga around. I wanted to be there for shorty, but she kept flipping the script on me. She wouldn't let me in and that was the shit that was fucking with me the most.

I had been spending more time at the shop and with Natalie than I had been with Pinky. I was starting to get sick of Natalie's whiney ass too! When we were fucking she was always demanding shit, and when we were at work she was always acting like since she was giving me the pussy, she didn't have to work. The only thing she was working was my nerves! Natalie was causing me more headache than she was worth, and it was making me miss Pinky even more. I wasn't used to a female invading my space.

Pinky had managed to get herself together enough to finish arranging Khalia's funeral. Today was the day we would lay her to rest. Today would also be the first time I had seen Pinky since we had the falling out.

I left Shadow in charge of the shop for the day and planned on going to the funeral to pay my respects and see if Pinky was willing to talk rationally. I missed her; and it was time that we hashed this shit out.

*****

BLAQUE

I entered the funeral home and it was standing room only. It really was a sad situation and just being there tugged on my heartstrings. A large poster of Khalia in her cap and gown was set up near the front of the funeral parlor; it was draped in a sea of flowers. There were people, mostly her high school friends and associates, standing in every corner comforting one another. My eyes scanned the room to see if I could locate Pinky. I didn't see her. I made my way to an available seat and a familiar face caught my eye.

Detective Gatsby was trying his best to go unnoticed. It was hard for him to do so being that he was the only out of shape, white man in an all-black funeral. He hung around the exit of the funeral home and looked very much out of place. I didn't want to lose the only seat in the house, but I wanted to know what he was doing here. Before I could get pass the crowded row of people to make my way to him to him, a group of young women walked over to him. I fell back because I didn't know what their exchange was about.

The girls all looked to be about Khalia's age, and I recognized a couple of them as friends that she would go out with. As the approached Gatsby, his face turned beet red and worry spread across his chubby cheeks. After whatever words were exchanged between them, the Detective ducked out of the funeral home before I could speak with him. I went to sit back down in my seat; side stepping the people who were getting tired of me moving all around. I even heard one of the older women suck her teeth when I politely said, "excuse me."

It was already 11:30 a.m. and the services were supposed to have started at 11:00 a.m. It was typical black gathering. Nothing ever started on time. Another fifteen minutes had come and gone before Pinky entered in from the rear of the funeral parlor. She looked tired and worn out. Regardless of that she was still stunning. Her pink *Chanel* suit hugged her in the right places and her long pink locks hung in curls around her face. Out of respect for her sister, she pulled off the shades she was wearing. Pinky stopped to greet a few people who offered their condolences. I wanted so badly to go to her and pull her into my arms and tell her everything would be alright. I wanted to take care of her, but Pinky was so stubborn, she would surely reject me if I did.

I watched as she carefully made her way to her sister's casket. Once she got there her normally hard shell cracked before the world that was watching her. She began to cry. The tears were pouring from her eyes uncontrollably. I couldn't take too much more of this. I got up again causing the old woman to roll her eyes at me for stepping over her feet again. I approached the spot where Pinky was standing.

As I touched her shoulder lightly, she turned to see who was violating her last moment with her dearly departed sister. Once she saw it was me, she crumbled into my arms; sobbing loudly. We stood there holding one another for comfort. Seeing our emotions run high set off a chorus of tears throughout the entire funeral parlor.

Pinky and I stood there, for what felt like an eternity, holding one another until the preacher politely let us know that we should begin the services. On cue, Pinky took my hand, leading me to the front pew where only the family was supposed to be seated; and she never let it go for the rest of the service. We sat there clutching each other and Pinky made it through the funeral without too many more tears.

*****

Hours later we were sitting in Pinky's home. The repast was over, and even though I hadn't left her side since we connected earlier, she hadn't said much to me. The last guest was headed out of the door and I decided I would be the one to initiate the conversation. There was still much hostility hanging over us and we needed to address it so we could move on.

Pinky and I were seated on the couch and the lingering smell of all the food that had been dropped off was still in the air.

I broke the silence.

"Pinky, for whatever it's worth, I am truly sorry. I apologize for not being here for you when you needed me the most. I apologize for you having to deal with this. No one should have to go through this alone." I said sincerely.

Ever so softly, she leaned over and planted a kiss on my lips; it made me feel warm throughout my entire body. She didn't have to say anything more. With that kiss I knew she had forgiven me for my behavior. She laid her head on my shoulder and locked our fingers together.

"Neko, do you understand that I have to deal with this?" she asked.

I nodded my head up and down. I knew what she meant. She was going to get her own kind of justice for her sister. She was looking for street justice. I couldn't say I blamed her for wanting to eliminate the monster who had taken the only person she loved unconditionally.

"How are you going to do that?" I asked her not really wanting to know. I normally stayed out of her business when it came to anything dealing with her line of work, but this instance was different. "Do you have any idea who did it? Do you have any leads?" I asked her with curiosity.

She lifted her head and we were eye to eye.

"I have some information. I don't want to involve you in any of this because it may get ugly once I lock on to him. The less you know, the better off you will be." she said.

I couldn't help but wonder who her target was. I wanted to question her, but I knew how she operated. She moved in silence; and by herself, and I didn't want to do anything else to upset her. If it meant being left in the dark about it then so be it. As long as she and I were on good terms, that is all I cared about.

Dirty
DNA 2

CHAPTER NINETEEN

Chuck Brown and The Soul Searchers

"Go-Go Swing"

NiQue

I woke up to the sound of the baby's muffled cries. Motionless, I sat there coming down off of my high. I wondered why Joseah would allow the baby to continue to cry and cry. No sooner than I had the thought, the reality of it all came crashing down around me. There was no Joseah. I swung my legs over the side of the bed and raced out of my room and down the hallway to the baby's nursery. The door was closed, and I didn't remember closing it.

My heart started to beat faster, and I threw the door open and was horrified to find my daughter with her mouth duck taped. She was thrashing around and being that she was only-three-months old, she didn't have the ability to remove her make-shift gag. I rushed over to the crib and scooped her up in my arms and pulled the tape from her tiny lips, causing her to cry harder. I had no idea how long she had been in the nursery with her mouth bound, and I was scared of what else had happened to her while I had been unconscious from the strong drugs that were pumping through my body. I rocked her back and forth and she continued to cry.

"I'm so sorry YaSheema." I whispered to her.

I carried her out of the room with my emotions at an all-time high. I made my way to the kitchen to fix her a bottle and once again I was faced with what I had done.

BLAQUE

I had not cleaned up anything in the house since Joseah died in the kitchen. The dishes were right where she had left them; including the broken glass along the floor and Dread's unfinished breakfast was still sitting on the table. I stepped around the glass and made the baby a bottle. She settled down and I took a seat at the kitchen table while she greedily sucked down her milk. I felt out of place. I felt like I was going insane.

"You ain't crazy bitch you're just pathetic!" Pajay sneered.

My eyes popped wide open hearing her voice and I became furious.

"You should be happy I let you get some rest or that little bitch would have had you running back and forth. All her spoiled ass keeps doing is crying." Pajay said annoyed and sucking her teeth.

"Don't you ever put your hands on my child again!" I screamed growing more and more agitated by the second.

"Well, I guess you shouldn't have gotten so high trying to rid yourself of me then! The next time you leave that baby hollering, like she is crazy, on my watch it will be much worse than duck tape!"

I cringed, thinking of what could have happened. I needed to get away from Pajay once and for all before she ruined my life. Thoughts of Dread flooded my mind like a broken dam. What would he have done if he had come home and found his fiancé passed out, high as hell, and his newborn bound in her crib. I knew he wouldn't be too pleased with that. That nigga might fuck around and throw my ass out with nowhere to go. As much as I hated to admit it, I needed help and I knew just who to call. I don't know why I hadn't thought of it before.

Pajay was still going on and on about what she would do to the baby if I didn't do something about her always crying. I ignored her as best as I could; not trying to let on that I had intentions on her never having to hear my baby cry again.

The baby was now sucking on an empty bottle and I carried her and the car seat up to my room. I took her out and decided I would give her a bath. I had no choice but to do these things

Dirty

DNA 2

now since I overreacted and had let Pajay cancel Joseah. I wasn't used to caring for the life I had brought into the world, and I felt ridiculous attempting to get her ready to leave out of the house.

After twenty minutes of the baby squirming around, I finally got her dressed. She was asleep and laying on the bed. I didn't even want to go into the closet to find something for myself to wear in fear of Pajay doing something awful to her. I couldn't believe how paranoid this bitch had me in my own home. I took a chance and scrambled around in the huge walk-in closet and pulled out a pair of *Seven* jeans that still fit even after the baby weight. I also grabbed a cream-colored *D and G* blouse. I was on a mission to end this shit with Pajay today, and no matter what I had to do, I was willing to do it to keep my family safe and in the dark about that screwed up bitch Pajay. She had caused enough trouble.

For the first time, I was grateful that Dread was not home and that he was out of harm's way for the moment. I know he was dealing with his own shit with the police accusing him of killing that girl. That was another problem I was going to address; but first things first, I had to go and see Neko. I knew he would help me.

I finished getting myself dressed and picked up the baby and placed her in her carrier. She looked so peaceful. I proceeded out of the house. I strapped the baby in her car seat and got in the driver's side.

"So, where are we headed?" Pajay asked before we could get out of the driveway.

I didn't respond. I just kept driving.

"So, you ain't gonna tell me where we are going? You are gonna sit there and ignore me? Bitch, I know you hear me talking to you!" Pajay yelled.

I just kept my eyes straight and didn't give her the attention she wanted. Every time I heard her voice I cringed. I couldn't even turn the radio up because I didn't want to wake the baby. It

117

wouldn't have done any good anyway because no matter what I did to drown her out, she would come harder.

I pulled into the detail shop and swung the truck into a space next to a pearl-colored bubble Chevy Caprice that was sitting high on 22" shoes with deep dish rims. I shut the engine down and got out. I was moving so fast I almost left the baby in the backseat in her car seat. I went back and cursed myself for leaving her. I really had to make a better attempt at being a mother. I had to at least try until the smoked cleared and I could get another nanny.

I laughed at the thought of getting another nanny. Who in their right mind would want to work for the Evans family? I could hear the conversation playing out in my head.

So, what happened to your last nanny?

Oh, she almost found out I was boarder line crazy and she tried to tell Mr. Evans and we killed her for sticking her nose in our business. When can you start?

I unfastened YaSheema from her seat and made my way to the front of the shop. When I entered there was an annoying chime that sounded as I walked in. It signaled to the receptionist that someone was inside the office. The same chick I had seen a week earlier was sitting behind the desk filing her nails. She eyed me as though I didn't belong there.

"Can I help you?" Natalie asked.

"I am here to see Neko. Is he in?" I asked trying to ignore her raunchy attitude.

She looked at me like I was crazy. She scanned my entire body like she was sizing me up. I returned the stare. She was a pretty girl who wore too much makeup. She also could have done something better to the raspy weave she had in her hair. But she was a nice-looking woman if she lost that fucked up chip she had on her shoulder. She sucked her teeth, clearly pissed that I had interrupted the manicure she was giving herself.

Dirty
DNA 2

"He ain't here. What can I do for you?" she asked not really meaning a word of it.

I started to tell her she could kiss my ass. I wasn't appreciating the funky ass attitude she was throwing at me. Before I could tell her, what was on the tip of my tongue. Shadow appeared from the back office.

"Well, hello again." he said looking at me hungrily.

"Hi Shadow." I said turning my attention to him instead of the hating ass receptionist.

He looked puzzled and I realized where I went wrong.

"Oh, so you do remember me!"

"Yes, I remember you."

"Well, you sure acted like you ain't know who a nigga was the night I saw you at *Proud Mary's.*"

I had forgotten about that shit. I had to think fast. I didn't want him to think I was crazy. I smiled a flirtatious smile.

"I was probably drunk and couldn't remember my own damn name. All that matters is that I remember you now." I said batting my lashes.

This little game I was playing with him was working because he started to smile showing all of the gold in his mouth. I secretly wondered where he was from because no one in the DMV sported gold teeth.

"Now that you remember a nigga, when can I take you out?" he said still smiling like the Cheshire Cat from *Alice In Wonderland.*

"I am not too sure if my husband would like that."

"I ain't trying to date ya husband, I am trying to take you out."

This nigga's pick-up lines were lame. There was no way in hell I would have gone out with him even if I wasn't involved. I could see Natalie ear hustling from her desk. It looked like her manicure could wait long enough for her to get all in our business.

"Is Neko in?" I asked trying to stop the game of cat and mouse because I had come here on a mission and all this back and forth was not in the equation.

"No, he ain't in. You wanna leave a message? I'm sitting in for the boss while he is dealing with his folks losing her sister." he said explaining Neko's absence.

I could see Natalie damn near stop breathing when she heard Shadow mention a female in the same sentence with Neko. It was obvious she and the boss man were fucking around. I peeped her moves when I visited the last time. She had looked at me side-eyed like there was something going on with me and Neko.

"No, no message." I said turning to leave.

I was gonna have to catch up to Neko some other time. I hope it would be soon.

"It was nice seeing you again Shadow. I said making my way out of the front door.

I had made it all the way to the truck and was placing baby YaSheema in the back when I heard the door from the shop open and close.

"Excuse me, but can I speak to you for a minute?" Natalie asked.

"I don't have time to make friends right now. I am kind of in a hurry." I said over my shoulder.

"This won't take but a minute. What is your relationship to Neko? As a matter of fact...you don't have to answer that! I just want you to know he is my man and you better back off! I don't play well with others!" she spat.

I closed the truck door with the baby tucked safely inside. "Neither do I, and that is why I ain't gonna stand here and play this stupid game with you. Like I said, I have to go. I am in a hurry."

I tried to walk around to the driver's side door and Natalie was still on my heels.

"I know you and Neko got something going on and I'm gonna shut that shit down!" Natalie said.

This had to be the dumbest broad I had ever met. I thought to myself hoping she did not cause Pajay to stir. There was no need in her getting involved. The whole reason I was here was to try and wipe her off the face of the map; not to bring her out swinging.

"Look, I said it ain't that type of party. Neko is my brother and there isn't anything going on."

"I don't believe shit you say! Neko had one sister and she died. So, unless you came back from the dead you ain't his sister!"

Natalie and I were face to face like it was a showdown at high noon. Before I could speak up and try to end the confusion, Pajay spoke up from somewhere in the distance.

"Bitch I told you to fall back. You don't want none of this right here. Playing pussy with me could get you fucked in so many ways." Pajay said spitting fire.

It was too late! Once Pajay was on, she was all the way turned up. There was no bringing her back or calming her down. If I didn't try to diffuse this shit, there would be another body for me to cover up.

"Who are you calling a bitch? I will show you a bitch!" Natalie screamed striking me across the face.

"Pajay please don't do this! We don't need any more trouble. We got enough shit going on."

"Naw NiQue, this bitch got us fucked up and she is gonna pay. Who the fuck does she think she is? You tried to be nice to her and she tried to test your gangster. So now it's my turn!"

"Please Pajay, just let it go just this one time. I promise if you want her we can get her later. We just can't fuck with her right here and right now." I said pleading with Pajay.

I must have looked crazy as hell standing out there having a conversation with myself. Natalie finally backed off because she didn't know who I was talking too or what was happening as I stood there trying to reason with Pajay to let her go.

Natalie's sucker ass ran off back to the office.

I hopped in the truck because I knew she was going to tell Shadow what had just happened, and I didn't need him seeing us carrying on in the middle of the parking lot like that. If and when it came down to it, I was going to have to lie to protect myself. I cranked up the engine and the Hemi came alive. I backed out of the space and roared down the street.

"This is the shit I am talking about! You keep letting people do and say whatever they want to us and you don't do shit about it. You should have let me body that bitch for being disrespectful." Pajay was ranting and raving out of control and I couldn't think.

"*You let that stank bitch hit you! Haven't I taught you better than that? Haven't you learned anything from me?*" she continued yelling.

I finally got tired of hearing her fuss and curse and decided to give her a taste of her own medicine.

"If it hadn't been for you, I wouldn't have been there in the first place. Had you not tied up my child, I wouldn't have gone to Neko's shop. I hope you are satisfied now. That bitch saw you acting all wild and she is definitely gonna tell. Who knows who will be sitting at our door waiting on us. Did you ever stop to think that it looks a little strange for a grown ass woman to be babbling and talking to herself?"

There was no response. So, I laid it on really thick.

"I bet you never stopped to think that if they lock me up, they are gonna lock your stupid ass up too! If they give me shock therapy, you are gonna get everything they give me!"

There was still no response. I was hoping I had scared her enough that she would go about her business and leave me alone.

I drove around aimlessly for thirty minutes before I decided I wasn't doing shit but wasting gas. I pulled over at a park and

DNA 2

tried calling Dread's cell. I was tired of this game we were playing, and I needed him. The call went straight to his voicemail again. I sat there feeling crazier than ever. I didn't see an end in sight with regards to my unwanted visitor Pajay. She kept me wrapped up in so much drama it wasn't funny. Then there was all the other shit going on: my future husband who was wanted for murder; then there was the death of the nanny, and to top it all off, I couldn't just get up and go, I had the baby to look after. Something was going to have to give if I wanted to keep what little sanity I had left.

BLAQUE

Dirty

DNA 2

CHAPTER TWENTY

Trouble Funk

"Pump Me Up"

Neko

I had taken the last few days off from the shop to help Pinky. Shadow was more than capable of handling the shop while I wasn't there, so I had left him in charge. I was eyeing Pinky lying on her stomach asleep. Just as I was about to go and make a play for some pussy, my phone started to ring.

"Wassup Shadow?" I said looking at the caller ID. I left out of the bedroom, so I wouldn't disturb Pinky with my conversation.

"Hey bro. I hope you and shorty are aight over there. I just wanted to tell you, you had a visitor at the shop this afternoon."

"A visitor like who?"

"You know that shorty NiQue; she came by looking for you."

"Did she say what she wanted?" I asked concerned.

"Naw she ain't say what she wanted. Your other shorty Natalie got to lunching out in here too. Yo' you're gonna have to check her ass! All I know is she ran outside behind NiQue and when she came back in, she was furious and was talking in that Patois shit. All I could make out was something about the bitch being crazy and wait until she talked to you." Shadow said trying to line up the events in chronological order.

"I had to fuck around and send her home for the day; she was wildin' so hard in here! I don't know what old girl laid on her outside, but Natalie ain't like it." Shadow continued.

"I will handle Natalie when I get back to the office. Shorty is getting carried away. NiQue and I are friends and nothing more.

125

I don't know why Natalie bugs out like that. I'm going to have to stop breaking her off if she is gonna keep this shit up!" I said careful not to be too loud. I didn't want to wake Pinky. I damn sure didn't want to wake her while I was talking about smashing another woman.

"Aye man, you are gonna have to do something because if those two bump heads again, it may take the jaws of life to pull them apart." Shadow said laughing.

"I can't help it if Natalie is on me! That playa shit runs in my family. Matter of fact, while I am bumping my gums with you I could be all up in some guts. I gotta go. Hold that shit down around the shop and don't let Natalie act up too much. Imma call her later when I can get away to talk to her and let her know she better get right or get gone. Thanks for looking out though!"

I wanted to know what NiQue came to see me for. I also wanted to know what the hell had happened with her and Natalie. Just as I was going to call Natalie and put her in her place, Pinky walked out of the bedroom. She had on some little boy shorts that half of her creamy round ass was hanging out of; looking at her made me re-think calling NiQue or Natalie.

"Why are you out here?" Pinky asked pressing her body against mine.

"I was on the phone with Shadow. He was giving me a run down on what was going on at the shop. I didn't want to wake you. You looked so peaceful."

I couldn't help myself and kissed her. Her mouth was warm and inviting. I could feel my nature rising in anticipation. Pinky was a vixen and I loved fucking with her. She should have been more than enough to satisfy me. She could tell that she was arousing me, and she wrapped her hand around my erection— stroking it through my boxers. I had missed our sessions of wild animalistic sex. Just the idea of me sliding into her sugary sweet pussy was making my manhood swell.

Dirty
DNA 2

Pinky immediately dropped to her knees and took me into her mouth right in the hallway of her condo. Looking down at her angelic face as she took me into her pouty lips was sending me over the edge. I stood thrusting my stiffness in and out of her mouth and she was beckoning for me to push her to the limit. If she kept this up I was going to cum and I damn sure didn't want that. I had waited weeks to feel her and she wasn't going to ruin it by making me cum before I was able to bang her back out.

Stepping back from her I pulled her up on her feet and backed her up into the wall. We were as eager as two high school students that had to do their business quick before their parents came home and busted them getting freaky. We moved with so much urgency and desire. Pinky stepped out of her boy shorts giving me one hell of a view of her delectable body. Picking her up and using the wall to brace us, I wrapped her legs around my waist and entered her tight tunnel.

"Oh, God Neko! I missed you baby." Pinky moaned over and over in my ear.

I dug deeper into her secret place, matching each of her movements thrust for thrust. The more I pounded the more she moaned. She was driving me crazy with desire. If anyone had seen us fucking up against the wall like that they would have surely turned that session into a porno to be sold to the highest bidder. Pinky was on her Kim Kardashian shit with it, and I was just trying to keep up.

"Ne...Sssssssss Ne...Neko, I love you!" Pinky screamed tightening her pussy muscles around my dick. I couldn't hold it anymore. I came and we both slid down the wall collapsing on the floor panting and sweating.

"Dammit girl! A nigga is gonna have to start working out fucking with your ole flexible ass!" I said.

I kissed her forehead and we both made our way to her room. I opened the windows to let in the fresh air and out went

127

the thoughts of Natalie, NiQue and the conversation I was supposed to have with them both.

I eyed Pinky as she jiggled her ass inviting me to another round. Before I joined her in the bed I powered off my cell phone because I damn sure didn't want anyone to knock our groove.

Dirty

DNA 2

CHAPTER TWENTY-ONE

Reaction Band

"Drop That Thang"

Dread

Crack and I were on I-85 north heading back to the DMV. He had rented a piece of shit Camary that wouldn't draw any attention to the Feds. So far everything was working out in our favor. We didn't speed, and we didn't even twist up any of that good Georgia bud we had packed away in our bags. We were trying to get back home without any incidents or issues.

I thought it would have been better if we left during at night to avoid the cops; but Crack insisted that we leave during the day so when we finally arrived in the DMV it would be well after midnight. We were pretty much on schedule when I checked the dash. It read 10:12 p.m. and we were due to touchdown in DC in about two hours.

I tried calling NiQue again, and every time I got her voicemail it made me want to fuck her up. I needed her to know I was on my way home and I wanted to make sure there weren't any cops posted up outside of the house. I would hate to get caught before I found out who was trying to fuck up my life.

Crack was cruising listening to some demo of some young cats that were trying to get put on. I had my game face on and was anxious to get home and handle this shit. I wasn't a sucker by far, and the media was making me out to be not only a sucker, but a murderer too.

"You aight man?" Crack asked.

"Yeah. I'm aight. Just ready to get home and handle this shit.

"Have you heard from your girl? How is she holding up?" Crack asked keeping his eyes trained on the road.

"Your guess is as good as mine. I haven't heard shit from her." As I answered Crack I couldn't help but wonder myself what NiQue was doing, and how my daughter was. I hadn't heard shit from them since all of this shit started.

We had had been driving for almost seven hours and were about to hit Richmond when I heard the sirens and looked back and saw the lights flashing in the rearview mirror. Panic surged throughout my body.

"Oh shit! We weren't speeding or anything. Maybe they are pulling us over on some bullshit. Just let me do the talking and don't say shit!" Crack said pulling the car over to the side of the road.

Being from the hood, he was already prepared for the routine. He slowly reached in the console between the driver and passenger seats and obtained his wallet along with the rental car paperwork as the officer approached the window.

"Good evening officer. May I ask why you pulled us over?" Crack asked calmly.

I tried to avoid eye contact with his cracker ass. My appearance was a cop magnet. I looked like what most people would classify as thug, hood or ghetto. It was times like these that made me wish I didn't have these dreads, expensive clothes, jewelry and most of the attitude of a street nigga.

The officer was looking from me to Crack and then he settled his gaze on me. He had his hand on the butt of his gun and I knew his country trigger happy ass was going to shoot if we didn't comply with any demand he was going to make.

"Can you give me your license and registration; and will the passenger please step out of the car and place your hands on the roof of the car where I can see them," he demanded.

"Officer, may I ask what this is all about?" Crack asked again handing the officer his license and the paperwork from the rental car company.

DNA 2

"Come on now son, I think you already know why I am pulling you over. If you don't know then you will find out sooner rather than later." he said never taking his eyes off of me. His country accent reminded me of one of those old western movies. There was no mistaking it. This pig knew who I was, and he was going to bust my ass. I wasn't going to make it back to DC without being in cuffs.

Before I could even blink, Crack had swung the driver's side door open and hit the officer in the midsection with the door; knocking the cop on his ass. Crack jumped out of the driver's side of the car. My shock finally wore off and I started to react. I ran around to where the cop was trying to get himself up off of the ground. I sent my fist crashing into his face, knocking him back on the ground. Crack removed his gun from its holster and tossed it on the side of the road.

"You still ain't telling me why you pulled us over officer." Crack taunted the officer who was rolling around the ground holding his nose that was gushing with blood.

"Fuck man! You broke my fucking nose. I was just following orders. Half the God damn country is looking for his ass!" The cop said pointing at me with blood dripping from his nose.

"Please don't kill me!" he said whimpering. His eyes were wide, and they were begging for us not to harm him.

Crack grabbed the officer up like a ragdoll and stood him up on his wobbly feet. He grabbed the officer's cuffs and keys. He cuffed his hands behind his back and walked him to the rear of the patrol car and shoved him in the backseat then he locked and slammed the doors. He jogged back to where I was standing and looked at me like I had lost my mind.

"Why the fuck are you still standing there? Get in the fucking car and let's go! Are you waiting on his backup to come and get you? We barely got out of this shit. I don't know about you, but I am getting the fuck out of here! We still have about two hours before we hit DC. Hopefully this bought us some time to get home." Crack said scooping up his license off of the ground where the cop had dropped it along with the rental car information.

We could hear the cop screaming for help in the back of the cruiser. I finally got my ass in gear and got in the car and Crack pulled off before I could even shut my door.

"Shit, they know we left Georgia and are headed back home. What are we going to do?" I was in a panic and couldn't think straight. How the fuck did they know we had left?

"I got an idea. NiQue told me that detective that had been snooping around when YaYa died came past the house the other day. I bet he knows something about this shit." I said aloud.

Crack had pulled off of I-85 and had decided to take some country back roads since we were less likely to be detected. I snatched up his cell phone and frantically dialed NiQue's number. I even tried the house which was something I didn't want to do. I didn't know if they had the house phones tapped or not, but I had to gamble to find out what I needed to know. After several rings and no answer, I officially gave up on NiQue. She was either running the streets or avoiding me; and either way she wasn't holding me down like she should have been.

"Dunny, what's the game plan?" Crack asked, concentrating on the roads and watching every approaching vehicle like a hawk.

"The plan is to get home and find Detective Gatsby. Fuck it, they are already looking for me, I might as well go the one place they wouldn't expect me to go...to the police station!"

Crack smiled a sick ass smile to let me know he was all in.

"Let's do it then. Fucking around with you Dread, Queen is going to kill me! I think I am more afraid of her than these sucker ass cops." Crack said referring to his wife who was going to go berserk when she found out what had happened. Queen stood about 4'11", but she was fiery and didn't play that shit when it came to her husband. If she found out about this shit she would probably be ready to beat the shit out of the both of us. As far as I know, Crack had been avoiding her, so she couldn't ask him too many questions about the police looking for me. She would have demanded that we brought our asses home and went straight to our lawyers. Queen was from uptown DC, but the way she carried herself you would never know it. She was about her money and her family; and if you fucked with either then she would be like a lioness protecting her cubs.

With a plan in motion I felt a little more at ease. I cranked up the music and, "Out of Luck" poured through the speakers. Secretly I hoped I wasn't out of luck!

BLAQUE

CHAPTER TWENTY-TWO
Junkyard Band (JYB)

"Loose Booty"

Detective Gatsby

I was sitting at my desk as usual. I was on pins and needles. The results from the DNA would be back any day now. I had already planned on taking out half of the Forensics Team if I had to in order to keep my secret.

The phone rang from somewhere under the piles of garbage I had on the desk. I pushed paper and food containers to the side trying to locate the ringing phone.

"Detective, Gatsby, speak to me." I answered.

I immediately started to panic once I heard the voice on the other end.

"John, they got away. They jumped me when I pulled them over."

"How the hell did they get away? Why didn't you shoot them?" I asked my cousin Patrick who was a rookie cop on the force in Petersburg, Virginia.

"When I ordered the guy, Ronald, out of the car, the other guy in the car hit me. They took my gun and cuffed me and left me in the back of my squad car. Thank God someone noticed my car on the road and got me out of there. Sorry John."

That was all I heard before I slammed the phone on the cradle. I didn't want to hear any more. I was starting to wonder if this dude Dread had an "S" on his chest because he kept getting away from me no matter how many obstacles I put in his path. It was time for me to really take matters into my own hands. Shit was getting thick and unless I wanted to take the fall for that girl's death, I had better do something about his ass quick.

I fumbled around my desk trying to locate a phone number I wished like hell I didn't have to use. I found the piece of paper that had coffee stains and all kinds of other shit on it. I dialed the number and waited for who I knew would answer.

"Yo," the voice on the other end of the line said.

"Smash." That was all I had to say. The voice on the other end knew exactly what it meant, and I knew all hell was going to break loose.

I didn't even wait for a response because I knew there would be none. I hung up the phone and gathered my things. I knew what I had set into motion couldn't be taken back. It was time to make my exit for the day. I snatched up my belongings, including my picture of Anona. It was my favorite. She had a beautiful smile that could move mountains. Her eyes sparkled like diamonds. She was my version of this life's perfection and she was no longer here. I knew she was disappointed in my actions. I could feel the tears welling up in my eyes.

"Baby look what I have become. I know you are looking down on me from heaven and I know you are ashamed of my behavior. Why did you leave me? My life ain't been shit without you Anona. Please forgive me." I said aloud.

I wiped the tears from my clouded eyes and headed out of the door. There was nothing I could do to stop the chaos I had already created.

****

I was sitting in a café around the corner of my apartment. I was pushing french fries across the plate. I wasn't really hungry. The indigestion and heartburn from my nervousness were making it so I didn't want to eat anything. Suddenly my cell phone rang, startling me.

Dirty
DNA 2

"Hello." I said into the phone.

"Smashed. It's done." Then the line went dead.

I wanted to run out of the café, but I had to remain calm. I had to keep my wits about me. I waved to the waitress who took her time making her way over to me. I got the check and waited for her to bring me my change. I wasn't giving her rude ass a tip either. I sat there looking around nervously like someone was going to come for me. I knew no one was coming from me, I was just paranoid.

The waitress finally brought her slow ass back to my table and handed me my change. She stood there like I had forgotten something. I got up from my seat and walked past her. She sucked her teeth and mumbled what sounded like, "cheap ass mutha fucker" under her breath. Paying her no attention, I headed out of the door, got into my car, and drove home. I all but ran up the steps to my lonely apartment. I grabbed the bottle of *Pinnacle* off of the kitchen counter.

I turned on the television and plopped down in my worn-down leather recliner and unscrewed the cap to the plastic bottle. I took a swig of the cheap vodka and fished around in the couch for the remote. Once I found it, I flipped through the channels until I found what I was looking for.

A reporter appeared on the screen.

"Bryan, can you tell me what's going on down there?"

Sarah it looks like the 5th District Police Department is burning to the ground. I am sure you can imagine the chaos out here right now. The fire has engulfed the entire building. The firefighters you see behind me are working feverishly to put out the flames.

They have had to pull out of the rescue efforts because the fire spread so fast and furious. The fire chief said every attempt was made to preserve life, it was just too dangerous to continue the search and rescue mission without jeopardizing the lives of the men and women battling the blaze."

"Bryan, do they know what started the blaze?"

"No Sarah, but my sources tell me that apparently an accelerant was used to jumpstart the fire. The fire is so ferocious and so out of control that they are afraid there are no survivors here at the 5th District. This is a tragic day indeed. My sources also tell me that the police chief has called an all hands-on deck. She has called in backup from each district and has also put in a call to the mayor to bring in reinforcements from the National Guard.

Sarah, you have got to wonder what type of animal would start a blaze like this and not have a guilty conscious. We will keep you updated on the situation as it unfolds.

I turned the television off and sunk deeper into the chair. I felt the smile pulling at the corners of my mouth and I didn't even fight the urge to break out into an all-out grin. I guess the Forensics Team would have to dig a little deeper to catch a killer. I hated that so many innocent people were harmed to keep my ugly secret, but it was survival of the fittest out here. I couldn't go down for a mistake.

I spent the rest of the night trying to figure out my next moves. I had to figure out how to catch Ronald Evans. He had proven to be elusive time and time again, but he would slip up, and when he did I would be right there to make sure he fell hard on his ass!

Dirty

DNA 2

CHAPTER TWENTY-THREE

Experience Unlimited (EU)

"Buck Wild"

Neko

I woke up in the middle of the night and Pinky was gone. That didn't surprise me. She said she had to go and handle some business. I took the time to make the phone call I needed to make to Natalie and straighten this shit out with her. Even though it was 1:00 a.m. in the morning, I knew she would take my call. She never denied me.

I sparked a J and went to the living room to make sure that if Pinky came home I could end the call before she got in the front door without her knowing I had been talking to another woman. I took a seat on the plush couch and called Natalie. Just like I suspected, she answered on the first ring.

"Wassup shawty?"

"Hey Neko. I am glad you called because we need to talk." she said giving up much attitude.

"Natalie what is this I am hearing about you going on my folks in my place of business. That shit doesn't sit well with me. I told you before that NiQue is nothing more than my friend. She was my sister's best friend and there ain't shit between us." I said before she could even get a word in.

"Baby, I'm sorry about all that but there is something else you need to know. That bitch is crazy! I know I shouldn't have spazzed on her like that, but you know I get jealous when it comes to you." She cooed into the phone.

139

I hated when she did that shit. She was a grown woman and had no business acting like that. I could hear someone knocking on her door.

"Baby hold on and let me get that." Natalie said.

I couldn't make out much that was going on in the background, but I could hear Natalie asking whoever her visitor was what they were doing there. There were sounds of a scuffle and then I heard Natalie scream.

"Please someone help me!" she screamed.

Her screams continued until they were no more and there was nothing but silence. I held the phone pressed to my ear trying to hear if someone was still there. I was rushing around the condo trying to put on clothes and find my keys, never disconnecting the call. There was a loud dragging sound. I could hear what sounded like a woman laughing and then the phone went dead.

My adrenaline kicked in to overdrive. I went to Pinky's closet and pulled out a chrome .357 Magnum, stuffed it into my waistband, and I rushed out the door. I was calling Natalie's phone as I made my way through the DC streets, but she never answered. I feared she was hurt and I needed to get to her. I can't explain why I felt like I needed to help her being that she was nothing more than my employee and my sexual gratification from time to time, but I was getting fed up with losing people. It was fucking with my manhood that everyone I came in contact with mysteriously turned up dead.

I drove beyond the speed limits praying that I didn't get pulled over. I pulled up to her house and hopped out of the car with the keys still in the ignition and the engine running. I ran as fast as my feet would carry me to her front door that was slightly ajar. I pushed the door open and called out Natalie's name. There was no answer, which heightened my fear. I had seen enough foul shit over the past year to last me a lifetime. I had learned my lesson and never walk into some shit blind. Natalie could have pissed anybody off and they came in and fucked her up and left her for dead. I didn't know what to expect.

I walked into the house and noticed that the lamp that normally sat on a table by the door was lying broken on the floor. I tiptoed further inside and started inching my way towards the back of the house and that's when I saw what I didn't want to see.

Natalie lay behind the couch in a nightie with a knife sticking out of her chest. I moved closer to her and saw some ole horrific shit that you normally only see in movies. Her tongue had been cut out of her mouth and it lay pinned in place on top of her bloody chest. Next to her body was a note written in big black marker. It read: *Loose lips sink ships.*

I back paddled and almost slipped in the trail of blood that was on the floor. I regained my footing and tried to fight the urge to throw up. I couldn't hold it anymore and rushed out the front door where I came in and threw up on the steps.

Once I finished letting my dinner loose on the steps I started to panic. I didn't know if anyone had seen me or if the killer was still there. I knew one thing, I wasn't going to wait around that mutha' fucka' to find out either.

I felt bad just leaving her there, but what was I supposed to do? I wasn't getting wrapped up in none of this shit. I hopped back into my ride and threw the car into reverse. I backed out watching the entire block. I half expected the police to pop out of any one of the cuts or alleys and bust my ass. It didn't happen.

I didn't exhale until I had pulled my car onto the entrance ramp for I-295. I thought about calling the police, but how could I explain that shit to them? How would that play out? I just happen to be stopping past my employee's house at the wee hours of the morning and I stumbled upon her half-naked body with her tongue detached and pinned to chest with a knife. That shit wasn't going to fly. They would bust my ass immediately!

BLAQUE

My mind was frantically racing. I made it back to Pinky's house and her car was parked in her assigned space. I whipped my car into the guest space next to hers and killed the engine. I rested my head on the steering wheel and tried to gather my thoughts.

I exited the car and entered the condo. I could hear Pinky in the shower. She was reciting the lyrics to, "Hope You Niggas Sleep," which I found odd. Or was it because I was already paranoid? I flopped on the pink leather couch and waited for her to exit out of the bathroom.

I couldn't help but wonder where she had disappeared to in the middle of the night. What had she done that she needed to come back in the house and take a shower and what was with her song choice?

When Pinky came out of the bathroom she jumped as though she were surprised to see me there.

"Oh shit! Hey baby." she said visibly startled.

She eyed me suspiciously. I knew I must have looked half crazy; but, so did she. If she knew what I had just seen she would have understood why I was looking at her like she was a suspect.

"Hey. Where did you disappear to? I woke up in the middle of the night and you were gone." I asked her trying to be as casual as possible. I was watching her face carefully to see if I could read her expression. Then it dawned on me, Pinky was a paid killer. Her life consisted of taking people out then lying if necessary to cover it up. Reading her expression would prove to be hard.

"Oh, I had some things to handle. You know how that goes. When money is to be made I gotta go and get it." she said not making eye contact with me.

I felt fear creep up through the pits of my stomach. I had all kinds of crazy shit racing through my mind. Had Pinky found out I was fucking around with Natalie and made her a target?

142

DNA 2

Had she gone over there and made an example out of her? I couldn't be sure by Pinky's demeanor.

I nodded at her last statement about her making money and for the first time I didn't feel safe in the house with her. There was no telling what she would do to me if she had in fact found out about me and Natalie. She might wait until I got comfortable and fell asleep, then killed me.

"You aight Neko? You look like you have seen a ghost." she asked watching me closely.

"Naw ma' I ain't feeling too well. I think I am coming down with something. Maybe I should head on home. I don't want to be coming down with a cold or something and give it to you."

I could see the disappointment make its way to the surface of her thoughts.

"I was hoping I could thank you for everything you have done for me over the last three weeks. I know I ain't been easy to deal with. Losing my baby sister has me all fucked up. Neko you are the only person I got left in my life that I care about and I started thinking about how I would feel if I didn't have you in my life." she said.

I couldn't help but feel like this whole scene was a set up. Pinky was not the clingy, mushy type, yet here she was acting super possessive.

"I hear you baby. I just don't want to get you sick." I said. I even threw in a fake cough to throw her off. I didn't want her to know that I was trying to get away from her. I knew what Pinky was capable of and I didn't want to end up one of her targets.

I got up and cautiously walked over to her and gave her a weak hug. I left her standing there with hurt and disappointment in her eyes. I walked out the front door and broke out to a full run when I got outside and away from her. I knew I must have looked like a bitch running to my car, but at least I was still alive. There was no way I was going to fall victim to Pinky. I had had enough shit happen to get caught slipping like that. I cranked up my engine and headed for my own home and prayed I was safe from Pinky there.

Dirty
DNA 2

CHAPTER TWENTY-FOUR

Familiar Faces

"Party Party"

NiQue

I woke up and my head was pounding. I felt strange. My body was sore like I had been working out. I was stiff and could hardly swing my legs over the edge of the bed. When I finally was able to push myself to my feet I got a good look at my reflection in the mirror and screamed. My arms and upper torso was covered in blood. I stripped out of my clothes frantically. I was searching for the source of the blood. When I got all the way down to my underwear I realized that it wasn't my blood all over my clothing and body. I fell back on the bed and put my head in my hands and started sobbing. Pajay had done it again! She had done something fucked up! What was scary was I had no idea who had become a victim!

Just when I started trying to figure out who she had butchered, I began to panic. I looked around the room to see if she had left behind any evidence of who she had hurt. I looked down on the other side of the bed and the baby was there safe and sound in her big wicker bassinet. She was sleeping and from the looks of it, she hadn't heard me scream when I first got a look at myself in the mirror and saw that I was drenched in blood.

Seeing the baby safe made me feel much better, but the fear within me kicked into overdrive. I could feel Pajay in the room and I knew she was watching my every move. I flew to the bathroom to get the darkening blood off of my body. I turned the shower on as hot as it would go and got in. The water was so hot that it burned my skin, and yet it wasn't hot enough to wash away the guilt I felt. I may not have known who I had hurt, but I was almost positive that they didn't deserve to be hurt or even worse, die.

"You look like the modern day 'Carrie' in there washing away the pig's blood!" Pajay laughed wickedly.

I almost jumped out of my skin. I don't know why I thought I was alone. Even when I thought I was alone, I never really was. That bitch was always lurking around waiting to turn shit out.

"What the fuck have you done? Whose blood is this all over me?" I asked her knowing it wasn't going to be easy getting an answer out of her.

I turned off the shower and stepped out. My entire body was red and raw from the combination of scrubbing too hard and the water that was way too hot for anyone to shower in.

"Does it matter whose blood it is? As long as they don't fuck with us anymore, that is all you should care about!" Pajay said. She was doing just what I knew she would do—dance and skate around my questions.

I was staring at myself in the mirror and I wished I could reach inside myself and drag this bitch Pajay out. I was getting tired of playing with her.

I didn't know who she had fucked around and killed or hurt this time, and she was gonna toy with me before she told me who it was. I needed to know who she had hurt because I needed to make sure I didn't need to watch my back. Pajay didn't think out any of the shit she did. She reacted and caused me problems. There was bound to be a mess for me to clean up somewhere. That is exactly what she did—make messes like a toddler and I always had to clean that shit up.

"Why is it every time something fucked up happens, it has something to do with you? You are always causing trouble and I swear this is the last fucking straw!" I screamed.

Dirty
DNA 2

Pajay just laughed at me because she knew that my threats were falling on deaf ears. She didn't give a fuck about anything but herself. She didn't see things like she should have. She didn't realize that if they locked me up they were going to lock her stupid ass up too!

"I'm going to ask you one more time. Whose blood was that Pajay? I need to know so I can protect us. If I don't know, what if the police come after me and I say something that incriminates us? I wouldn't know what to say because you ain't told me shit!" I said trying to flip the script on her, so she would see things my way.

"Let's just say I got rid of a whiney bitch who was asking for it. She was talking so much I cut her tongue out so she would shut the fuck up forever!" she laughed wickedly as though she had told the best joke ever.

I was stunned, and I could feel my body shaking from the thought of taking yet another life. For a long time, I used to think I was crazy. It was *she* who was crazy. Only someone insane would cut out another human beings tongue, and think it was a joke.

I couldn't help but think back to when I was younger and Pajay did crazy shit and everyone thought I was weird.

****

Summer 1987

"NiQue come down here right fucking now!" I heard my brother Mike yell from the lower level of our home in Trinidad NE.

I knew by the tone of his voice he wasn't happy. I slowly made my way down the steps. I knew whatever he was yelling about he wasn't pleased with me. When Mike wasn't happy he often let me know by spankings and making me say I was sorry in a not so traditional way.

BLAQUE

I was notorious for getting in trouble. The only time I seemed to stay out of trouble was when my best friend YaSheema "YaYa" Clayton was around. When she was around my brother would act like a different person. It wasn't until many years later that I found out why he acted like an innocent saint when YaYa was on the scene. She was my only outlet to the abuse I was getting from who I thought was my brother Mike.

When I reached the bottom of the steps, Mike and his girlfriend Janet were waiting for me. Mike had a look of displeasure on his face and Janet had been crying. Her eyes were red and puffy. I knew whatever I had done was something serious because Janet who was normally as sweet as summer rain, wouldn't look at me. My presence only made her cry harder. Janet was always kind to me, until that day. She used to save me from Mike when he was mad. She was the closest thing to a mother I had, and I hated for her to be angry or upset with me over my actions. She would braid my hair and read stories to me before bedtime. Janet would always let me play in her makeup and try on her "big girl" clothes as she would call them. I loved Janet and to see her crying pained me.

I stood before them trembling. My eyes darted between the two of them trying to get a feel for what I had done. Mike's antics caused Janet to sob even louder and it was scaring the shit out of me!

"What the fuck is wrong with you NiQue?" he growled. He pounded his fist into the wall causing both me and Janet to jump.

I wanted to run to Janet and have her protect me, but from the way she was crying, I knew she wouldn't. I didn't say anything. There was nothing I could say, so I stood there. I didn't even know what I had done to make them upset.

"I don't know what you are talking about Mike. Whatever I did, I am sorry." I said backing up from the two of them. My eyes begged for forgiveness. I was sorry, and I didn't even know what I was sorry for.

"You know what you did! You're just gonna stand there and act like you ain't have nothing to do with this shit?"

I was so confused. He was talking in circles making my head hurt, and I just wished he would tell me what I had done so I could get the punishment part over with.

Mike grabbed my wrist and yanked me to the living room and pushed me on the couch. He turned on the VCR and popped in a tape. I still didn't know what was going on. I tried again to look to Janet for help and she avoided making eye contact with me.

When the tape started to play I saw why they were beyond upset. In the tape, I was totally naked, wearing nothing but a huge grin. There were several boys of all ages in the room with me. As the tape continued to play, it showed the boys taking turns having their way with me. They were putting me in positions that the inventors of *Karma Sutra* would have been ashamed of.

Not only was I being gang banged on the tape, but I was doing so as a willing participant for boys in a rival drug crew that my brother and YaYa's father had a beef with. I didn't know how any of it happened or how I got there. I didn't know why I had done the things I was doing on that tape.

What baffled me more than anything else about the video was that after I allowed my body to be used for the gang bang, I walked over to the front of the camera, licked my lips and blew a kiss at the camera as though I were proud of humiliating not only myself, but the family too.

I looked away from the screen trying not to watch the horror of it all as it unfolded on the screen. Janet had long since stopped watching the spectacle I was making of myself. Mike was totally engrossed in the madness and I could have sworn that while the tape played he would rub his hand up and down the shaft of his dick as though the whole scene was exciting him.

"What do you have to say for yourself? You ain't shit but a whore NiQue and you ain't gonna be shit but a whore when you get older!" Mike screamed.

He was putting on a show for Janet and I knew it. The whole thing on the tape had turned him on and I knew once Janet had gone about her merry way he would be making me say, "sorry" in the way that Mike had taught me so many years before.

Whenever I got into trouble Mike would make me do things to prove that I was sorry for the bad shit I had done. He would force me on my knees and shove his dick down my throat and tell me hum the words, "I'm sorry" until he came in my mouth. That wasn't the worst part of it. He would force me to swallow every drop of his baby batter and would laugh at me when I would gag and throw up.

I knew after the incident with the boys on the tape I would be doing way more than humming my "sorry" this time. Mike was going to make sure I paid for embarrassing him! I didn't know what to expect, and I sure wasn't looking forward to the punishment either. I knew what he was doing to me was wrong but what was I supposed to do about it?

Finally, Mike dismissed me to my room. I sat on my bed and waited in silence. I knew once Janet was gone it was going to be on.

"You shouldn't let him control you like that!" I heard the voice say.

"Well, what am I supposed to do? You know he is really mad and he is gonna make me pay for what you've done! He always blames me for the stuff you do!" I whined through mountains of tears.

When I first heard Pajay speaking to me she sounded muffled like she was speaking to me through a closed door or from under water. I didn't know if she were real like the others who had come before her. I used to think that someone was playing a trick on me when the voices began. I would hear my name being called and there would be no one there. As time went on, her

150

voice became crisp and clear and I knew there was something sinister about her. She wasn't nice, and she was always willing to do shit just to get a rise out of people. She always claimed that she was doing the horrible things she was doing to protect me.

I dozed off and I woke up when I heard the door to my bedroom creak. I knew there was no way for me to pretend that I was asleep. It was time for my punishment. The others who had dwelled in the corners of my mind used to help me get through the punishment Mike dished up. They taught me how to shut down and feel no pain. Pajay acted like she loved the shit he was doing to me and I couldn't figure out why. I knew what Mike was doing to me was wrong and no man should force himself on a woman, but Pajay reveled in it. Anything sexual sent her into frenzy.

I could feel Mike's presence standing over me.

"Just fall back NiQue. I got this. Don't worry we will make his ass pay for this shit one day." Pajay said.

She was almost excited for the punishment to take place. I didn't question her. I just lay there and let her take over my mind and body and when I woke up, it was all over. The sun had risen, and it was a new day. I was alone in my room. There was no Mike and no Pajay. The only clue I had that something had happened that shouldn't have, was that my body hurt. My pussy ached, and I could smell Mike's *Joop* cologne and funk all over my body and bed. Something had happened. I didn't know if I had been a willing participant or not, but something had gone down! Knowing that Pajay had been there through it all meant that there was no telling if I had let him do horrible things to me willingly, or if he punished me by force. I could never be sure, and I wasn't sure I really wanted to know anyway.

****

Winter 1997

I was glad I was getting older and Mike had slacked up on the punishment shit. I think because he knew I was old enough to tell, he wasn't into it as much. But when I would get caught breaking curfew, then on my knees I would go, head bobbing back and forth bringing my twisted brother to ecstasy.

Pajay always promised that one day she would make him suffer for the shit he was doing to me. My only escape was spending time with my best friend YaYa. Her family welcomed me with open arms. I had longed to have a family like theirs. They were rich and powerful. Don't get me wrong, Mike had money because he worked for YaYa's family, but they had something Mike and I definitely didn't have for one another— love. I hated his ass and he acted like I was a burden.

I spent more time with YaYa and her father than I did at home and that suited Mike just fine. He only had one rule, I better not tell Darnell Clayton shit about what was going on in our house. He claimed it was none of his business and he didn't want to fuck around and have to kill me for running my mouth.

When YaYa's dad would ask me, how was my home life. I thought about telling him it was fucked up on so many levels. Then I thought about Mike's threats and knew he would act upon those threats if I was disobedient. Mike had a reputation in the streets of being a goon and he didn't take too kindly to niggas testing his gangsta'. I was not going to put myself in the position of being on his shit list. Besides, who was to say Mr. Clayton would believe anything I told him anyway.

I was spending more and more time with YaYa's family than my own and that was fine by me! I could identify with YaYa. She was being raised by her father. Her mother had left years before after her father had put her out when he found out she was using drugs and fucking around on him with more niggas than he could count. YaYa's mother was a real piece of work. I had even seen her at my house creeping out of Mike's room. Her mother was scandalous, and it was a wonder that her father hadn't done more to her than put her out. I was surprised that he hadn't killed her for her behavior. YaYa said the only reason her father let her mother live was because she was his baby's mother; if it had not been for that, he would have deaded her ass years ago.

I could relate. My mother had left me years ago too. Then I found out she had killed herself. Why, I don't know, but my life had been lonely and cruel, and she wasn't around to change any of that. My mother didn't want me, and my brother harbored such ill feelings towards me that he would rather torture me than love me. That was my sick, cruel, and twisted world.

In spite of all that, I made it to high school. I had a reputation of being "easy" because of the shit Pajay kept doing. I knew even my best friend thought I was fucking anything moving. It wasn't easy to deal with the whispers and the stares. I did what I could to get by. The girls hated me and the boys all flocked to me in hopes of getting some ass. None of them knew Pajay was the easy one. I was still a virgin. I hadn't given myself to anyone willingly, Pajay had.

Pajay was a gift and a curse all rolled into one. She would defend me when I couldn't take the abuse, and then she would do something crazy causing people to look at me like I was unstable.

One morning I decided I didn't feel like dealing with the pressures of school, so I ditched. I didn't have anywhere else to go so I went back to my house. I only had a slim window to double back home before Mike would come back home after his cash pick-ups for YaYa's father. I sure didn't want him to know I had ditched. He would have taken the opportunity to get his rocks off for me ditching class.

I entered my house and went to my room. I watched television until I heard Mike come in. Easing across the room, I turned the TV off and pressed my ear against the vent that I used to spy on my brother's conversations. He didn't know I could hear all of his business dealings and everything he said when he was in his office on the lower level of the house. I positioned myself, so I could hear his drama. With my ear pressed firmly against the vent I could hear he was on the phone.

"Darnell she is your responsibility, not mine. I was doing you a solid by keeping her here. She is starting to cramp my style. If you want me to keep playing big brother to your daughter, then I suggest you run me some more money. She is wilding out over here and I don't know what to do with her. I never know what the fuck NiQue is going to do next. She keeps lying, saying that it ain't her doing this crazy shit. Besides no one believes shorty is my sister but her! Niggas in the hood are looking at her all funny and you got me playing super save a hoe!" Mike said.

I knew I should have backed away from the vent. I had heard too much! Any fool could see that Mike and I didn't look anything alike, but I chalked it up to what he said about us having different fathers. I never doubted that he was my real brother.

I continued to listen because Mike was yelling and cursing, and I was afraid if I moved he might hear me. To be honest, I was too shocked to even move!

"Wait a fucking minute did he say Darnell? Darnell who? I know this nigga ain't talking to who I think he is talking to!" Pajay said.

Oh shit! Pajay was taking in every detail. She didn't miss a fucking beat.

The tears flowed silently down my cheeks as I listened to the only person in the world that I thought I had in my corner talking about me like I wasn't shit. I wanted to go and get my so-called brother's gun and put two bullets in his head with it.

I was trying to shake having bad thoughts because if I kept having them I knew Pajay would hear me and react. The last thing I needed was her getting mad and doing something off the hook before I could confirm what I needed to know.

"I can't believe you are going to sit there and let him talk about us like that. If you don't handle this shit, you are just what he said about us, crazy!" Pajay continued.

I bit my bottom lip until I bled, holding in the anger and hatred I felt for everyone. It was bad enough I ain't have a mother or father for damn near my whole life; but to know my entire existence was a lie was enough for me to say fuck it and let Pajay loose on all of those involved.

"Fuck this, they are gonna' tell us something! If Mike ain't ya' brother, then who is he? I know one thing; it sure does explain why he wanted to sample the pussy instead of acting like your brother!" Pajay said, breaking into my thoughts.

I could hear Mike demanding money. He was threatening to tell me that everything I thought was real was just a bunch of concocted fabrications, put together to keep me from finding out who I really was. Little did he know he had done just that. He didn't have to worry about blackmailing anyone to keep their dirty secrets because he had said a mouthful and I had heard it all!

"For a street nigga, he sure does run his mouth like a bitch! Doesn't he know the first rule is to trust no one and check his surrounding before he gets to bumping his gums? I don't give a fuck if he is at home. Niggas these days act more like females than the bitches." Pajay continued in my ear.

I didn't know why I couldn't know who my father really was, but I was going to find out no matter who had to die if they got in my way! Playing with my whole life and feeding me bullshit was not something I was going to take lightly. Pajay was more than willing to do whatever she needed to do to make sure that happened.

After a few more minutes of Mike fussing at the person on the other end of the phone, I heard the front door open and slam shut. Mike had left back out and I wished I had taken my ass to school instead of ditching and hearing the shit I had heard.

I didn't know which was worse, living as though I hadn't heard what I had heard, or knowing that niggas around me had been keeping secrets for years. I sprawled out across the bed and cried until I fell asleep. When I woke up a few hours later, Mike was standing over me with a lustful look in his eyes.

"The school called and said you didn't show up to class today! You know there is going to be punishment for that shit, don't you?" He unfastened his pants and released his massive dick as he spoke the words, and I knew another punishment was coming.

I nodded my head and dropped to my knees and took my punishment like the soldier I had become. Mike didn't know there weren't going to be many more days like this where he was going to be able to abuse me...at least not if I could help it!

****

Winter 2010

I managed to not only survive Mike's shit, but I was able to find out all the information on my father I needed.

I did a long stint of cutting class and getting high after that. When I started experimenting with Xtasy I was doing it for the high. Then I started to notice that it kept Pajay too high and suppressed to get into anything dangerous. I began to use the drug regularly to keep her out of the way. The wounds that had been opened by learning that my father was paying this nigga Mike to molest me was fresh. If I didn't stay high, then Pajay might get out of hand and kill Mike before I got confirmation that Darnell, his employer, was indeed my father.

Mike was a bitch-made mutha fucker just like Pajay said! He talked too much and left too much shit to chance. I went through Mike's shit a few years back and found all I needed to know about my mother and father. Mike had kept all of the documents and my birth certificate right in his room. I guess he thought he had instilled enough fear in me that I would never go through his shit to find out who I really was and where I came from.

Mike had more than my birth certificate naming Darnell Clayton as my father; he had a written contract between him and Darnell. The contract stated that Mike was to be paid several thousand dollars a month to care for me and guard the fact that I was Darnell's child.

What was shocking about it all was that the name on the birth certificate was Pajay Clayton. All this time I was thinking that the voice in my head wasn't real and it really was. Along with my birth certificate, were medical papers from a doctor who diagnosed me with multiple personality disorder and a manic depressive since the tender age of three. The papers suggested that I be placed under a doctor's care and that I be medicated to try and sedate the other personalities that were roaming around freely in my head.

One day I made copies of all of those papers and stashed them for safe keeping. I knew some of it would come in handy. The doctor's diagnosis wasn't the part that threw me for a loop. It was the name that was listed as "mother" on my birth certificate that had me intrigued me the most. My mother's name was Donna Reynolds. She was the sister to Christa Reynolds, Darnell's bitch, and my best friend's mother!

My father had chosen to keep YaYa around because she was perfect, and she didn't have the voices controlling her like I did. I played along with their little game while I devised my payback on all of them. I had also found out I wasn't the only child Darnell had thrown away for his precious YaYa. I had a brother too. His name was Neko Reynolds. Christa gave birth to him after Darnell threw her out.

BLAQUE

As I began to put all the pieces together in my head, it was apparent to me that Darnell had gone to great lengths to hide me from the truth, and I was ready to expose him for the liar he was. I confronted Darnell and he wanted no parts of me. He denied knowing what I was talking about. After he shot down my hopes of having a real relationship with him, I figured out how to get back at them all and make them pay for hurting me. Pajay and I spent countless hours putting it together. I made sure that Darnell's past would catch up to him and hit him where it hurt the most—with YaSheema. Since he loved her so much, I was going to use her to get to him.

I started by finding my drug-addicted aunt Christa, and my brother Neko. I had them come back into Darnell's life. I wanted to watch him squirm while he tried to figure out how to keep Neko a secret. When that didn't work as planned and he accepted Neko into his life with open arms without offering me the same opportunity, I started picking Darnell's life apart by way of his precious daughter, and my sister, YaYa.

YaYa never saw it coming. I set her up and tried to drive her crazy by making her think that she was being stalked and hunted by some unknown person. I played my part as the loyal best friend and used our friendship as a way in. I tried to have her boyfriend, Papi, kill her so I wouldn't have to get my hands dirty. He was so fucking stupid and into too many other things. He ended up dead before he could take her out. So, I took matters into my own hands and killed Darnell and his whole camp myself. One by one I got rid of anyone who knew anything about me and finally I got rid of YaYa who, just like my father, was loyal to no one but themselves.

I kept my baby brother Neko alive only because he didn't know about any of the family secrets. He didn't know that he and I shared the same bloodline. That was the only reason I spared his life. As far as I was concerned, he was an innocent pawn in Darnell's game of chess.

$\mathcal{D}irty$

DNA 2

****

There couldn't be such thing as a God. If there were, I wouldn't have been cursed with Pajay. A kind God wouldn't allow someone to have other people living inside of them constantly doing evil things and pushing evil thoughts into their head. If there is a God, He has never shown me any kind of love and He damn sure hasn't given me any breaks in life. I didn't believe in God or anything spiritual. Sure, I had prayed from time to time to see if this Mighty God that so many people worshiped would appear and save me from myself. He never showed up, so I gave up and stopped praying altogether.

BLAQUE

CHAPTER TWENTY-FIVE
Junkyard Band (JYB)
"Hee Haw"
Dread

Crack and I made it to DC without further incident. We stuck to the back roads and tried not to draw any attention to ourselves.

"Are you sure you want to go through with this? I think we should call Queen. She might be able to get us in with the attorney." Crack said trying to talk me out of what I had intended to do.

"If you don't want to go through with this you don't have to. You've already done enough. You are risking your own freedom so I can keep mine." I said only half meaning it. I didn't want to do any of this shit alone, but I didn't want to drag anyone else into my mess with me.

"I ain't saying I ain't want to do it. I think we need to think this shit through before we go to the police station. They are looking for you so what's stopping them from shooting you on sight?"

Crack was making sense but it was too late to try and do this the right way when everyone else was playing dirty.

We crept through the city I loved so much hoping that we would make it to the police station without getting caught up in the process. We were about two blocks away when we saw the barriers and plumes of smoke billowing from somewhere in the distance. There were news trucks and reporters everywhere. When we got a little closer to where the smoke was coming from we saw men and women dressed in fatigues and big tanks stopping any traffic from proceeding any further. Crack pulled the car over and looked at me like I knew what the hell was going on. There were people milling about all over the place.

"Aye, come here for a minute shorty." Crack called out to a young girl who was standing out on the block watching the happenings. The girl cautiously walked over to the car. She put a twist in her hips when she got closer. She must have thought we were trying to holler at her.

"What's going on around here?" Crack asked her.

The girl was cracking sunflower seeds between her teeth and spitting the shells on the ground. I watched her to make sure she didn't know who we were or try to alert anyone of our presence.

"You ain't heard? Some nut fucked around and blew up the police station, killing everybody inside." She spit a shell on the ground and focused her attention on me.

"Oh shit, ain't you that rapper everybody been looking for?" she said with excitement.

"I don't know what you are talking about baby girl. You must have me confused with someone else." I said looking around to make sure no one had heard her. No one had.

She smacked her lips and leaned into the car.

"You are him! Can I have your autograph? Can I call my friend and you tell her who you are? She ain't gonna' believe this shit!" The girl said whipping her phone out and feverishly pushing buttons. "I have all of your stuff; you have got to at least take a picture with me!" The girl continued, not giving up.

She was starting to irritate me and I wanted nothing more than to get away from her. Normally I enjoyed the reactions of my fans, but right now I didn't want any unwanted attention. Shorty was so star struck she was going on and on.

"You have me mistaken for someone else. I ain't no rapper baby. I was just trying to get home. I live just up the block and I was trying to get through here. Do you know how long they have been here?"

Dirty
DNA 2

"They have been here for hours and they ain't going anywhere anytime soon! The whole place went up in a ball of fire with close to one hundred people inside. That includes police, and just random niggas being held until they were to be transported to Central Cell. I mean, can you imagine just walking in to file a missing person's report and BOOM, the whole place is on fire? That is some gangster shit right there. I bet you could write a whole album off of that one."

Crack was smiling, but I knew what he was thinking. He was thinking that calling this dumb bitch over to the car to fish for information was more trouble than it was worth!

"So Dread, can I get my autograph and my picture now or what?" she asked while tossing more seeds into her ever running mouth.

I wondered how many sisters in this world would be more attractive if they just shut the fuck up!

Crack made a face at me. I looked around and got out the car slowly, being mindful that I was less than a block away from a police station and Crack took the picture with the sunflower seed assassin.

"Can I call my friend and you tell her who you are? She is never going to believe this shit!" the girl said.

"Naw baby, we have to go! I don't have time to talk!" I said, trying to be as polite as possible so she wouldn't cause a scene. Any kind of attention right now would be bad. It was bad enough I was in the middle of the hood participating in a ghetto photo shoot.

I got back in the car and Crack made a u-turn in the middle of the street. With a relieved look on his face, he headed back in the direction from which we came.

"I guess it is a good thing that we ran into that crazy broad before we went any further and got caught up in whatever is going on around here." Crack said.

163

I slouched down in the seat wondering what to do next. I hadn't anticipated the shit going on at the police station. I was fully prepared to sit there and wait out Detective Gatsby. Looks like I wouldn't have to wait on him at all. He might have gone down in flames with the rest of the Feds that were hunting me if I was lucky.

"Where are we headed to now?" Crack asked with his eyes scanning the road and watching for anything abnormal. This whole ordeal had everyone around me paranoid and watching for everything.

"I guess you can take me home. There ain't nowhere else for me to go."

Crack shrugged his shoulders and drove me to where I had directed him. I watched the city I loved so much pass me by and wondered how someplace I represented to the fullest could turn its back on me. I never thought in a million years that I would be on the run in my city, for a crime I knew nothing about, and damn sure didn't commit.

Thoughts of seeing NiQue and my daughter consumed me and I smiled. I hadn't seen them in weeks and I really missed them. I was willing to risk my freedom just to see them. I didn't know if the police had the house staked out or what, but I was going home to them. I still hadn't talked to NiQue, so I didn't know what the situation was like on the home front. For all I knew them boys in blue could have been waiting to snatch my ass up and cart me off to jail. But that was a chance I was willing to take to see my daughter. I missed NiQue but, my heart was with my daughter.

We drove until the dilapidated buildings and housing projects filled with my people were no more and gave way to the lush foliage and single-family homes. Laurel was nothing like the city and I almost hated it. The white people were always eye-balling me here like I was a criminal; because of my appearance they always thought the worst of me. None of them knew I had worked hard in my career for all that I had for my daughter and future wife, or that we belonged in these neighborhoods as much as they did.

We pulled up to my house and I hesitated before getting out of the car. Crack must have sensed my hesitation and spoke up.

"Dread, you can stay at the house with me and Queen until this shit blows over. I don't know what I would do if your coming home causes you more static. Maybe we could lay low and figure something else out before you go in there. You don't know who is watching your crib," he said.

I shook my head.

"Naw man, I got this. I can't keep running from it. At least if they are gonna get me, I will be able to see my daughter and wifey before they take me down," I said.

I gave Crack a pound and exited the car. I walked up the drive and up the steps. When I got to the door I felt the tension mounting and the fear building. I hadn't seen anything out of the ordinary when I exited the car, but something in my gut was telling me to make a break for it to the car.

Before I could turn around and run back to the car, I felt the hot bullets ripping through my flesh. The last thing I remembered before my eyes closed was Pinky standing over me mouthing the words, "Got cha nigga!"

BLAQUE

CHAPTER TWENTY-SIX

Backyard Band (BYB)

"Fakin' Like"

Neko

I went to work and once inside the office I passed by Natalie's desk which was vacant. I stood there staring at the empty seat. It was empty and I knew why. It was empty because she wasn't coming in today or tomorrow, or the day after that. She wasn't coming in ever again and it was killing me inside. Natalie wouldn't be coming to work or going anywhere but six feet under; and I may have played a part in it.

As much as I disliked her smart ass mouth and her nasty attitude, she didn't deserve to have that foul shit happen to her. There was so much chaos in my life; a normal nigga would have buckled under the pressure. With the type of family I had been born into, I should have been able to handle shit like this, but dead bodies of loved ones was something you don't ever get used to!

I continued down the hall and into my office. When I opened the door, Shadow was waiting on me. I almost jumped out of my skin seeing him there. I forgot that nigga had a key.

"Damn my nigga, you look like shit Boss! What's good?" Shadow said giving me a once over.

"Man, I don't know if anything is good!"

The look on Shadow's face went from curiosity to concern.

"Pinky got you stressed homie?" Shadow inquired.

"Yeah man, more than you could imagine," I responded.

Shadow pulled out a bag of loud and started dumping the guts out of a blunt into the trashcan.

"Ain't nothing like some fuck it in your system to make all of your problems disappear." he said quoting Katt Williams.

He twisted up the blunt with the weed and sparked it and passed it to me. I inhaled, and thought about whether I should trust him and tell him what I knew about Natalie. Letting the smoke out, I decided that Shadow was a good nigga and would be able to help if I needed it.

"Man, last night I called Natalie to check her ass about the shit she's been around here pulling. Before I could dig into that ass about her attitude something happened. I could hear a scuffle and then I didn't hear anything else." I said before stopping and looking at Shadow to make sure I had his full attention. He was sitting damn near on the edge of the chair waiting for me to finish telling him what had gone down.

"I knew something fucked up had happened. She never came back to the phone so I slipped out the door and hit a hundred to her house." My voice trailed off. I closed my eyes and thought about the fucked up scene at Natalie's. I knew that shit was going to haunt me for the rest of my life.

"I found shorty dead on her floor with her tongue cut out and pinned to her chest! She had multiple stab wounds all over her body."

"What the fuck!" Shadow exclaimed. He had dropped the blunt on the floor and was coughing from the smoke.

"Yeah man, that shit got me all the way fucked up. That ain't even the worst part of it either."

Shadow raised an eyebrow and stared at me.

"Nigga it gets worse? How can it get worse than finding your shorty like that?" He asked sounding alarmed. He was fishing around trying to get the lit blunt off of the floor.

Niggas like Shadow didn't let too much shit rattle them, but he was fucked up with hearing this shit.

Dirty

DNA 2

"Yeah man, I found a note pinned to her chest with her tongue. It read: 'Loose lips sink ships.' The cryptic message made my insides churn."

"What the fuck is that supposed to mean? Who the fuck cuts out someone's tongue and pins that shit to their chest?" Shadow asked. He was staring at me like I really had the answers. I wish I had them because not knowing if I was sleeping with Natalie's killer was beyond torture. I had sat up all night long trying to figure out the same shit.

I took another pull of the blunt letting the smoke invade my lungs and the thought of what I had to do invade my mind. Even though Natalie was my side piece, there was no reason she should have gone through some shit like this and I needed to get to the bottom of it. I was afraid I knew who was behind that shit and that fucked me up even more.

Shadow looked at me while the weed calmed my nerves. He was waiting on me to give him the answers to questions I didn't know the answers to. I debated as to whether I should tell him who I thought was behind it. I knew once he got that information he would be ready to go to war with her and I wasn't quite sure it was her. The way Natalie popped off at the mouth all the time; it could have been anyone who killed her. I passed the blunt back to him and decided I needed to tell him because if something happened to me, he knew whose head to hit!

"Aye yo Shadow, I think Pink had something to do with that shit man," I said. I studied his face waiting for his reaction.

"Pinky? Why do you think shorty would even go there? I thought ya'll's shit was straight."

"Man there is some shit you don't know about her man. She is a fucking killer. Literally! My Pops and my sister had some ties to her when they were alive and in the streets. That's how I really met her," I confessed.

"Awww man, you got some problems my nigga. What are you gonna do if it was her?" he asked.

"I shrugged because I really ain't know what I'd do if I found out Pink was behind Natalie's death. After all I was the one creeping out on her.

Shadow snapped his fingers.

"Damn man, that reminds me! I almost forgot why I came to work early," Shadow said.

"Wassup my nigga, I know it wasn't to actually work because you never do that shit." I said chuckling even though nothing going on in my life was funny.

"Man fuck you! You ain't watched the news?" Shadow asked putting the blunt out and rolling another one.

I shook my head. I hadn't watched shit but my fucking back!

"They found that rapper nigga your sister used to fuck with, Dread, shot in front of his house. Ole boy had some hot ones put in his ass. Whoever did that shit was aiming to kill and they almost succeeded. That nigga is in ICU at Georgetown in critical condition fighting for his life. Man, whoever was trying to get at that nigga was on a mission!"

I was in a state of disbelief to say the least. I didn't say anything.

"You know the city is going crazy about that shit. He is like an idol to these niggas. That nigga going down ain't a good look for you my man. People knew you had a hard on for that nigga for that shit with YaYa. You better be careful, you don't want niggas putting that body on you. You might want to handle that!" Shadow warned.

Shadow made it more than clear that I had better watch my back. Someone was playing for keeps. I patted my pockets looking for my cell phone and remembered I had left it in the truck. I got up and jogged out to the truck and got it and powered it on.

There were thirteen voicemails and thirty text messages. I didn't have to listen to the voicemails or read the text messages to know they were from Pinky and NiQue. Too much had gone on for it not to have been them. Just the thought of that nigga Dread

170

being laid up in the hospital made me nervous. I got my hammer out of the glove box because for all I knew I may have been next on somebody's hit list. My gun was gonna have to stay on my hip. Someone was playing dirty. I knew one thing; I wasn't going out without a fight!

I headed back inside the building, but not before looking over my shoulder. I didn't know what the fuck was going on and I wasn't going to get caught slipping. I decided I would call NiQue and Pinky later. I punched in the numbers to the only person who may have known something about what was happening. I called Detective John Gatsby. I knew if Pops could see me now he would be rolling over in his grave. Pops was a policeman's worst nightmare, and here I was trusting a mutha' fuckin' cop.

I tried his office and there was no answer. Then I tried his cell and again there was no answer. I made my way back in my office and sat in my high back leather chair behind my desk. Shadow hadn't moved a muscle besides rolling another blunt packed with *Pink Panther.*

"You ready to blow some more trees or are you gonna wallow in your own pity around this mutha fucker?" he asked like the true pothead he was.

"Man fire that shit up, I'm trying to get high!" I said. What else was there to do?

I was trying to call Gatsby repeatedly and I finally gave up.

"Man why you look like that? The weed ain't good enough or something?" Shadow asked attempting to lighten the mood.

There really was no way to make any of this seem any better than it was.

"No, it's all good. I am trying to reach this Fed who was working on my family's case and he ain't answering. He might be able to give me some inside information on who tried to gun down that nigga Dread. He might be able to tell me if they had any leads on Natalie's killer too."

I took the blunt from Shadow's hands and took a long pull and held it until I was sure there was no more smoke to when I exhaled.

"Neko are you sure that Fed is still alive? Didn't he work in the 5th District? Oh, shit you said you have been out of touch with the real world! You ain't heard huh? Some crazy mutha fucker blew up the 5th District Police Department. That shit has been all over the news. The news reported that there were no survivors. Maybe he got caught up in that shit. If he was there that day that shit happened, then sorry to tell you but homeboy probably didn't make it!"

This shit was beginning to be a repeat of the year before. Chaos and drama was surrounding me like the force of Hurricane Katrina; it was fucking up everything in sight.

I was back at the square root of one! I grabbed up the remote and started flipping through the channels to see what I could about the police station being torched, and if there was anything on the news or *BET* about Dread being shot and whether they had any suspects.

Where the fuck had I really been? Shit was happening all around me and I hadn't seen or heard about any of it.

In the midst of me flipping through the channels my phone started to ring. I picked it up and almost panicked like a bitch when I saw Pinky's face flash across the screen. I rejected the call.

Shadow was heading out of my office and going to open the shop being that Natalie obviously wasn't coming back. That was some shit I was going to have to handle too! I was going to have to hire someone to replace her. I decided right then and there I was definitely hiring a dude to fill her spot so temptation wouldn't be an issue. I was putting a killer on my team because shit was getting real. I knew, from firsthand experience, that when a nigga slipped up, he is his own worst enemy.

A young nigga I knew from the street named Head was the first person that popped in my mind. Not only was he a smart lil nigga from the street, but he was heavy with his trigger finger. This nigga was thorough and he wouldn't turn down the chance to bang his hammer if it was called for.

My phone rang bringing me out of my thoughts. I knew who it was before I could even get good a look at the number or the face that appeared on the screen. I normally would have been happy to receive a call from Pinky. Today, I wanted nothing to do with her ass. At least until I figured out if she was the one who was responsible for what happened to Natalie.

BLAQUE

Dirty
DNA 2

CHAPTER TWENTY-SEVEN
Backyard Band (BYB)
"Rowdy Rowdy"
Detective Gatsby

Well, I'll be damned! That bitch lived up to her promise. She said she was going to take that nigga out and she did it! Well almost. That asshole Dread was laid up in a hospital fighting for his life. He was unconscious and on life support. The doctors said the probability of him making it was slim to none.

I could feel the smile pulling at the corners of my mouth. I would have been happier when that bastard was dead. Him being in a coma would have to do for now, at least until we finished his ass. I didn't have shit to complain about! I tossed the newspaper I was reading on the floor and opened the blinds to my dark apartment. I had been hiding out, listening to the police scanner, and hoping no one knew my ass was involved with what had happened at the police department. With all the chaos going on at the station, no one knew if I was dead or alive. They were still pulling bodies from the building that had burned to the ground killing everyone inside and even taking the lives of some of the firefighters who tried to control the blaze.

It was time for me to pay Dread a visit in the hospital. I needed to be sure he didn't come out of the hospital and if he did he was going to be in cuffs! I owed Head big time for making that shit happen at the precinct, and if I didn't take care of that debt he would make sure everyone who would listen know I was the one who gave the order to turn the lights out at the 5th District.

Head torching the place is going to cost me a pretty penny. It was all worth it though as long as no one knew I had killed that young girl. I was willing to kill whoever I had too in order to keep my secret a secret.

Head was a crazy mutha fucker that I busted a while back. He was up on some murder charges and I helped him get off. He was being accused of killing some local thugs and I saw the fire in him. He was one of those people you wanted on your team for when you needed a job completed! I called on Head when I needed people taken out and didn't want to get myself involved. He didn't care who he had to kill. He was ruthless. He would kill the target, the kids, the wife, the dog, the neighbors, and anyone else who tried to get in his way and stop him. Like I said, he was worth every dime I had to spend to employ him and he was definitely someone I would not stand up as far as payment. If I didn't pay him, and pay him on time, he would see to it that I ended up in a box.

I may have kept Head out of jail, but if I crossed him he was going to make sure I met my maker sooner than I wanted too; and I was not prepared for that. I would rather have him on my team than against me.

I also needed to pay Ms. York a visit. I wanted Dread dead and I didn't want to get my hands dirty. I would rather help her finish his ass off then get my hands dirty killing him myself. I had just skated out of enough shit. There was no need to put my ass back on the line when I was in the free and clear. If Ms. York was harboring ill feelings towards him for what happened to her sister then she would have no problems with finishing this, once and for all.

I knew she was thirsty for the kill. It showed in her eyes the day she had met with me in my office. I had seen that look many times before. I had cuffed and arrested killers for more than half of my life. I could sense she was a killer. Call it my intuition, but I could sense she was hungry to see that man die and she wanted nothing more than to be the one to pull the trigger. I couldn't confirm that she was the one who had put those hot ones in

Dirty
DNA 2

Dread, but I knew she had something to do with it! Just the thought of her pulling the trigger and rocking his ass to sleep got my dick hard. Something about pain was a turn on. Then to top it off, Pinky was a lot to get excited about. She was built like she was drawn.

I stopped getting dressed and took a seat in my recliner. The lustful thoughts of Pinky were too strong for me to ignore. I gripped my dick, stroking myself to pleasure while thinking about her thick frame on top of me performing acts of gratification I knew she would never do. Once I finished, I wiped my sticky hand on the underwear that were down around my ankles. I shook the wet boxers from around my feet and looked around the floor for a dry pair; seeing none, and I picked the ones wet with my semen up, and headed to the back to iron them dry.

I can't remember when I started to not care about shit anymore, but I do know it was somewhere between the death of my wife and child and the murders I committed against my own parents. Somewhere in that timeframe is when I stopped giving a damn. My soul was already to be delivered to the devil and I didn't care about shit anymore but living from day to day. My appearance was something that was trivial, and I didn't give a fuck about it unless I had too.

I plugged the iron in; immediately thoughts of how my life might have been if my wife and daughter had not been taken away from me, began to consume me. I almost felt bad for what I was doing to Dread. because like me, his whole world was being snatched away from him and there was no real explanation as to why it was happening.

I finished ironing the dirty garments and threw them on my oversized body and headed out the door to meet Head.

BLAQUE

178

Dirty

DNA 2

CHAPTER TWENTY-EIGHT

Critical Condition Band (CCB)

"Bazooka Bottom"

NiQue

When I heard the gunshots outside of the house I scooped the baby up and ran to the front door. I was scared as hell that the police had found out Pajay had done something and were after me. I don't know why I ran in the direction of the gunfire. Something in me told me to get my ass in gear and prepare for the worst.

"Didn't anyone teach you anything? You ain't' supposed to run towards the gunfire. You're supposed to go in the opposite direction!" Pajay said harshly.

Before I could get my hands on the door knob I stopped and thought about what she had said. I should have been turning around and ducking for cover. I didn't know who was outside my door firing. Something told me not to open the door, but to at least look out the peep hole first so I would know what was happening. Cautiously, I followed my instincts and looked out the peep hole. I didn't see the police, but what I did see shocked the hell out of me! I saw Crack running up the walkway at full speed. What was he doing here? I wondered.

I swung the door open and was stunned to see Dread sprawled on the front porch, his blood oozing down the steps. I couldn't even pinpoint where he had been hit. There was blood everywhere and the holes left in his body were enough to make the hardest of hood niggas fall to their knees and pray.

What shocked me even more than my soon-to-be husband laying shot on the front steps of our home, was the pink

179

motorcycle I saw that sped from around the back of the house. The bike was moving so fast across the lawn it was ripping up the freshly-manicured lawn. I couldn't see the figure on the bike. They were dressed in all black and the black helmet concealed their face. I could tell from the build of the person on the bike that it was a woman.

I knew this was a hit, and only person I knew of who would have enough balls to walk up on my property and gun down my man didn't actually have balls at all! I didn't know of any nigga on the streets who rode a pink Ducati. It was Pinky. She was one of my late father's paid shooters and she was one of the best! That bitch came with a high ass price tag, but she was one of the best if you had a mark to eliminate.

I stood stark still; looking in the direction of where the bike had sped off too when a second bike came from the same path that the first one had come from. I don't know what made me stand there trying to figure out the identity of the second assassin.

"That bitch is dead! Dead, dead, dead!" Pajay said, taking the words from me as if she were reading my thoughts.

"NiQue! NiQue! Take the baby and go inside the house, lock the door, and call the police! Do you hear me NiQue?" Crack said snapping me back into reality.

I looked around and saw my man lying in a pool of blood and I started to cry. I knew something I had done had caused Pinky to target him and now it was going to be war. I did as Crack said and rushed inside the house while he stayed out front with Dread. My fingers could not move fast enough as I called the police; and unlike being in the hood, they arrived within minutes of the call. When I heard the sirens in front of the house, I rushed out to see what was happening. Once again I was on display for the entire neighborhood to see. My neighbor who had rushed to my assistance when the police were here because of Joseah's death, was on her porch again. She was clutching her chest as though she were having a heart attack watching the whole thing unfold.

Dirty
DNA 2

"Look at that fake bitch! She wasn't looking at us like that when we really did kill someone." Pajay hissed in my ear

Other neighbors were standing around, and some snatched their children up and went inside, peeping the action from the safety of their homes. They had never seen anything up close and personal in real life as what was happening on my doorstep. If they were talking about me before then they were really going to have a mouthful now. Shit like this only happened in the hood. It did not happen in their pristine neighborhood. Sure you may have an occasional incident, but two within weeks of one another was unheard of.

"Miss, are you going to ride to the hospital with us, or are you going to follow behind us?" the EMT tending to Dread asked me.

I didn't say anything I just stared in the direction from which the bikes had come. Crack draped his arm around me and tried to comfort me. I didn't need comforting; I needed and wanted revenge for what had been done to my man. It was a direct violation and it needed to be handled.

"Don't worry NiQue! We will find out who ordered this hit and when we do, it's lights out for their asses!" Pajay said.

"You don't even have to worry about that because I am prepared for war." I said back to her aloud, forgetting that I was in mixed company. At that point, I didn't give a fuck and I welcomed the evil within named Pajay wholeheartedly.

Crack stared at me and kept asking if I was alright. I nodded my head 'yes' just to get him to leave me alone and stop staring at me as I held a conversation with who he thought was myself.

The paramedics asked me again would I like to ride to the hospital with Dread. I declined. I could hear them discussing if I needed to see a doctor. They thought I was in shock. That couldn't be the furthest thing from the truth! I was fully alert and aware of what was happening around me. I just had a different agenda. They were trying to save a life, and I was trying to take out whoever was trying to destroy mine! I walked into the house and exited with the baby. I got in my car and headed in the opposite direction of where the ambulance was taking Dread. I was so hell bent on making niggas pay that I didn't stick around long enough to find out which hospital they were transporting him to.

I mashed my foot on the gas and headed into the city. I heard Notorious B.I.G.'s song playing in my head over and over! *"Somebody Got To Die."* Pajay loved every moment of this shit and she was doing nothing but adding fuel to an all ready simmering fire! She lived for the chance to shine. Now was her chance, and I wasn't going to stop her. I was encouraging her to do what she did best—cause chaos.

CHAPTER TWENTY-NINE

Junkyard Band (JYB)

"Shifty"

Pinky

I raced through the streets with my partner in crime right behind me. We were dipping and weaving through the traffic trying to get as far away from the scene as possible. For the first time, I had killed for my own personal gain. There was no money involved, and no contract for my services. This was strictly personal. I pulled my bike into the garage in a warehouse in NE, DC and killed the engine with my accomplice following suit.

Shaking and trying to gain my composure, I removed my helmet and threw up on the floor of the dank warehouse. My stomach was churning. I knew it was nothing but my nerves. I wasn't used to this feeling. I was usually as tough as *Teflon*. Not this time. I couldn't believe I was having issues with taking a life. Normally, I would have gone on this mission alone, pulled the trigger, and never felt a thing. This time was far different from any time I had ever had to end someone's life. When I pulled the trigger I didn't get the same satisfaction. Something deep inside was telling me I had made a grave mistake. I don't know when I developed a conscious. Maybe it was somewhere between the death of my little sister, and me finding out I was pregnant.

I was starting to have mixed emotions about everything I did. I knew I wasn't going to be able to keep the baby. My lifestyle wouldn't let me. I would always have to look over my shoulder trying to figure out if someone was going to try and harm the baby for my past business decisions.

"Are you ok Pinky?" My partner in crime asked me.

"Yeah, I must have had something to eat that didn't agree with me." I said lying. I didn't want anyone to know about the life I was carrying inside of me. Anyone could use it as a weakness and get at me when I least expected it. In this business you trusted no one and discussed nothing. Even with the ones you loved the most.

That is why I loved Neko. He never questioned anything I did. He simply went with the flow of things. He didn't look down upon me for the path I decided to take in life; and for that, I was grateful. Who in their right mind would want to date a woman who was a stripper and a hit woman? Either she was fucking niggas or fucking them up! There was no in between.

"Aye yo Pinky, you did that shit! Damn, four straight chest shots. Did you see how that nigga hit the pavement? That nigga looked like he had seen death. I bet he wished he would have never gone home today! He really did have a homegoing service." Head laughed.

"Why are we here?" I asked him. I wanted to get the fuck out of that warehouse. My stomach was feeling queasy again and I felt like I needed fresh air. I could feel the bile trying to make its way up and out again. I forced myself to hold it in until we could get out of there. I was sure that once Head handled his business and we could get out of there, I would feel much better. The smell of mildew was surrounding me.

"I have to see a man about a horse." he laughed.

I am glad he thought his joke was funny because I sure didn't. I didn't like to meet with anyone about anything in places like this unless it involved my money! Plus, I didn't know who he was meeting, and in our line of work I didn't like to meet anyone I wasn't familiar with.

Head walked over to me and rubbed my back.

"You don't look so hot baby girl. Maybe you should take a few weeks off. If you have any work coming up let me know…I can get it done for you. I got this thing coming up, but it is on some legit shit. My boy got me a nine-to-five gig. So I should be free to help you with any contracts you get.

Head was a stone cold killer, but he had a soft spot for me. I wanted to talk to someone about what I was going through, but I knew that could be dangerous. Head pushed my wild pink dreads from my face and kissed me on my lips. There was no way I could tell him I was pregnant. He would try and talk me out of aborting the baby. Besides, I didn't know if it was his baby, Dread's, or Neko's. I had been playing a dangerous game, and I was going to fuck around and lose if Head or Neko found out I was pregnant.

This whole situation was a mess and I needed to get a handle on it as soon as possible. I didn't need any more complications. I wanted to go back to my normal routine. I've been calling Neko and he has been avoiding me. I think he knows I have been creeping out to be with Head. The last night we were together, I had left out and when I returned he was gone. He showed up again and then he disappeared. I know Neko loves me, but being that I used to be employed by his father, I am not willing to find out if he had the same temper his father possessed. I would hate to have to put a bullet in Neko's ass if he turned out to be as treacherous as his late father and sister.

Neko had never shown any signs of being like Darnell and YaSheema Clayton, but I knew he could potentially be just as dangerous. Every time I thought of how kind Neko was to me, it would be overshadowed by the thoughts of how fucked up his sister and father were before their untimely deaths. Those two were cold-hearted. They employed me to pull many jobs and even when a nigga tried to make peace with them they were still going to war with them. I was motivated by the money, and they were motivated by gaining respect.

Head had wrapped his arms around me trying to get my full attention by planting a trail of wet kisses on my neck. Although I really liked Head, I was in love with Neko. I guess you could say I was in lust with Head. He would bang my back out, twist my body into all kinds of positions, and send me home satisfied as hell. That was the benefits of having a younger lover.

I didn't like the fact that he was demanding. He didn't want me to dance anymore. He wanted me to work strictly on my hits and nothing more. What he didn't know was I had no intentions of leaving the entertainment world behind. It wasn't the money that kept me dancing. It was a way to keep all of my money legal. There was no way I would be able to only pull jobs and keep the Feds off of my ass if I didn't have a way to explain why I had so much money! Head was too young to understand that and his immature attitude bothered me.

There was a knock on the steel doors to the warehouse and Head and I separated ourselves from one another. He walked over to the door. When I saw who it was on the other side of the door it almost took my breath away. There stood Detective Gatsby. When our eyes connected and locked on one another, Head took notice to it. I decided to speak first before Head said something that incriminated me.

"Hello Detective," I said casually.

"Good afternoon Ms. York." he said glancing in Head's direction.

"The two of you know one another?" Head asked, baffled that we knew each other and spoke so casually.

I nodded my head and hoped that both of them would follow my lead.

"Detective Gatsby is investigating my sister's death," I said.

I could see Head's expression soften when he heard my explanation. He believed me!

"How is my sister's case coming along?" I asked, trying to find out if he knew I was the one who had pulled the trigger on that bastard Dread.

"The case is still open, but I know exactly where to find our main suspect. Someone tried to off Dread a little while ago. It has been all over the scanners. Someone gunned him down on the steps of his house."

My heartbeat quickened like a Congo solo in a go-go song. I couldn't be sure, but I thought I saw that fat bastard Gatsby smile at me.

Head watched the detective and I interact as if he were watching a tennis match. He followed our movements, studying us, and dissecting our every word. Even though Head was young, he was no fool. He could sense there was more to it than just my sister's case.

"Aye Gat, let me holla at you outside!" Head said gruffly heading in the direction of the doors.

He and Detective Gatsby made their way out of the warehouse and I assumed they handled whatever business they needed to because Head was back inside within a matter of a few minutes.

"How do you really know that greasy mutha fucker Pink?" Head asked me.

"I just told you he is working on my sister's case. Why?" I pried, trying to find out how they knew one another. They definitely had some type of affiliation with one another. If Detective Gatsby knew Head then that meant he was crooked. There was no way Head would be dealing with a cop just to be chummy with him. Either Head had turned informant, or the good Detective was playing for the wrong side of the law.

"Stay away from him Pink. That mutha fucker is off the chain and not to be trusted." Head demanded.

I gave him a questioning look. I didn't like to be told what to do by anyone. I didn't give a fuck how good the dick was. Besides, the Detective had given us some information that I needed. Dread had managed to survive. I swore the slugs I put him were enough to kill him. Now I was going to have to pull a move to make sure that nigga didn't come up out of that coma. I know he saw me before he closed his eyes. I didn't know if he would remember I was the one who shot him, but I wasn't going to take the chance in finding out.

Head spoke up as if he were reading my thoughts. "Pink what are we gonna do to finish off our little problem sleeping in the hospital? We sure as shit can't just gamble and hope this nigga dies! We have to finish his ass and we have to do it soon."

When Head took control of a situation there was something so sexy about it. A few minutes ago I wanted nothing more than to get out of that warehouse and away from the sickening smell. Now I wanted Head to fuck me so could clear my mind. I unzipped my black leather rider's jacket and pulled my tank top over my head, exposing my breasts to him.

"I know you don't think fucking is a solution?" Head said licking his lips as he admired my partially nude body.

"No, but it will make me feel better!" I said seductively.

I stepped out of my boots and leather pants. I knew he wasn't going to deny me. He may have tried to front like he wasn't going to take me in that warehouse, but I knew better. If he even tried to deny me I was going to get what I wanted by force.

Head moved closer to me; kissing and sucking on my breasts. They were swollen and sore, but his touching them ignited a fire that had to be extinguished; and could only be done one way. He dropped to his knees and fingered at the lacy fabric of my thong. His touch made my body quiver. Ripping my thong off he went to work, he lapped at my flower as though he were a kitten taking his first drink of milk.

I tried to keep my composure as I stood there. My legs almost gave way as he pushed his tongue deep into my pussy, causing me to moan louder than I intended. I looked down at my young lover and decided I wanted a full session and he was going to give it to me. I rocked my hips, riding his face and mouth until I climaxed.

My legs were shaking uncontrollably and almost buckled from the intense orgasm. Since getting pregnant it was as if my orgasms were intensified. Head got up off of his knees and removed his pants and shirt displaying his chiseled body. He had the body of a God. His milk-chocolate complexion and bowed legs were delicious looking. When he released his massive ten-inch dick from his pants, my center throbbed in anticipation. I was all set to bend over and let him hit it from the back when Head used his motorcycle jacket as a make shift blanket and laid it across the floor. He laid himself on the floor and extending his hand up to me to help me down to the floor to join him.

I didn't want to sex him on the floor of the warehouse, but I definitely wanted to sex him. I took his hand and mounted him. When I took all ten of those inches inside of my walls it felt like I was going to cum with that one stroke. I started to ride his pole slowly getting my body used to him. Once my kitty was ready, I rocked back and forth. Our bodies made music of their own. Up and down. He was watching my every move as I bounced up and down on his dick. He grabbed at my waist and thrust himself upwards, pushing himself as deep as he could go. I felt like I was in heaven and I didn't want it to end. I wound my hips in a circle and he thrust his stiff member in and out of my pussy. I tightened my muscles around him. I wanted him to know how much pleasure he brought me. I felt my orgasm building again and he began to tremble beneath me. I knew he was just as close as I was.

"Oh God baby, I'm about to come!" I yelled out.

Our grunts and moans bounced and echoed off of the warehouse walls. I clawed at his chest trying to find something to hang on to as I came. He followed my lead and spilled his seed in my creamy treasure. I collapsed on his chest breathing heavy. I immediately started to feel guilty after we finished fucking. There was no way I was going to be able to keep this baby. I didn't know whose baby it was, and I didn't have it in me to hurt either Neko or Head. The tears started to well up in my eyes. I started to think about the inevitable, and it pained me to have to kill the baby growing inside of me, but I had no other choice.

BLAQUE

I got up off of Head and started to pull my clothes on my body slowly. I turned my back to him in case my tears couldn't be controlled. I didn't need him seeing me cry and I wasn't going to be questioned about it either. I put my game face on with every stitch of clothing I pulled on to my body. I still had a matter to handle which was Dread. He was still alive and I couldn't leave him breathing. He had seen my face!

I had never missed my mark and this was a bad time for me to start.

Dirty
DNA 2

CHAPTER THIRTY
Northeast Groovers (NEG)
"Dip Dip"
Neko

Pinky had been calling my phone back to back for the last two days and I still didn't know what I was going to say to her. I was in the office waiting on Head to arrive. We had talked a few days back and he was amped to work for me. He was given the name Hot Head for his temper. Somewhere along the lines his nickname was shortened to Head and I guess it stuck. It was fitting for him because once his temper flared, there was sure to be trouble.

I heard the chimes signaling that someone had entered the front area and rose to my feet to greet whoever was at the door. *Damn, I'm not used to this shit!* I had to do everything myself and I hated doing it. I missed Natalie. She was a nuisance, but she took care of the shit around the office I didn't want to do. Shadow helped out as much as he could, but being my receptionist wasn't his job. He had other shit to do. Even though Shadow was my right-hand man, I didn't want him to know that I had planted Head there as protection. He may have thought I was soft for hiring a young gun. I had some of my late father's traits in me; more than I liked to admit, but I didn't like to get my hands dirty when it came to busting my guns. I was going to avoid that shit unless I had no other choice.

I made my way to the front and Head was standing in the reception area looking around.

"Wassup my nigga?" he said giving me a pound.

I started thinking maybe I had made a mistake hiring him. I had already had one hood bitch running the front area. Now I was having a hood nigga replacing her. His appearance screamed, "street." Not saying there was anything wrong with that, I grew up in the streets and I was far from a sell-out; but this nigga had on skinny jeans, a pair of colorful *Nikes* and a shirt that matched none of the colors in his shoes. I know I had specifically told him the attire was "business casual," not wear what the fuck you want! I knew I hadn't really hired him to be the front desk help; however, I needed him to at least look the part. Everything about him said, "young, street, nigga!"

I could tell he felt my disapproval because he tried to pull his tight jeans up and cover his boxers that were peeking out. I didn't have any problems with the way he was dressed if he were going out to the club, but I did have a problem with him not looking the part in the office.

"Sorry man, I was in a rush this morning when I left the house." he said trying to cover up the fact that he wasn't dressed properly.

"It's cool man. It's your first day. I don't want anyone to know why you are really here. You have got to blend in. No one can know why you are here. They need to think you are just the front desk help. Let me show you where everything is." I said, leading him around the office showing him where everything was and what he would be doing.

By the time I got him acclimated with the office and his duties it was already after noon. Shadow came in after I had shown Head the compartment that I had built into the underside of the desk. It housed two 9mm Glocks. I instructed him on how to make the compartment open and close. I already knew he didn't need the shoot first and ask questions later spiel. He was hot headed and eager for something to jump off.

I had never been trigger happy unless the situation called for it. Head and I were the same age and we were totally opposite from one another. All I wanted from life was to make money, drive fast cars and fuck fine bitches. I had plenty of ends in the bank. I just needed to stay alive to enjoy it and keep the bitch I suspected of killing one of my many females off of my line.

Head and I wanted the same things, but we had different ways to get it. He wanted the money; but he would take a nigga's head off to get it instead of trying to make it legally. He was every ghetto's nightmare. I figured keeping him around to be on watch for Pinky, or whoever had gunned Natalie down, was one of the best things I could have done. He was one of the only people I knew hood with it who didn't mind shooting a bitch if that was the case.

Shadow and I went to my office and left Head to himself.

"Who is that clown ass nigga you got at Natalie's desk?" Shadow asked taking a seat in the chair directly across from mine.

I shook my head. You would have thought this was Shadow's establishment the way he was questioning me.

"His name is Head, and I owed him a favor so I hired him to help out around here if you don't mind boss!" I responded sarcastically.

Shadow almost doubled over laughing.

"This niggas name is Head? You can't be serious? Check this shit though, he looks familiar. I can't put my finger on where I have seen him before, but I have seen him around. What's his real name?" Shadow said getting serious.

I shrugged my shoulders. I didn't know Head's real name and I ain't care to know either. I tried to change the subject before Shadow got too nosy about who Head really was.

"Did you do what I asked you to do about Natalie?" I asked Shadow, giving him the eye. Shadow was a good dude, but he would get so wrapped in his drama with his baby mommas that he would get sidetracked. I had to check him for forgetting to handle important shit because he was too busy chasing ass and making babies.

"Yeah, I went to the police station and filed a missing person's report on Natalie. They said they were going to send someone over to her home to check it out. They are short on manpower with that shit happening at the 5th District. Who knows when they are gonna go over there and handle it, if they even handle it at all. The city is all fucked up behind that fire." Shadow said.

My mind started to wonder who was going to find Natalie and if they found her would they know I had been there.

Gorilla Zo's song, "Hood Nigga," rang on my cell phone; breaking the silence and my thoughts. I saw it was NiQue. I had been meaning to call her, but hadn't gotten around to it since finding Natalie's body. I answered the call and immediately knew something was wrong. She was crying and inaudible.

"Neko, they shot him! They shot him and they don't think he is gonna make it!" she wailed into the phone.

"Wait NiQue, I can't understand a word you are saying. Who was shot?" I was beyond scared now. NiQue was normally a soldier. There wasn't too much that rattled or shook her up! I don't recall her shedding one damn tear at my sister's funeral and YaYa was her best friend. I don't remember her crying at her brother's funeral either. Yet here she was crying and screaming in the phone. Shit had to be drastic for her to sound like she did.

"Neko just get to Laurel Regional Hospital and I will fill you in on the rest when you get here." she sniffled. Then the phone clicked and went dead.

I tried to call her back and she didn't respond. I left my office with Shadow on my heels. I didn't know if I should tell Head to ride to the hospital with me or not. I decided against it and had Shadow ride with me instead. Something told me that this was going to be a sensitive matter and that having Head accompany me was something that would not sit well with NiQue who could be temperamental when she wanted to be.

DNA 2

I left instructions for Head to reschedule all of the work for the day being that both Shadow and I would be out and there was no one else to close the books for the day. I didn't fuck around with my money. I only trusted one person with my ends and that was Shadow and he had strict instructions on how to handle my dough.

He had to count the transactions in my office and in my office only! He never knew why I had that demand. I had cameras installed in my office so that if anyone wanted to get cute and try anything funny, they would be caught on candid camera. I trusted Shadow, but after the shit I had been through with my own family, I left nothing to chance anymore. Plus, before Natalie died, I had filmed us having a few sessions in my office. She never even knew that she was being filmed. I did that for my own special treat.

Thoughts of what happened to Natalie danced around in my head again. It made me leery of not taking my hired muscle with me. I let the thoughts go, and Shadow and I gunned it all the way to Laurel to find out what had happened with NiQue and the mystery person that she referred to who had been shot.

"Whoa my nigga…don't you think you should slow down before you get us pulled over or worse yet, fuck around and get us killed? You are doing 90 miles an hour on 295. Don't you think that is a bit much?" Shadow asked hanging on to the, "oh shit bar" in the ceiling of the car.

I ignored his comment, but I did let my speed drop down to 80 mph. I shot him a dirty look as if to say, "Are you satisfied now" and then I kept on pushing the pedal on the way to the hospital.

Horrible thoughts filled my head and I was trying to prepare myself for the worse. I didn't know who had been shot and the only person that kept coming to mind was Pinky. She was the only person that me and NiQue both knew and cared about.

Even if I suspected Pink of taking out Natalie, I wouldn't know how to react if something bad happened to her. I loved that crazy bitch; and I damn sure didn't want to lose her. Thoughts of Pinky were replaced with thoughts of my sister, YaYa. I wasn't there when she died and I should have been. I couldn't lose anyone else in my life. I refused to!

Determined to get to that hospital in record time, I mashed the gas and the car jolted forward. I glanced at Shadow and with my eyes, I dared him to make a sound. He didn't know about my past and I wasn't going to tell him why it was so important for me to be there for NiQue. All he needed to do was be there for me if and when I needed him to be! Everything else was secondary.

We pulled into the emergency entrance of the hospital. I hopped out the car, forgetting to take my keys or shut the doors. I had barely put the car in park. Once inside, I found NiQue pacing the floor right outside of the operating room doors. I grabbed her and she fell into my arms crying. Her body was shaking and convulsing.

"NiQue, who is in there? Who has been shot?" I asked bracing myself for the answer.

NiQue had her head buried in my chest and she was just as hard to understand now as she had been earlier when she called urging me to come. She finally pulled her head off of my chest and wiped at the tears that were running out of her red, puffy, eyes. She looked so lost and helpless. I wanted nothing more than for her to stop crying long enough to tell me who we were here to see.

"Neko, thank you for coming. I didn't know who else to call," she said. Her voice was shaky and I knew she was stalling to tell me what was going on.

"No problem NiQue. You already know I am here for you no matter what! I've always got you. You are the only family I got left." I said, meaning every word. She really was the only family I had left, and I was going to do whatever I had to do to make sure she was straight.

Dirty

DNA 2

She smiled weakly and tried to fight back more tears that were building in the corners of her big brown eyes.

"NiQue, who is in there? Who was shot?" I asked trying to remain as sensitive as I could, but I needed to know what the fuck was going on and this back and forth shit was getting me nowhere fast.

"I knew if I had told you over the phone, you wouldn't have come. Please don't be mad!" She was stuttering and stalling and I was getting pissed.

"Someone tried to kill Dread. They gunned him down on the porch of our house," she finally managed to say through her sobbing.

She looked so sad and everything in me wanted me to feel something for what had happened to him, but I couldn't. I didn't like the fact that NiQue had been caused so much pain, but what could I say? I didn't trust the dude and I didn't like him either. She knew that, and I wasn't the only one with those feelings, at least, so it seemed.

"What! Who the fuck even knew where ya'll lived?" I yelled at her and she jumped, startled by my reaction.

My loud outburst cause the other people in the waiting room to throw me dirty looks. I lowered my voice and directed my attention back to NiQue who looked like she was on the verge of a meltdown. She was biting her bottom lip and looking at me nervously. Before she could answer me, the doctor came out of the double doors and scanned the room until his eyes rested on NiQue.

BLAQUE

Dirty
DNA 2

CHAPTER THIRTY-ONE
Trouble Funk
"Tilt"
NiQue

I was a wreck when the doctor came out of the operating room. I was glad I had Neko for support. If I had to face any of this alone with just Pajay by my side, there is no telling what would have happened.

"Ms. Watkins, my name is Doctor Rhina Diaz." the doctor said giving Neko the once over.

He was doing the same to her. Some things never change. He was looking at the doctor with lust in his eyes. She was a beautiful Latino woman with long curly hair and curves that I am sure made other women envious. She didn't look a day over twenty-five and she definitely didn't look old enough to be a doctor. I had concerns about her being the one tending to Dread's delicate situation.

"See they are all the same. He is just like your no good ass father. He is thinking about fucking her instead of being here to support you." Pajay said from somewhere in the back of my mind.

"Shut up and let the doctor speak!" I said aloud, forgetting I wasn't alone and was indeed in the company of other people. I had messed up big time because both the doctor and Neko were staring at me like I was crazy.

"I'm sorry. I am stressed out. Please pay me no mind. This whole thing has me frustrated." I said trying to smooth over a potentially bad situation.

The doctor remained suspicious of my behavior and my outburst, but she continued speaking.

"Ms. Watkins we were able to remove three of the four bullets that penetrated Mr. Evans body. The fourth bullet, we could not remove. The bullet is lodged dangerously close to a main artery and if we were to try to remove it, it may do more damage and possibly cause internal bleeding and eventually death. He experienced a lot of blood loss and is in recovery right now. He is stable, but he is still in critical condition. I have to tell you he is a very luck y man. If the bullets would have penetrated his chest area a little more north of where they penetrated, it could have been deadly. I need you to understand that he is not out of the woods yet, and he has a long road of recovery ahead of him, but in time he should heal fine. Right now we have him in a medically-induced coma for his own protection. Any sudden movements could make the bullet shift and damage his heart."

Doctor Diaz had given good news and bad news all rolled in one. Dread had survived, but he still had a long fight ahead of him. I let out a sigh of relief knowing that he would be ok for the meantime.

"Thank you Doctor Diaz. When can I see him?" I asked hopeful that my man would fight his way through this.

"We have to run a few more tests while he is in recovery and then we will be moving him to the Intensive Care Unit. Once he has been moved you will be allowed to see him. If you don't have any other questions, I have to get back to my patient." she said smiling.

I wasn't sure if the smile was because she was happy that she had saved Dread's life or if she was showing off for Neko who was still exchanging lustful looks with her.

His grey eyes roamed all over the good doctor and it was upsetting me*! Like father...like son!*

"Thank you doctor!" Neko said, licking his lips reminding me of L.L. Cool J. He was doing way too much to make the good doctor notice him and it was sickening. He was supposed to be here to support me, not trying and bed the doctor who was saving Dread's life.

Doctor Diaz nodded and left the same way she had come in. Before I could address the issue of Neko playing *Mack Daddy* with the doctor, two men approached us.

I could smell a pig a mile away. I knew they were detectives. "Oh shit, here we go!" I said to Neko.

"Ms. Watkins may we have a word with you for a moment?" the shorter of the two fifty-something-year-old men asked me.

They reminded me of those cops in those old movies. They wore expressions of disinterest on their faces with each word spoken. I secretly wondered if there was a class that taught Feds facial expressions as a form of training. They never smiled. They never seemed to really care for the people they were supposed to be providing a service to. They almost always had a fucked-up disposition and I hated dealing with the police on any level. Instantly I wondered who was going to be the good cop and who the bad cop was.

"Sure, you can have a moment of my time, but can you make it quick. The doctor said that we would be allowed in to see him once he was transported from the recovery room."

"Ms. Watkins, we will be brief. My name is Detective Ross and this is Detective Miller. I am working Mr. Evan's case and Detective Miller is working the case that stems from the death of a young woman named Khalia York."

At the mention of Khalia's name, Neko's jaw clenched up and he dropped my hand which he had been holding as we stood in the hospital emergency room.

"I know why you are here." I said addressing Detective Ross.

"I just don't know why he's here! Dread didn't kill anyone!" I said getting loud and pointing at Detective Miller. "Dread wouldn't hurt anyone; let alone kill a woman! What would he do some shit like that for? Do you even know who he is? He could have any woman he wanted! Why would he kill one?" I said defending my man.

"Ma'am that is what we are here to find out. Since the 5th District fiasco, I have been assigned to the case. I am here to make sure Mr. Evans doesn't try to run before he can be questioned," Detective Miller said.

I laughed at his statement of Dread running. How the hell was he going to run if he wasn't even conscious? Running could kill him at this point, and surely they knew his condition was bad.

"Excuse me officer, did you say he is a suspect in Khalia York's murder?" Neko barged in.

"That is Detective, not officer…and yes, he is our number one suspect in her death. We found DNA evidence at the crime scene. Before we could get a positive ID on the suspect, we believe he had the 5th District torched and burned to the ground killing everyone inside to cover his tracks."

I stood there in disbelief. I knew Dread had nothing to do with the fire at the police station. He was in Georgia at the time that shit happened. There was no way he could have done the shit they were accusing him of! The detectives were staring at Neko now. I didn't know why at first until I caught him looking at me funny.

"Sir, you seem to know something about Ms. York's case. Would you like to tell us what you know about it?" Detective Ross spoke up.

"No sir, I ain't got shit to discuss with you about it. Pinky…I mean, Chyan York is my girlfriend and a close friend of the family. I didn't know you all had suspected Dread of her sister's murder. Does she know that you think Dread had something to do with it?" Neko asked.

"Mr. I am sorry I never got your name…" Detective Ross said pulling out a note pad preparing to take notes.

"That's because I didn't give it to you and I ain't gonna' give it to you." Neko said smugly.

Dirty
DNA 2

I stood there trying to process the shit I was hearing. They all had me fucked up and I didn't know who to trust. Neko was sleeping with Pinky, and she was the motherfucker who had shot Dread. This shit was unbelievable.

"What do you mean Pinky is your girlfriend?" I barked at Neko.

A look of confusion danced in his grey eyes.

"What does that shit matter? Pinky and I reconnected at YaSheema's funeral. We have been seeing each other ever since," he said confused as to why I had gotten smart.

I hadn't gotten the chance to tell him that it was Pinky I had seen driving away when Dread was shot!

"He probably helped set Dread up! You know he didn't like him anyway! He has been acting funny since we killed that bitch YaYa." Pajay crept in.

My head was swimming and I couldn't control Pajay, or anything else happening for that matter. I hadn't had a pill and I could feel my temperature rising.

"You need to let me deal with all of their sneaky asses. You can't trust any of these motherfuckers! They rolled up to your house and tried to take out your man. I know you aren't going to stand by and just let them get away with this shit! If you do, you are more of a fool than I thought you were! Fuck this…let me get um! Your own brother is in cahoots with that bitch and you ain't said two words about it! I told you to kill his ass when you killed his no good ass mother, sister and your lying ass daddy! You are gonna fuck around and let them take everything from us!" Pajay seethed viciously.

I fought with Pajay for control. She was no easy opponent. My mind was already made up, I was going to let her have her way, but she was gonna have to hold off until there were no witnesses. I was getting sick of the members of this family trying to take everything from me! I thought I had finished off the ones who didn't want me. I was a fool for thinking Neko would be different from YaYa. He was just like my father! He didn't care about anything but himself and his dick! He didn't care

203

whose life he ruined just like Darnell! They were all careless, selfish bastards and they would be dealt with!

Just as I was about to walk away so Pajay wouldn't do or say anything stupid, that guy from Neko's shop walked through the doors of the ER .

"Damn man, you left the car in the driveway they are about to write your ass a ticket. The ambulances can't get through." His voice trailed off when he saw that we had company.

Shadow's eyes darted back and forth between me and Neko and he must have sensed something wasn't quite right.

"Look NiQue, keep me informed about what's going on. I'm out!" Neko said.

He nodded his head towards Shadow who was more confused than ever.

"Let's go!" Neko muttered between clenched teethed and walked out the glass sliding doors with Shadow jogging to catch up to him!

I was left all alone with the policemen, and I didn't have too much more to say to them either. Maybe they felt like it wasn't the appropriate time to push me further, because they handed me a card and told me to be in touch. I couldn't have been happier either. I had some shit to handle and I didn't need them around while I handled it. I scooped up the baby's carrier and decided it was time for me to leave too! I didn't want to be questioned and they damn sure weren't going to make me answer them. I wasn't going to wait for Dread to come out of recovery. I was going to finish this shit with my family and kill anyone who had anything to do with them.

CHAPTER THIRTY-TWO

Raw Image Band

"Tight'n Up"

Detective Gatsby

This shit was working out better than I thought. After my meeting with Head, I decided to pay my friend Dread a visit in the hospital. It was time to finish that shit once and for all. I got to Laurel Hospital and was pleasantly surprised to see Neko Reynolds walking out of the hospital. I was hoping he had stuck a knife in my headache's throat so I wouldn't have to worry about Dread anymore. I was getting mighty tired of that man slipping through my fingers. No one should have the type of luck he had. It was like he had nine lives or some shit like that. He had to have used them all by now. There was no way he could make it out of this hospital alive. I was going to be sure of it this time. I wasn't about to leave shit else to chance. I was done with trusting that someone else was going to get this shit done. Although it would have been nice for someone else to kill that bastard so I didn't have to, the chances of that happening were slim to none, so I was going to have to eliminate him myself.

I got out of the car and immediately noticed I was walking into the hospital with no gun and no badge.

"Fuck!" I said as I turned around and headed back to my messy car to get what I needed to gain entrance to Dread's room. I knew he was going to be under heavy guard. Not just for the shit he was being accused of, but because an attempt had been made on his life. I couldn't just mosey in there and think that whoever was guarding him was going to let me waltz in there with no credentials.

I was fumbling around in my car, looking for my badge under the junk, when I felt a sharp pain in the back of my neck. At first I thought I had been stung by a bee. I swatted at the area so whatever it was would go away. Then I felt it again. Unless I was being attacked by bees, the chance of being stung again wasn't happening. I turned around and there she was. NiQue Watkins was standing there with a knife in one hand and a baby carrier with a sleeping child in it at her feet.

Something about the wild look in her eyes told me she wasn't here to be social. The knife she held loosely between her fingers had blood on the very tip of it. Quickly I realized that her knife was what I had felt penetrating my neck. I moved my hand to the spot where she had poked me. When I brought my hand in front of my face to survey what she had done, my hand had blood on it! This bitch really is crazy!

I looked up at her from where I was positioned in the car. She wore a bazaar smile on her face and panic started to take over me. I wanted to scream for help. She was not going to let me walk away from this. I could read it in her eyes. Something about her was different and it scared me.

She had already threatened to do me harm if she thought I was trying to ruin her life. This situation was proving that she only made promises in which she intended to keep. There was something dark and sinister about her. All of a sudden I was sorry. I was sorry for all of the pain I had caused her and her family.

"Detective Gatsby, funny seeing you here. I was just on my way to see you as a matter of fact. I think there are some things we need to discuss." she said in a hushed tone.

"What do we need to discuss Ms. Watkins?" I asked her, never taking my eyes off of the knife.

To say I was afraid would be an understatement.

Dirty
DNA 2

"First let me reintroduce myself. My name isn't Ms. Watkins. My name is Pajay Reynolds."

My eyes got wide. I knew that name. I couldn't place where I knew the name from, but it was significant from somewhere in my very recent past.

"Next Detective, I wanted to tell you a little secret."

She leaned close to me until her full lips pressed against my ear. I was petrified. No one had ever had me afraid like this before. "What secret?" I stuttered.

"I'm going to kill you, but I wanted to let you know you have been chasing the wrong person all this time! You thought Dread was the one who took out my family? Well guess what Detective? It wasn't Dread at all. He wouldn't harm a soul. It was me! I killed them one by one and you should have left us alone! You should have minded your own fucking business and this wouldn't be happening to you right now. You were so fucking determined to be the hunter. Now you are the hunted and you are my prey!"

I tried to shield my face, but it was too late. She sent the blade straight through my hand and into my left eye, pinning my hand in place. I screamed out in pain but with all of the sirens from the ambulances pulling into the ER entrance I am sure no one heard me.

When she pulled the knife out she also pulled my eye out right along with it. I screamed again as I watched her pluck my eye from the tip of the blade and I watched in horror with my good eye as the other one rolled under the car beside us. The wailing from the coming and going of the rescue vehicles drowned out my grunting and moaning. I had never felt anything like this pain.

"Please Ms. Watkins, I'm sorry. Please don't do this! I can make this right! I can get him off! I swear I can make it all go away! Do you want to be known as a cop killer Ms. Watkins? What will happen to your daughter if you get caught. If you do this she will have no mother and possibly no father." I moaned loudly. The pain from the wound was damn near unbearable. It hurt so much I was woozy.

"Fuck that baby and fuck you too! I told you my name is Pajay. Ms. Watkins doesn't live here anymore. She checked out and I checked in!" she laughed as she drove the knife into my ear.

I slumped over and prayed. I knew my prayers weren't being heard by anyone but the devil. I had done so much shit that even God wouldn't listen anymore. I was going to die right in the front seat of my car. Right where this bullshit with this crazy ass family began. My heart beat at a rapid pace and before I passed out from the loss of blood, I saw Ms. Watkins walk away, leaving the baby and the carrier right there next to me as my soul departed this world bound for hell no doubt. I had sold my soul long ago and now it was time to pay up! Lucifer welcomed me to hell with open arms.

Dirty
DNA 2

CHAPTER THIRTY-THREE

Rare Essence (R.E.)

"What Would You Do"

Pinky

Today was the day. I was headed to the abortion clinic. I tried to figure out how I could go about getting out of doing this and after coming up with no answers, I decided that it had to be done and I would start anew. I would go to the clinic and handle this shit and then try to move on. With whom, in particular...well, I hadn't decided that yet. Neko, Dread and Head all could have been the one that planted the seed within me. But I knew that once I uprooted that seed out of me, I would be left to choose between two out of three since I had tried to kill one of them. Actions like attempted murder kind of throw a monkey wrench in plans for a future with the one that was the object of the crime. So Dread was out of the picture. That left Head and Neko.

I loved Neko with everything I had; but he was acting strange. He was not returning my calls and in doing so, was fucking with my head. I would call him and he would send me to voicemail. It was frustrating. I loved him and I could feel that I was losing him. I had never felt like this for anyone before and it was maddening. I know he and I started out as fuck buddies, but I thought we had grown past that. We had become closer after the loss of my sister than I thought we ever would. We had built a strong bond, then one day something happened. I don't know what...but it did, and he has been avoiding me ever since.

I hate that I got my emotions all twisted up in him. That mentality was unlike me. It was fucking with my judgment. I wished like hell that I knew the baby was Neko's, then I could tell him and maybe he would stop avoiding me. Neko was the settle down and marry type. There are some men that you just fuck and some that you marry. Neko was in the latter category and I could see myself growing old with him and having a family.

Head, on the other hand, was young and wild. He excited me in ways that no man had ever done before. He lived life on the edge and our sex life was off the chain. He was the kind of man you fucked and just recognized the relationship for what it was. He would have most likely turned his back on me if he found out I was pregnant and a real bitch knew that from the start. I was a real bitch.

Head was attracted to the side of me that reminded him of himself. A child would slow down his bigger-than-life lifestyle. He would have most likely carted me off to the clinic himself if he found out his seed had taken root.

I wanted to kick myself for the shit I had done. I wanted both men in my life for different reasons, but I knew that would never happen. In my perfect world I would have had both of them.

I pulled into the *Planned Parenthood* parking lot and fought back the tears that were forming. I could take a life for the right amount of money. I could shake my ass if the price was right. But I couldn't control my emotions about what I had to do for anything in the world and it was beyond pathetic. That alone forced me to do what I knew I had to do! How was I going to take care of a child and make decisions about a life when I couldn't make a decision about my own?

"I will never get myself into anything like this ever again!" I said aloud.

I got out of my car and my feet felt like lead as I slowly walked up to the doors of the clinic. I wanted to turn around and get back inside my car and drive off and face the consequences of not knowing whose child it was. It wasn't like I didn't have the money to raise the child on my own. I was more than capable of doing it by myself. Besides, women raised babies everyday on their own, it's nothing new; but me doing it was something different

Then the thoughts of my own father not being there for me and Khalia crept their way to the corners of my mind. He was never there, and he didn't want anything to do with us. I definitely didn't want the same life for my child.

I don't know how I pushed myself into the clinic and to the front desk; but I did. They had me fill out forms and take a seat. The room was packed. There were women of all ages in the waiting room. I felt bad for all of us; but for different reasons. Some I could tell were regretting the decision that had brought them here. Some were accompanied by their husbands and boyfriends, and some looked like this wasn't their first time visiting a place like this. All of us looked sad and confused at having to be waiting to do what we were here to do.

I wound up sitting next to a bitch who had been there more times than not. She kept looking at me like she wanted to talk and I buried my face in a *Parent's* magazine that did more damage than good. Seeing the pictures of all of the babies made me want to get the fuck out of there; and not now, but I wanted to get out of there *right* now! The tears welled up and poured from my eyes without further notice or explanation. I couldn't control them.

"Is this your first time?" the woman asked me.

I wiped my tears and nodded my head, 'yes.' I was too emotional to speak.

"It ain't that bad. It's over real quick and you will be back to your old self in no time." she said snapping her fingers in the air for emphasis. Her words nor her actions made me feel better.

"This is my fourth time having one done. They are probably sick of seeing my face in here! I might be a card carrying *Planned Parenthood* member." She continued with no remorse; almost boastful of her history.

I stared at her in horror as she casually talked about having an abortion like it was as easy as returning a pair of shoes that she didn't want. I felt sick to my stomach; and wanted to grab hold of that bitch and punch her in her mouth for being so trifling. But who was I to talk? I was a murderer too. The only difference was she didn't see it that way. She looked at the abortion as a method of birth control. I looked at it as her being just as devious as I was. It was all murder in my eyes. A life was going to be taken. It didn't matter how it was going to be done. Just because the baby didn't have a name didn't mean there wasn't going to be a crime committed in that clinic. I looked around at the faces of the women and knew that we were truly some fucked up creatures.

"Ms. York. Chyan York," the nurse called my name from a doorway.

I was glad she had called my name when she did because I was two seconds from bolting to the door and saying, *fuck it!*

I followed the nurse to a little room where they did an ultrasound and I found I was three months pregnant. I cried watching the little gas bubble float around on the screen. By process of elimination due to the time line, the man I had believed had killed my sister was not the one who had fathered this child. Dread was eliminated from planting the seed.

The nurse handed me a paper cup with water and two pain tablets.

"Why do I have to take this now?" I asked the nurse.

"It keeps the pain down to a minimum when you wake up. I see you opted to be asleep while having the procedure done. It is easier that way," she said.

I guess she could see the concern on my face.

"You know it is not too late to change your mind honey. It is never too late! You can take your stuff and go if you want to." the middle-aged black nurse urged.

Dirty
DNA 2

It was as if she could read my mind. I wanted to tuck my tail between my legs and run. Instead I stayed. I nodded my head at her and popped the pain pills and chased it with the water.

"I have to do this. I don't have a choice," I said weakly.

I hated being so weak. I had prided myself on being strong and now here I was being reduced down to a river of tears.

"I understand darling. Just make sure you are doing this for the right reasons, no matter what they be." the woman said as she left the room.

No sooner had the nurse left before another one came in with a wheelchair. I got off of the table and into the chair. The new nurse, who needed practice on her bedside manners and who was rude as hell, wheeled me to another waiting room.

I was instructed to climb up on a bed. A doctor came in and gave me the run down on what was going to happen. I tuned him out and nodded at him to make him think I understood what he was saying. I sure was glad I had dropped another $350 in order to be sedated. Another doctor and the friendly nurse joined him. She glanced over at me again. Her eyes were begging me not to go through with it. I could see the plea in her eyes. I did my best to ignore her because there was no turning back. It was do or die for me. The nurse started an IV line and the doctor she had accompanied in told me to count to one hundred. The doctor pushed some fluid into the IV line. I got to number fourteen and that is all I remember.

*****

I woke up and my body was in so much pain I cried out for Neko. I screamed for him to come to me. What I got in return were nurses who gave me another shot of morphine. I lay there high, confused and sobbing. I wanted to get up and get far away from this place but I was in no condition to do so. The doctor came in to check on me. He was followed by the same nurse who had been so friendly to me before. This time she avoided all eye contact with me. I could feel the disappointment in her eyes. I knew she wished I had changed my mind before going through with the procedure. This time it was me who looked at her, begging for this woman who knew nothing about me, to forgive me for what I had done.

The doctor wrote me out a few prescriptions and told me that I would be back to my old self in no time. He didn't know that was the furthest thing from the truth. I was never going to be the same. Not after this shit. Nothing in my world would ever be the same.

I guess it was really imbedded in my blood to be a murderer. I was a natural born killer. It didn't matter who the mark was. Anything I touched withered and died. I was such a sorry bitch that I had even killed my own unborn child for my own selfish reasons and I felt low behind it. I valued nothing; not even the life I had created.

Dirty

DNA 2

CHAPTER THIRTY-FOUR

Rare Essence

"Sweet Miranda"

Neko

I sat in my office wondering if I should call Pinky. She had tried to call me repeatedly for the last four days and I had continued to avoid her. I loved her deeply on a level only she and I could understand, but I couldn't be 100% sure she wasn't out to get at me for fucking with Natalie.

Head stuck his head in my office to tell me that he had to leave early. Something about his girl wasn't sitting to well with him and he wanted to check on her. I hadn't met the bitch who had tamed him, but I wasn't going to be a cock blocker either. I couldn't imagine him with anyone. She would definitely have to be as wild as he is to put up with him. He said he would be back before I was supposed to leave work for the day and that if I needed to leave before my normal time I should hit him on his cell phone.

I let him know that was fine with me and then Head and his girl were out of my thoughts as they drifted to NiQue and her strange behavior that day in the hospital. I hadn't heard from her since that day. I didn't have a clue to what the fuck came over her when she found out I had been dating Pinky. She looked wild and confused when she found out, but that shit was for the birds and I wasn't concerning myself with her or what she thought about who I was fucking.

There still hadn't been any word from Gatsby and I assumed he had perished in the fire. I had barely gone home during that time, and I didn't plan on going home if it meant I may run into Pinky.

The office phone rang taking me from my thoughts. I had forgotten that I had let Head leave, which meant the phones were going unanswered.

"Hello this is Neko." I said.

"Oh, so you can't answer the phone when I call you on your cell phone, but yo' ass can answer your office phone! What the fuck is up with that nigga?" Pinky said in a manner that dictated she meant business. From the harshness in her voice I could tell she was pissed. This was not a good sign.

"Hey Pinky. I'm sorry I haven't returned your calls. I've been so caught up in some other shit around here that has been demanding my time; I forgot to holla back at you."

Before I could finish my lie, she cut me off.

"Neko, I want you to know I hate you for not answering my calls. If I didn't care about you, your ass would have been cancelled a long time ago. You can believe that. You don't know what I have been through and I will never be able to forgive you for making me go through this shit alone." she sniffled into the phone.

"Pinky, I am sorry for whatever you are going through, but my receptionist ain't been in the office in days and no one can find her." I said trying to let her know I suspected her of killing Natalie. I was trying to get a rise out of Pinky to see if she would let on to the fact that she had killed Natalie.

"I don't give a fuck about your slut ass receptionist. Neko, you weren't there when I needed you! I have been calling you, and calling you, because I was pregnant, you selfish bastard!" she screamed at me.

I thought I hadn't heard her correctly. *Did she say she was pregnant?*

"Pregnant? Did you say you are pregnant?" I asked her.

Dirty
DNA 2

Shadow walked into the office and looked at me to make sure everything was ok. I'm sure he was getting used to all of my drama by now. I put my hand up to let him know to stay right where he was and be quiet.

"No. What I said was, 'I *was* pregnant!'" she corrected me.

"Pinky what do you mean, *was?*" I asked confused. My mind was all over the place. Had something happened to her to cause her to lose the baby? Had she miscarried?

"I said exactly what you heard. I *was*—but because your selfish ass ain't answer the phone, I was forced to handle shit on my own. I didn't know where we stood, so I handled the situation," Pinky said. Her voice cracked and I knew she was crying.

"Pinky, I wish you would tell me straight up what you did!"

Shadow's eyes got big as saucers at the mention of her name. He may have been more uneasy about me speaking to her than I was.

"Neko, I went and had an abortion. I didn't know what else to do. You didn't answer the phone and you made me feel like you had cut me off. So I didn't want to keep a baby from a man who didn't want its mother. I figured you had moved on, and I didn't want to raise the baby on my own, so why should I have the burden of being the only one who cared for a child?"

My ears had to have been deceiving me because I knew this bitch hadn't just said she killed my baby when she hadn't even bothered to ask me what I wanted to do about it. I knew we weren't speaking, but Pinky had taken things too fucking far this time! She had made a decision, for my life that I wasn't so sure I approved of. I couldn't contain my anger. I knew I was dead wrong for what I said next, but I wasn't able to hold it in.

"You killed my baby? Is there nothing you won't destroy? You kill niggas for pay; and now you killed my seed just because you had a chip on your shoulder! You killed my baby because I didn't pick up the fucking phone? You must have lost your

217

fucking mind!" I screamed at her. I knew my words were ripping through her like cannons.

"I lost my mind a long time ago Neko!" she continued to cry.

A part of me wanted to go to her, and a part of me didn't want to be anywhere near her. I might put my hands on her if I did. She was mad as hell that I hadn't been there for her and she retaliated by killing my child. She didn't even wait to hear from me. There was no doubt in my mind now that she had killed Natalie. If she would stoop so low as to take an innocent child's life to get under my skin, she was more than capable of killing Natalie to fuck with me too.

As far as I was concerned, Pink was a monster and she may have done me a favor by having that abortion. I may have loved her, but some things were unforgivable. Some things you just couldn't look past. This was one of them.

"Yeah Pinky, that was a choice you made on your own by killing my baby, and that is a decision you will have to live with by yourself!" I shouted into the phone and hung up.

I was pissed that she had killed my baby so easily and didn't think enough to tell me that she was pregnant. I looked up and Shadow was standing there staring at me. I knew he felt the same way I did about children. If he didn't, he wouldn't have so many.

"If she was pissed at you before my nigga, you can best believe she fuckin' hates you now! You better watch your ass slim. You know that old saying, '*Hell hath no fury like a woman scorned.*' I think it is safe to say that bitch is a little more than scorned. She is pissed. There ain't no telling what she is gonna' do now," Shadow said.

I sat there listening to what Shadow was saying and he was right. I may have done some shit I couldn't undo. The phone rang in my office again. I motioned for Shadow to answer it. I was too mad to talk to anyone. I especially didn't have anything more to say to Pinky.

Dirty

DNA 2

"Reynolds's Rides and Detailing." Shadow said into my phone.

I watched Shadow closely, waiting for him to give me a sign that it wasn't who I already suspected it was. Shadow's face twisted in horror; he hung up the phone and looked at me with a fear in his eyes that no grown man should have.

"Who was that?" I asked him.

"Man, I don't know who that was. But whoever she is, she ain't happy. She said she was coming for your ass."

I was sick of niggas thinking I was a joke. They must have forgotten whose blood ran through my veins. Female or no female, I would take her ass out. Pinky was on some different shit by threatening me. I would kill her ass and not have second thoughts about it! Even though I had settled down and laid low, I was far from a scared ass nigga. If Pinky wanted to take it to the streets with me, then that's what we would do!

BLAQUE

Dirty
DNA 2

CHAPTER THIRTY-FIVE

Rare Essence (R.E.)

"Come Back Baby Come Back"

NiQue

I woke up in my old house in NE, Washington, DC. I hadn't been back here since the shooting of my brother more than a year and a half earlier. No one knew I still had the place. I kept it just in case shit with Dread and I didn't work out; I wanted to always have some place to lay my head. I was more than happy to have it now.

I couldn't go home after Dread's shooting. Pinky could have easily come back and sprayed the place with me and the baby inside. I wasn't sure if anyone had seen what had happened to Detective Gatsby. If they had, surely they would be looking for me at my house.

I looked around and didn't see the baby. I went from room to room looking for her. She had to be hungry and wet by now. Why wasn't she crying?

"She ain't crying because she ain't here idiot!" Pajay said annoyed—and as usual—reading my thoughts.

"What do you mean she 'ain't' here? Where is my daughter? What have you done with her?" I asked afraid that Pajay might have killed her. I didn't put anything past her.

"I swear you are the dumbest bitch on the planet! You can't remember shit, and you would be nothing without me guiding your footsteps!" she said viciously. *"You need to stop playing innocent like you didn't give me the ok to handle everything. You said you were tired of fucking around with your*

family, so I left her ass right next to where I left that sorry ass, no good Detective." Pajay lied.

Her laugh made me cringe as it bounced around in my head.

"Yeah Pajay, I said, 'my family' meaning Neko; not my daughter! Do you know Dread would kill me himself if something happened to her?"

"I am sure she is fine! We left her at the hospital in the parking lot. I am sure whoever found that private dick, found that annoying ass baby too! And Dread...please! You better pray he makes it out of ICU first; and then you can worry about the police not hauling him straight to jail before he even gets released from the hospital. You got other shit to worry about besides that kid. Like I said, 'she's safe!'" she scoffed. *"You couldn't exactly handle this 'other' business dragging that funny looking kid around; now could you?"* she asked.

I don't know why, but I knew she was lying about my daughter. There really wasn't anything I could do about it. I had to hope that Pajay had left her where she said she had and hopefully the baby would be ok.

"So what's next? If we started this shit, I guess we should finish it," I said defeated.

I would have to worry about trying to get my daughter later. Pajay was right; I couldn't get at Neko and Pinky if I had to worry about the baby getting in the way. Dread was in the hospital. He would never know what was happening anyway. I just prayed that I would have her back before Dread was healthy enough to realize that she was gone.

"I am glad to see you're seeing things my way! Now who would you like to settle the score with first...your dear ole brother, or his bitch?" Pajay laughed maniacally.

Just thinking about Pinky suffering made feel better about not having my daughter. Pinky had pulled up on the wrong nigga on the wrong day, and she was gonna feel some heat behind it! I don't give a fuck what her reasons were for shooting Dread; she had officially started a war.

Dirty
DNA 2

"I think we should do something special just for the two of them! They need to die slow!" Pajay said. Her laughter echoed around in my head and it was causing it to throb.

For the first time I didn't stop her, nor did I want to! I wanted her to do whatever she could to make them pay for what they had done to me! I was no longer in the business of forgiving and forgetting and trying to make amends! I was in the business of making those who hurt me suffer. I guess genetics are a mutha fucker!

I picked up the phone and called Neko's office. He was going to feel just what I had felt my entire life; pain. I thought he would have been the one to answer the phone being that Pajay had taken his receptionist's pretty tongue and her life too. Neko was just like our father as far as I was concerned. He didn't care about anything unless his dick was involved. He had shown me his true colors and I could not allow him to be spared this time. He had betrayed me, and now he was going to get a better understanding of the term *Bad Blood.*

I let the phone ring several times. I almost hung up when that fool Shadow answered. I figured I would leave the message with him and he would relay it to Neko. It didn't matter who got the message as long as I got my point across. I was coming for them and they had better get an army if they thought they were going win this battle.

"Fuck them all!" I said aloud.

"You finally have the right fucking idea! It took your simple ass long enough to see things my way!" Pajay said.

I laid my body back across the bare mattress in the house where I grew up and began to drift off into an uneasy slumber. I had a mission that was far more sinister than anything Pajay and I had ever pulled off before, and I needed to be well rested and alert to make sure this went off without any issues. One slip up, and not only would I expose my ugly truths, but I would end up either caged or dead. I had no room for errors.

BLAQUE

Dirty
DNA 2

CHAPTER THIRTY-SIX

Northeast Groovers (N.E.G)

"Hell Mary"

Pinky

I would have never thought Neko would have treated me so cold. After the way the conversation had gone earlier, I didn't regret my decision to terminate the pregnancy. Neko had hurt me and I took pleasure in hurting him back. Fuck him! I was finished fucking with Neko. There was no use in crying over it. I had done what I had done and there was no taking it back even if I wanted to. The baby was gone and I felt empty and cold inside.

I was in my favorite spot, a café by the harbor in Oxon Hill, Maryland. I had called him to come and meet me. I didn't want to be alone. I had been feeling lonely since I decided to end the pregnancy. Being cooped up in my home had led to nothing more than me crying for far too long. I was sick of crying. It was time for me to get back to business. I had been neglecting contracts and I hadn't been back to the club since my sister's death. It was high time I shook all that shit off and got back to my grind. I had never been a weak woman and I sure as hell wasn't going to let the shit happening to stop me from doing what I did best.

I blamed the pregnancy for my inability to finish my personal mission of making sure someone would be burying Dread. I needed to see Head. He was the only person I knew that was willing to go all in with me on killing Dread, or anyone else for that matter.

While I was deep in thought Head pulled up on his bike. Damn he was sexy! All I could do was think how glad I would be once I was no longer under a doctor's care, and he could fuck me and make me forget all about the feelings I had for Neko. My saying was that in order to get over a man, the best thing to do was to get on or under another one!

"What's up Pinky?" Head said kissing my forehead.

"Nothing much, I wanted to spend some time with you!" I said smiling at him.

Head looked bored and uninterested in me saying that I wanted to spend time with him. I wondered what that was about.

"Did I catch you at a bad time? Were you busy? If so, you could have just told me that and what I wanted to say to you could have waited," I said. I was trying to keep him on my side of the fence. I needed him to help me eliminate Dread.

"Naw, you are good. I was at work though. You know I took this legal gig and I've been kind of busy with that," he said.

"Well, we needed to talk about finishing that job we started. We cannot leave it unfinished. Too much is at stake if we do." I said reading his face to see if he was following me.

"I got you Pink. I need to holla at Gat to see if he can get us into the hospital without anyone knowing what we are up to. You know they might have that nigga under lock and key for all this shit he is twisted up in. We can't just go in with guns blazing in a hospital. We will end up getting knocked for sure," he said pausing when the waitress came to take his order.

"I don't want that *detective* involved in this Head. He knows too much about me. I got the feeling he can't be trusted." I said truthfully

Something about that Detective was more than sneaky; it was downright devious.

"Well, how do you suppose we get in that hospital and get at your boy then?" He asked. He sat there waiting on me to respond and I had no answer. I had no idea how I was going to get past the guards I knew were protecting Dread. After all, he had just survived someone trying to murder his ass, and they didn't know who or why. It only made sense that he would be in protective custody at the hospital. I thought it all over for a few moments longer and decided that maybe having Head contact Gatsby wasn't such a bad idea.

"Go ahead and make the call and see what he is willing to do to help us get at Dread." I said giving in.

Head seemed like he didn't care either way. His eye was trained on the waitress who had taken our order. She was giving him suggestive glances and he was doing the same in return like I wasn't even there.

In the past few weeks I hadn't been myself. Before all of this shit happened, I wouldn't have cared about him looking at another female. I was never the jealous type. Now I was feeling insecure. Was he looking at her because he thought she was prettier than me? Was her ass phatter than mine? It wasn't just my appearance that I was feeling inadequate about; it was also my ability to handle a job. I had fucked up and Dread was still alive. I had never missed a target before and now was a horrible time to start missing my mark!

"You know you could at least wait to eye fuck that bitch once I leave the table!" I said. I was feeling insecure and unsure about myself and his behavior wasn't helping.

I was so sick of niggas playing with me. First the shit with Neko, and now Head was ass watching right in front of me like I wasn't even sitting there. I was so upset with his blatant disrespect that leaving was the best thing for me to do if I didn't want to wind up with a murder beef. I gathered my shit and got up without saying a word; leaving him and his roaming eye having his ass sitting right there. Had I continued to sit there, I may have gotten mad enough to blow his head clean off in a café full of patrons.

I had made up my mind that I was going to have to do this shit on my own. I was a loner before Neko and Head; and I could do it all over again. This emotional shit wasn't me and it was leaving me feeling vulnerable. Anyone could catch me slipping giving the way I had been acting lately. I was too wrapped up in this heartfelt shit and it was becoming dangerous. I was going to get my head blown off if I kept this weak shit up!

I wanted the old me back. I missed the bitch that didn't care about anything but making money and pleasing herself. Once I started caring about niggas who didn't give a damn about me that is when my life got turned upside down. I needed to get my shit on track and stay in my own lane. I wasn't meant to love anyone. This "love" shit only complicated the simplest of things. I guess that is why I had never let anyone get too close to me, and I never got too close to anyone else for fear of them using that shit against me. That was just what had been happening lately. I let my guard down, and Neko fucked me over. I started to feel something other than lust for Head, and he was too wild to care about anything!

My mind was spinning with thoughts of how much I was allowing things to fall apart all because I had been stupid. In the midst of cursing myself out, I hopped on my bike and was about to pulled on my helmet. Just as I was prepared to ride off, Head caught up to me before I could pull away.

"Pink what the fuck is up with you? You have been tripping lately. What's wrong? You ain't ever tripped off of nothing like this before." he said looking at me as if I were a science experiment.

"Nothing is wrong baby. As a matter of fact, everything is just right. I had to check myself. I will get up with you later." I said icily.

I pulled my helmet on and sped off leaving him standing right there with a confused look on his face. It was time for me to take my life back! Those bum niggas had done enough of playing with my heart, and as far as I was concerned, they could all go straight to hell!

Dirty
DNA 2

*****

I had spent the remainder of my day trying to figure out where to start. I wasn't exactly sure what to do next. I drove to the 5th District to see if I was able to catch up to Detective Gatsby, but the place was chaotic. There were people busying themselves with the clean-up of the fire. I thought maybe I would find him out there assisting with the clean-up effort. After an hour or so of no Detective Gatsby, I gave up. I hated being around that many law enforcement officials.

I tried his phone over and over and there was no answer. It was like he had dropped off of the face of the map. I didn't know any other way to reach him besides Head; and there was no way I was going to ask him to help me again! I was through with being a weakling. No matter how bad I didn't want to admit it, I was going to need help with locating Dread; and once I found him, I would need help gaining entrance to wherever he was.

I found myself a few times wanting to pick up the phone and dial Head, but I stuck to my guns and decided against it. I was just going to have to come up with another way to get this shit done. Either I was going to have to wait until the good detective got back to me, or I was going to have to play nice with Head since he seemed to have a direct line in reaching Detective Gatsby. Until I decided which was better for me to do when it came to waiting it out or swallowing my pride and calling Head, my hands were tied. My ego wouldn't allow me to contact Head; so I waited— unbeknownst to me—on a call that was never going to come.

BLAQUE

CHAPTER THIRTY-SEVEN

Rare Essence (R.E.)

"Give Um' What They Want"

Neko

Head came back to the office right before it was time to close up the shop for the day. He looked like he had been through some shit, so I let the young nigga go home. He said his lady friend was driving him crazy. She had been acting strange and he didn't know why.

I could understand where he was coming from. All the females in my life, past and present, were fucked up; from my sister YaYa, to Pinky, to Natalie, to NiQue. They all were fucked up. Oh, and we couldn't forget my mother who had her fair share of shit too. All of the bitches I knew had issues. I ain't talking minor issues either. They all had some serious shit that needed to be worked out. Therapy may have helped them, but even that wasn't guaranteed.

I chuckled to myself thinking about that part in "Baby Boy" where the big head ass nigga said that women were unstable creatures. He spoke nothing but the truth! They were always moody, always whining about something, and they could be deadly if you didn't handle them with care. As soon as I thought about anything being deadly, I immediately started thinking of Pinky. I started to become enraged all over again. I wanted to kick myself for not telling Head I had an issue that we might have to address.

My thoughts were interrupted by the sound of someone walking down the hallway towards my office. I instantly stuck my hand in the top drawer of my desk and wrapped my hand around the cool steel of my Beretta. I never pulled it out; I just waited to see who was coming down the hall. If it wasn't anybody I cared to see, I wouldn't hesitate to squeeze the trigger. *Fuck what ya heard!*

The uninvited guest stuck his head in the door and I pulled the gun and trained it on his dome.

"What the fuck is wrong with you man?" Shadow said in a high-pitched voice.

I had obviously scared the shit out of him with a gun aimed at his head. Fuck that, he had scared the shit out of me as well. I let out a sigh of relief. Had I not been thinking, and been on some ole "shoot first" type shit instead, Shadow would have been a done deal!

"Nigga, what the fuck is wrong with you creeping through here? I thought you were gone for the day. I thought I was alone, so I had to be prepared" I said putting the gun back in the desk drawer.

That is when I noticed Shadow was carrying a baby carrier.

"Oh, hell naw nigga, I know damn well you ain't get another bitch pregnant and now you are babysitting and bringing babies to work!" I laughed.

Shadow didn't laugh with me. He didn't even crack a smile.

"No, this is a special delivery just for you," he said sitting the carrier on the desk.

"You must have lost your mind! I don't have any babies!"

"I never said it was your baby, I said it is a special delivery for you," he said repeating himself.

I was baffled.

"What the fuck are you talking about Shadow? If it ain't my kid, and it ain't your kid, whose kid is it, and where the fuck did it come from and why is it here? Don't give me no shit about no stork or no crazy shit like that either." I said trying to diffuse the situation.

"Man you need to stop fucking around!" Shadow said seriously.

I peeked inside of the carrier and at first glance I just shrugged. It was just a baby. I looked at the baby again and noticed something I hadn't seen. The baby had grey eyes just like mine. She had flaming red hair and she looked like a mixture of my late sister YaYa and Dread. I felt like I was hyperventilating. I sat down and leaned back in the chair and tried to calm down. I gripped the sides of the chair tightly and tried to breathe as normally as I could.

"Shadow, whose damn baby is that and where the fuck did it come from?" I asked him trying to catch my breath.

"Boss, you ain't ever going to believe this shit! I almost got all the way to Tya's house and found out I left my keys to my baby momma Marie's house at the front desk. I turned around and came back here to get them. I pulled up out front and your girl NiQue was peeling out from the parking lot. I saw the carrier on the steps. Who thought that bitch would be crazy enough to leave a baby out front? Yo' when I got to the steps, I had no idea there would be a sleeping baby inside! What kind of shit is ole girl on? She got to be on something for her to leave a fucking baby on the steps of a business like that!" Shadow said getting hyped over the situation.

"I don't know man. She was acting crazy that day in the hospital. Maybe the shit going on with Dread is making her bug out," I said. I rubbed my temples. NiQue really had lost her mind. She left her daughter on the steps of my business like she was trash. I knew she was going through it with Dread, but to drop a baby off like it was a package was ridiculous.

"What are you going to do with the baby?" Shadow asked me.

"There has to be a reason that she left her here with me. I guess I am babysitting until I can find her crazy ass mother," I responded.

"You don't know shit about babies. Do you even know how to change or feed her?" Shadow questioned me.

"Shadow, my dude, that is what you are here for! All those damn kids you got, I am sure you can give me a crash course in taking care of this one until I find her mother." I laughed uneasily.

*****

Shadow showed me the basics of taking care of a baby. I was nervous. I didn't have a clue about what I was supposed to do. I wanted him to take her, but what was he going to do with another baby? He already had enough of his own to take care of. If he brought home another baby his girl might flip the fuck out; whether it was his or not. That was Shadow's pattern every few months, he would turn up with another kid and Tya would kick his ass out. She would take him back, but not before he had spent several nights sleeping in the office.

I gathered my up my things, grabbed the baby, locked up the office and left. I felt so awkward with a baby in my care. I made a quick stop at *CVS* and got what I thought I would need for taking care of her until I could locate her crazy mother. Then I headed to my house. In doing so, I let my guard down. I had forgotten about the threats Pinky had been making because I was so focused on taking care of the baby.

I never even knew I was being followed.

After several hours of trial and error with trying to feed the baby and change her, I finally got her fed. I had to call Shadow a good four times just so he could walk me through the process of how to put a diaper on her. Not to mention the fact that she peed on everything during my attempts. I couldn't do anything but laugh. I gave her a bath and put her down for the night.

234

Dirty
DNA 2

As I was watching the baby sleep it dawned on me that I had never seen Dread and NiQue's daughter before now. It was eerie looking at a baby that reminded me so much of my sister. Sure she looked like her father, but there was no mistaking who she really favored. She favored YaSheema. It was like looking at a miniature version of my sister.

I tried calling NiQue to find out what the fuck was up with her, but she didn't answer. I waited on the voicemail to pick up because I had a lot to say to her ass for leaving her daughter at my shop. I didn't mind keeping her, but the way she went about it was just trifling and she was going to hear about it too!

"Aye, yo NiQue, what the fuck is up with you leaving a baby on my property like this? Look…take whatever time you need to do whatever it is you need to do, but I wanted you to know that was some heartless shit you just pulled! What kind of mother does some shit like that? You are lucky we got some kind of bond or I would have dropped her off somewhere and called them people on you! Man, hit me when you get yourself together. The baby is fine and you will be lucky if you ever see her again at the rate you are going!" I said slamming the house phone down on the cradle. I flopped down on the bed hard; causing the baby to stir. I couldn't figure out how her mother could just drop her off and not look back. She hadn't even bothered to call to check on her daughter.

"Some fucking parents you got baby girl." I said to the baby who had returned to a peaceful slumber on my king size bed.

It was by sheer chance that Shadow had seen NiQue leaving, or we might have never known whose kid she was. I couldn't help but wonder if NiQue had snapped. Had she lost her damn mind leaving her daughter exposed to the elements?

Seeing the baby sleeping made me think of Pinky and our baby that she had aborted. I started to call Pink and try and work shit out with her, but I wasn't so sure she would be receptive of my call being that our last conversation wasn't so pleasant. After thinking about it for a few minutes I swallowed my pride because I really did miss ole girl. I didn't know if she was the one who was out to get me or not, but I dialed her number anyway. She answered on the first ring.

"Pinky, please let me say what I need to say first ma. I know I said some really nasty shit to you the other day, and for that, I apologize. I couldn't believe the shit you were telling me. The whole thing with you and the baby had my mind fucked up. I can't blame anyone but myself for what you had to do. My own insecurities were keeping me from being there for you when you needed me the most."

"Neko, I'm sorry that I didn't talk to you first about the baby, but you wouldn't answer me when I tried to reach out to you. I didn't want to be alone raising a baby. I ain't too good at caring for myself; I knew I would be a mess trying to take care of a baby alone," she sniffled.

I felt so bad for not being there for her. I put all of my suspicions of her to the side and threw caution to the wind.

"Pinky, do you mind stopping through? I think we need to talk about this face to face. I don't want to discuss this over the phone." I said hoping she would accept my invitation.

"I will be on my way in a few minutes," she said.

"Good, I will be here waiting for you."

"Hey Neko...I love you," Pinky said.

"I love you too Pinky." I said as I hung up the phone.

I was excited about seeing her. I really did love her. I prayed that we could work out our differences and that she wasn't the one who had killed Natalie; mostly because I really wanted to be with shorty. Not having her around was fucking with me.

Dirty

DNA 2

CHAPTER THIRTY-EIGHT

Huck-a-Bucks

"The Bud"

Pinky

I couldn't contain my excitement. Neko had called! I know I had said I wasn't going to give him or Head another thought, but there was something about Neko that I couldn't let go of. He gave me my space, he was there when I needed him the most, and he understood my need to be independent. He wasn't the typical nigga. He didn't trip about either one of my jobs and I loved him for loving me just the way I was. I was a walking, talking, oxymoron! A hit-woman with a heart! I am sure there was never such a thing before me, and there would never be one after me.

I got in the shower and a lathered my body with my favorite lavender-scented body wash. It was Neko's favorite too.

I slid into my pink leather pants with no panties, black tank top and pink leather rider's jacket. I gave myself a once over before grabbing my keys and helmet as I hit the door.

I hopped on my bike and sat there enjoying the crisp, fresh autumn air. There was nothing better than taking a ride on my Ducati in the fall. Somehow DC seemed a little brighter to me. I felt brand new.

I cranked up my bikes engine and pulled out of my condo complex. I enjoyed riding my bike. It made me feel free. I could get ghost in a matter of seconds, and no one could catch me! As I came to the intersection right before Neko's neighborhood, the light turned red. I tried to brake, but nothing happened. I tried repeatedly to reduce the speed of the bike but my brakes failed me. At the speed I was going there was nothing I could do. I swerved around the cars that were directly ahead of me and the bike kept right on going into the intersection where the traffic had the right of way on my left and right sides.

"Oh God!" was all I was able to scream before a SUV smacked into the side of my bike throwing me twenty feet into the air.

Dirty
DNA 2

CHAPTER THIRTY-NINE

Chuck Brown

"Stormy Monday"

NiQue

"Serves that bitch right!" Pajay said laughing hysterically.

I nodded at Pajay's statement.

We watched as the pink bike that Pinky was operating careened out of control and into traffic. There was so much joy and satisfaction in my dark heart watching her body, and her bike, being tossed high into the air and smacking the hood of a car coming from the opposite direction. The sounds of people screaming, and tires screeching to a halt, were like music to my ears. There were people running from all directions to help Pinky's sorry ass. What they didn't know was it was a complete waste of time. That bitch was dead before her body ever hit the hood of the car and rolled into the street.

"Two down and one more to go!" Pajay said as though she were making a tick on her mental tally sheet.

I nodded my head in agreement and drove past the grizzly scene. I didn't need to stick around. I knew Pinky was gone. I had to hand it to Pajay…fucking with Pinky's break lines was genius! No one would ever suspect us of that shit.

I made my way through the cars that were rubber necking trying to see what had happened. Next stop, Neko's shop. I had plans of my own! Plans I hadn't even gone over with Pajay. I pushed my foot all the way down to the floor of the Mercedes and the car launched forward.

"Where are we going? Neko's house is in the other direction" Pajay said.

"I know where his house is. Just sit back and enjoy the ride! I got a special surprise for you! I'm going to show you that I am far from weak! Imma show you that I am in control of this!" I said trying to quiet her. I didn't want her to ruin my surprise. It was going to be better than anything we had ever pulled off!

I cranked up, "Hailie's Song" by Eminem and kept pushing my car, ignoring every question Pajay asked.

When we pulled up to Neko's shop, Pajay started really questioning me.

"What are doing here? We were supposed to be going to Neko's house. We ain't supposed to be here!" Pajay said over and over again.

"Shut the fuck up and watch me work!" I said to her.

I got out of the car and went to the trunk and pulled out a container of lighter fluid and one of those big lighters used to ignite a fireplace.

My phone rang and I don't know what made me answer it, but I did!

"What!" I screamed into the phone.

"Ms. Watkins this is Detective Ross."

It took me a few moments to figure out who the fuck he was and what he wanted. Then it dawned on me that he was the detective who was handling Dread's case.

"Yeah, what do you want?" I snapped at him.

"Ms. Watkins, can you come in to the station? We have some very important developments in your fiancés' case that we would like to discuss with you in person," he said with urgency.

"Detective, I am in the middle of something, can this wait?" I said agitated.

"No, this cannot wait. We were able to obtain the DNA sample report that was run by a detective in the 5th District before it was set on fire. The detective uploaded it to the city wide database before he was killed in that fire," he said gaining my undivided attention.

240

Dirty

DNA 2

I stopped walking towards the building and listened to what the man on the other end of the phone was saying to me.

"Ms. Watkins, Mr. Evans is innocent! The DNA was a match to Detective Gatsby," he said.

I gasped and dropped the can of lighter fluid at my feet. I watched as its contents slowly started to spill and run out on the ground around me.

"Ms. Watkins? Are you there?"

"Yeah, I am here. Did you say that Gatsby killed that girl?" I asked not sure I had heard him right.

"Yes, ma'am. We also have reason to believe that Gatsby started that fire in the 5th District to cover his tracks. Your fiancé has been cleared of all charges. However, we do have another issue to sort out."

I was smiling from ear to ear. My smile quickly faded when I thought about how Pinky and Neko tried to kill my man for some shit he didn't do. I wanted Neko dead more than ever! He should have trusted me instead of that pig ass cop! I told him that cop was no fuckin' good and now look what happened. Neko trusted everyone but me, and he was going to find out that believing everyone else was a mistake. He was going to feel this shit!

"Ms. Watkins, Ms. Watkins are you there?" the detective asked.

"Yes. I am here." I responded, still in deep thought about how I was going to make Neko pay for this shit!

"Mr. Evans will be a free man once he recovers. We do have one other issue though. We won't be able to lock Gatsby up."

"I know…I mean why not?" I said, trying to cover up the fact that I had almost incriminated myself!

"His body was found outside of the ER where we met you the day your fiancé was shot. He was stabbed in his neck, face, and ear."

Unsuccessfully I tried to muffle my laughter.

"What is so funny? I don't find any of this funny! Is there something you aren't telling us?" he asked.

"No, why would I know anything about that?" I said real confident like.

"Because we find it very strange that the same cop that may have been trying to frame your fiancé was found dead in the same hospital, miles away from where anyone knew him…except you!"

"So what are you trying to say officer? Are you trying to say I had something to do with that pig getting what he deserved?"

"That is exactly what I am trying to say Ms. Watkins," he said.

I laughed in the phone until I realized that Pajay had told me before that she had left my daughter at the scene of the crime. No wonder this Fed was pressing me out. Maybe they had my daughter and were trying to set me up.

Pajay barged in, "*Hang up the phone bitch! Don't you see he is trying to catch you in some shit!*"

I disconnected the call and paced back and forth in the empty parking lot. I started to panic.

"Pajay, what about my daughter? Didn't you say you left her there with Gatsby? Why didn't that cop mention my baby?" I asked her frantically.

"*Bitch, let's do whatever you came here to do and let's get the fuck out of here! They could have traced that call and be on their way here to bust our asses. We don't have time to be worried about that fucking baby!*" Pajay said avoiding me.

"Pajay, where is my daughter? You said you left her where someone could find her. Why hasn't anyone tried to return her to me yet?"

I picked up the lighter fluid from the ground and was emptying what was left from the container in a path leading to the front entrance of the detailing shop. I walked back to where I had originally stood and dropped the empty can on the ground.

"*Hurry up and do it! We can't be out here all night worrying about that fucking kid!*"

DNA 2

Dirty

I clicked the lighter and touched the flame to the puddle that was on the ground. Instant satisfaction filled my veins as I watched it race up the path I had created with the fluid. In a matter of seconds the front of the business was engulfed in flames. When I was satisfied with the destruction, I got in the car and pulled off. It was time for me to pay my brother a visit. I was going to end all of this shit once and for all, and I was going to end it tonight!

BLAQUE

CHAPTER FORTY

Trouble Funk

"Trouble Funk Express"

Neko

I had fallen asleep on the bed next to the baby when the phone rang waking me. I checked the caller ID, hoping it was Pinky calling to let me know she was on her way. It was Shadow.

"Wassup Shadow?" I asked sleepily into the phone.

"Man, you will never believe the shit I just saw. I was headed back to the shop and when I got there your folk, NiQue, the one who left her kid, was here. She was talking to herself, ranting and raving about ending shit tonight. Man, shorty is crazier than a mutha fucker. She fucked around and set the shop on fire. The whole building went up in flames! You need to get down here right now!" Shadow said out of breath.

"What the fuck are you talking about Shadow? Why would she set the place on fire?" I asked, sitting up being careful not to wake the baby.

"She was on her phone, and at first I thought she had come back to get her baby, but then she went to the trunk of her car and started to pour lighter fluid all around the joint! Whoever was on the other end pissed her off and then she set the place on fire. She kept yelling at someone named Pajay!" he said in a panic.

"Pajay!" I damn near screamed into the phone.

"Did you see this Pajay person Shadow? Did you see her?" I asked Shadow who was holding a conversation with someone in the background.

I could hear the sirens and the commotion. Hearing the name, "Pajay" sent chills up my spine. I hadn't seen, nor heard anything from the mystery sibling since YaYa's death.

"Naw man, I didn't see anyone but that crazy bitch who torched the place!"

I started to put on my clothes and gather the baby's stuff. I had to get to the shop. I needed to see how much damage had been done.

"If NiQue was talking to Pajay, then she had to be there somewhere." In my confused state, I couldn't help but scream at Shadow.

"I'm trying to tell you there was no one out here but me and that crazy broad."

"Aight man, I am on my way down there. Let me get the baby dressed and I am on the way. Just stay there until I get there!" I told Shadow.

"Aye Neko. Be careful man, that bitch got some serious issues. I knew there was something wrong with that bitch the day I met her; and right now, she just proved that shit!"

"I'm on my way!" I said and hung up the phone.

I scooped the baby up and headed for the door. As I flung the door open and was surprised to see NiQue standing there with two very familiar gold Desert Eagles in each of her hands. They had belonged to my father's best friend Oscar before he had died. I almost dropped the baby; I was so shook up seeing her there.

"Hello Neko. You look surprised to see me!" she said waving the guns around wildly.

The way she was acting let me know she had come to do me harm. This was no social visit and it was no coincidence that she had Oscar's guns.

I backed up from the doorway and she followed me inside.

"Were you going somewhere Neko? Maybe you were going to visit your whore of a girlfriend? Or maybe you were going to what 'used' to be your shop!" she laughed.

246

Dirty

DNA 2

I backed up further into the house and frantically looked around for something, anything that I could use to protect myself. It was obvious NiQue had lost her damn mind.

Seeing NiQue, all wild eyed and crazy, was some shit I had never seen before and I was certain that the look in her eyes was murder. She looked like her soul was tainted with evil. NiQue was battling good and evil and it looked like evil had won.

Suddenly she started crying. I had no idea what was going.

"Wait, wait he has my daughter. Don't do anything to harm my baby!" NiQue yelled out.

I looked around to see who she was talking to because I saw no one else there but her, me and the baby. I clutched the baby tighter in my arms because I certainly wasn't giving her to her mother in that state.

Her voice switched up and the tone in it changed. It was as if she were throwing her voice. She was talking to someone I couldn't see, but there was a sense that someone else was really there. NiQue was gone; and what I was witnessing was some ole Brandon Marshall from the *Chicago Bears* type shit! She needed to be on that straight jacket and padded room list. I didn't know how no one had put it together before.

"It was you all along!" I said aloud making the painful revelation.

NiQue stopped her back and forth banter with herself long enough to stare at me. She cocked her head to the side like she was sizing me up. She was on another level with it!

"Yeah, so what if it was me?" she laughed. Her laugh was so cold and demonic.

"If you and your trick ass girlfriend hadn't tried to set me up and shot Dread this would have never happened. Your girlfriend tried to kill my man over some shit he had nothing to do with. Yeah. I found out your boy, Detective Gatsby, was more crooked than you could have ever dreamed of. Remember those cops from the hospital that questioned you the day that Dread was shot?" she paused and waited on a response from me.

247

I didn't answer her for fear that if I answered her incorrectly, she would use the guns she was brandishing. I could see that she was getting annoyed with my silence, so I decided to answer her by nodding my head up and down.

"Well, they told me your friend Detective Gatsby was the one responsible for killing that girl at your whore's club."

My mouth fell open with the information she was feeding me. My eyes never lost their focus on the gold guns in NiQue's hands. She was waving them back and forth in the direction of me and the baby.

"NiQue, I don't know what you are talking about! Can we calm down and talk about this?" I said trying to reason with her. From the look on her face there was no being rational with her. She reminded me of one of those crazy broads from that show, "Snapped."

"Calm! I am calm!" she screamed causing me to jump. I almost dropped the baby on the floor.

"Oh, and Neko if you think I give a fuck about you or that piece of shit baby you're holding, you're wrong! You know over the years I have learned that family ain't shit, including ours!"

"What do you mean, 'ours?' NiQue you were just my sister's friend. We aren't related. The only family I had died last year."

She was getting under my skin talking about my parents and my sister. I know she had lost the only family she had too, but she was hitting a sensitive spot with me.

She moved even closer to me. I could smell death on her.

"Let me clue you in on a little secret Neko because your ignorance is starting to anger me! You aren't really this fucking stupid are you?" she laughed.

"Look at that baby you're holding. I know you cannot deny who she really looks like. Have you even bothered to even look at your niece?"

"My niece? This shit ain't funny! My sister and the baby died! Are you standing here telling me that this is YaYa's baby?"

Dirty
DNA 2

"No, you fucking moron! She is my baby and your niece! I think maybe you need to have a look at your family tree. You see, your father liked to keep secrets. I was one of them!"

It was her. She was Pajay. I don't know why I had never seen it before. I don't know why I had never put it together!

"You…you're Pajay!" I stuttered.

"Finally you fucking get it!" she said real animated like.

"But how? I don't understand!" I was totally confused.

"Maybe you should take a seat. I see explaining this shit to you isn't going to be as easy as it was when I had to break it to YaYa. As you can imagine, she was just as surprised as you are." she said smiling.

I backed up all the way to the couch and took a seat. I held the baby tightly. There was no telling what her crazy ass mother would do to me, or her for that matter. The way NiQue was acting I wouldn't put it past her to pull the trigger and kill us both. I looked around my home which seemed so unfamiliar at the moment. I felt like I was living in the *Twilight Zone*.

"Now that you're comfy, I guess I can fill you in on a few things before you die like the rest of our shady ass family! I'll keep it brief before that whining bitch NiQue shows up!"

She really was crazy. She was talking about herself in third person like she, and the person speaking to me, weren't one in the same. As I saw her in action, I believed there was someone else inside of her because the woman standing before me wasn't NiQue. I don't know who she was, but I didn't want to know anymore of her than I already knew.

"You are NiQue!" I interjected.

"No baby brother, NiQue was who our dear ole' dad put together to hide the fact that I was his child. Papa really was a rolling stone! He showered everything he had on YaYa. It was no coincidence you were reunited with your father. I set that shit up with your crack head mother. It still amazes me what an 8 ball of crack can make a nigga do!

Your mother had stayed away from our father until I found out about you. I tracked your mother down and offered her a way back into Darnell's life. She jumped at the chance to ruin YaYa's life since she felt like YaYa ruined hers. Your mother blamed YaYa for all of her downfalls. When I told her who I was, she didn't want to believe it, but after I dangled the drugs in front of her she was more than willing to do whatever I wanted her to do. Including getting me the information I needed which was the inside track on our father's connects. She watched his movements and reported everything to me, all while claiming to be rehabbing in his home."

As the woman standing before me spewed her venom, I was reminded of the day my mother introduced me to my father. He wasn't exactly happy to see us.

NiQue took a seat in the love seat across from me and continued; never lowering her weapons.

"Once I tried to confront our father, who had rejected me all the while embracing you, I had had enough, that was it! I decided that I was going to kill all of them. Daddy wanted you and YaYa and not me because I was his bad seed! I was the one who had a few problems; and because I wasn't perfect like his precious YaYa, he sent me to live with Mike who raped and molested me repeatedly."

I shook my head in disbelief. I knew my father was fucked up, but for him to hide a child like that because she was sick mentally was downright horrible.

"Why didn't you tell one of us what you were going through NiQue...I mean Pajay. Maybe YaYa or I could have helped you." I said sympathetically. I felt bad that she had gone through so much and it led her down a path of destruction.

"I told the one person who could have helped me—our father. When he didn't receive me with open arms like I wanted him to, well, I helped YaYa kill your mother. Once I got a taste for making people hurt, I couldn't stop. It excited me! So I decided to make daddy pay for not loving me the way he should have. I dismantled his empire strategically, piece by piece, and person by person starting with your mother!

See, daddy thought his empire couldn't be infiltrated from outside; but he never counted on me taking him down from the inside. It was easy too. I plucked them off one by one from your mother to your father, to Mike who impersonated the role of being my brother, to Oscar and finally YaYa!"

One tear escaped my eyes for the souls of all those I had buried. For the ones who were innocent in this fucked up game NiQue was playing. None of them deserved to die because of one man's flaws.

"Why did you kill YaYa? She didn't do anything to you. She was our friend." I said from a depth within me that needed to know. If this was going to be my last day on earth I wanted clarity on everything.

NiQue laughed. *"I killed her because she had it all! I didn't have shit but a fucked up life and a man who molested me for being different. YaYa had our father's love and she couldn't just be happy with that. She had to have Dread too. That was the last straw. Once I found out she had slept with my man, I was furious! She had to have everything and she got whatever she wanted.*

After I killed them all, I thought I would be able to go on without having to kill anyone else again; but you and your bitch Pinky tried to take the happiness I had finally found by trying to kill Dread."

"NiQue I didn't have anything to do with that! I swear I didn't. Pinky and I weren't even speaking until tonight!"

That made me wonder where the fuck Pink was anyway. She should have been here by now. This sure would be a great time for her to show up before my sister blew my fuckin' head off; and her daughter's too!

"Oh well, too bad you won't be speaking to her anymore except in your dreams because that bitch is dead! I saw to it before I set your shop on fire and headed over here to have a family reunion with you. By the way I would appreciate it if you wouldn't call me NiQue. My name is Pajay!" She laughed and cocked the hammer back on one of the guns.

I closed my eyes and prayed that God would see me through this. Before I could say amen, my door, which was still slightly ajar, was kicked completely off the hinges. I took the opportunity to make a break for it to the kitchen, with the baby still in my arms, while NiQue was distracted by our new guests.

From my position in the kitchen I watched the horror unfold before my eyes. The two detectives from the hospital had kicked the door off the frame and ordered that NiQue drop her weapons. She looked in my direction and smiled the deadliest of smiles. It sent chills up my spine. She spun around and opened fire on the police officers. She wasn't good with the kick back from the dual guns and missed her marks. They returned fire and filled her body full of lead.

I ran from where I had taken cover in the kitchen and put the baby on the couch before running over to NiQue. I didn't care how much foul shit she had done; she was still my sister. She needed mental help, not to be killed. She couldn't help what she was. It wasn't her fault. I scooped her up in my arms and pressed on the biggest hole in her chest trying to stop the blood that was pouring from the gaping hole.

Her eyes popped open.

"Neko." she coughed and sputtered, spewing blood.

"I'm sorry you had to find out about me like this. Baby brother, she…I mean Pajay, is gone. Thank you for saving me from her," she coughed. She smiled a weak smile like she had finally found the peace and love she had been killing and dying for. Her body went limp and my sister died in my arms.

"What the fuck happened in here?" Shadow said, entering what used to be my door as he found me there holding NiQue's dead body.

Shadow explained later that I had taken too long to get to the shop and the detectives had come to the scene because they had pinged NiQue's cell phone to the location of the fire. He informed them that he had witnessed her starting the fire. They asked him for my information and he led them to my house. They had gotten there right on time or else there was no telling what would have happened!

CHAPTER FORTY-ONE

Backyard Band (BYB)

"94 Dope Jam"

Neko

Everyone is gone. I can't seem to figure out the curse that was put upon my family. It was passed on from generation to generation. None of us did anything in life that didn't result in someone dying. Either I am extremely lucky, or the man upstairs wasn't ready for me yet. Over a two-year time frame I had lost my mother, gained two sisters, and found my father. And over that same two-year time frame I had lost them all and others close to me along the way. I was torn because I didn't know how to feel about my family. I loved them and missed them, but I also would have much rather not had any of them as part of my life. They could have left me in the gutter where they had found me if it would have meant I could live a normal life! Money is the only thing I gained out of any of this, and it wasn't worth it because I had lost so much more.

After NiQue died, there was no one willing to take the baby. Dread didn't want to be bothered with her because she reminded him of all of the wild shit he had gone through with both of my sisters, and my girl. He never came and got her once he was released from the hospital. He said he wanted to be left alone. He didn't leave any contact information or any means of finding him. Although some people thought he was cruel to abandon his child and not look back, I couldn't say I blamed him for not wanting anything to do with any of us! We ran through that man's life and fucked it up over the span of two years. Everything he had was tested and then taken. His career was in shambles and beyond repair. For him to try and live out what was left of his life, he had to leave it all behind. I am more than sure it would require years of therapy for him to trust anyone ever again. Both of my sisters ran through his life and tore it apart.

Pajay left nothing behind but death and destruction. She dismantled everything that could have been perfect. She brought down an entire empire and nothing was left of my father's legacy.

My father had hustled hard to create a business and make millions in the streets. He worked even harder at trying to conceal his infidelities. His secrets, denial, and betrayal had all backfired. Instead of him being able to maintain and control his dirty secrets, they were unleashed on the city by way of his children. It was his demise and ultimately his downfall. He should have been a father instead of trying to hide his other children and their problems. Money doesn't fix everything.

I don't blame my father for everything that happened, even though he played a huge part. My father spent countless dollars hiding Pajay or NiQue or whoever she really was, instead of getting her the help she deserved and needed; and for that he was wrong. He should have embraced my sister and sought medical attention for her. The fact that Pajay never got the love and the treatment she needed to cope with her mental problems left her unstable and deadly. Had he focused his energy on her, maybe Pajay wouldn't have taken control of NiQue.

On the other hand, NiQue knew for years that she was sick and needed help, but somehow, she thought that self-medicating with drugs would make her problems disappear. Her condition slowly deteriorated until Pajay had taken complete control of her. NiQue was filled with so much hatred and animosity in her soul from not receiving the love she was denied, that she allowed who she really was, Pajay, to lash out.

I wonder from time to time if NiQue could have been saved. Would medical treatment have done her any good? Or was she

Dirty

DNA 2

too far gone to help? I will never know the answers to those questions.

It has been six years since all of that shit went down. The smoke has cleared, and the dust has settled. I live a normal life now. Well, as normal as one can under the circumstances. I left my father's traits of bed hopping, the drugs, and the careless ways behind me. Those traits had played an intricate part in taking down everyone we loved, and I was trying to move forward with raising one woman, my niece, YaSheema Nicole. Besides, I don't know who would want to be involved with me. My jaded past was put on front street for the entire world to see. No woman in her right mind wanted anything to do with me. I was jinxed, cursed and they didn't know if any more of my family's shameful past would make its way into their lives and cause the reaper to rear his ugly head and make them a target. My life had turned into an Urban Legend.

I finally moved out of Washington DC. I had no other choice but to take my niece and leave. There was so much controversy swirling around me that it wasn't the type of environment I wanted for my niece. We needed to get away from all of the stares and people wanting to invade our lives and pick it a part. I am thankful that she was so young when it all happened that she doesn't remember any of it. I wish I could have been as lucky as her in that regard and have all of the memories taken away from me as well.

It's funny sometimes but I see my niece, YaSheema Nicole, talking to people who ain't there and it makes me wonder sometimes. I hope, for the life of me, that she isn't like her mother and hears the voices in her head. When I asked her about it she says it's her imaginary friend. I hope her imaginary friend isn't like Pajay, because if she, is I am dropping her ass off somewhere far away and I ain't gonna look back; niece or no niece! For the sake of everyone around us I will have her locked away with no regret.

255

BLAQUE

I have seen and lived what shit like this can do to not only an entire family, but an entire city!

YaSheema Nicole's mother single-handedly destroyed my entire family, the love of my life, my friends, and a man's destiny. There is no way I would stand by and watch it happen all over again. Call me cruel, but you didn't live through this shit...I did, and I ain't willing to do it again!

Made in the USA
Middletown, DE
01 March 2022

61809753R00154